NO OTHER LOVER WILL DO

Kandace stormed into her room and thought about calling the front desk to complain about that jackass. No matter how cute he was, she would not succumb to his smooth voice and killer body. At least she didn't give him her name.

Well, if I see him again, I'm just going to ignore the horn dog, she thought as she peeled off her wet suit and headed for the shower.

Still, as she stood in the shower, her mind wandered back to his haunting eyes, and despite herself, when she felt the lick of the water against her neck, she thought of his lips and tongue being there. Kandace quickly shut off the water.

Just as she finished drying off and rubbing lotion on her skin, there was a knock at the door.

"Yes," she said as she wrapped herself in the robe and looked through the peephole.

"Delivery for Kandace Davis," the hotel messenger said. Kandace opened the door and accepted the large white box.

Kandace looked at the box wondering who sent her a gift. There was no card on the outside of the box, so Kandace opened it. Inside, she found a red fur bikini. She lifted the barely there garment from the box and a card fell to the floor. She dropped the box on the bed and picked up the card.

I want to see you in this and then I want to see it on the floor. It was signed, *The Jackass.*

D1019806

Also by Cheris Hodges

JUST CAN'T GET ENOUGH

LET'S GET IT ON

MORE THAN HE CAN HANDLE

BETTING ON LOVE

Published by Kensington Publishing Corporation

No Other LOVER Will Do

CHERIS HODGES

Kensington Publishing Corp.

http://www.kensingtonbooks.com

DAFINA BOOKS are published by

Kensington Publishing Corp.
119 West 40th Street
New York, NY 10018

All Kensington Titles, Imprints, and Distributed Lines are available at special quantity discounts for bulk purchases for sales promotions, premiums, fund-raising, and educational or institutional use. Special book excerpts or customized printings can also be created to fit specific needs. For details, write or phone the office of the Kensington special sales manager: Kensington Publishing Corp., 119 West 40th Street, New York, NY 10018, attn: Special Sales Department, Phone: 1-800-221-2647.

Dafina and the Dafina logo Reg. U.S. Pat. & TM Off.

ISBN-13: 978-0-7582-4709-4
ISBN-10: 0-7582-4709-5

First mass market printing: February 2010

10 9 8 7 6 5 4 3 2 1

Printed in the United States of America

ACKNOWLEDGMENTS

It's hard to thank everyone who stood by my side while I wrote this novel. First, I have to thank Irene Russell for her insight and for answering my nursing questions. Thank you for being a good friend.

Thanks to my tattoo artist, Joe Hart, who allowed me to come and bounce ideas off him, and for the wonderful skin art.

To my family, every member, especially my mom and dad, Doris and Freddie Hodges, for all of the support and love.

Thank you to all of the members of the Cheris F. Hodges Book Club. You guys rock and I couldn't do this without you.

To the SBS Book Club, Sistah Friend's Book Club, the PWOC Book Club, Yolanda Cuttino and the Sistah Unlimited Book Club, thank you for everything.

And last but certainly not least, to the reader with this book in her (or his) hands. Thank you for allowing me into your world.

CHAPTER 1

Solomon Crawford turned his back to the buxom blond model lying beside him. She was on the cover of *Maxim* this month and he thought it would've taken him longer to get her in bed. In reality, it had only taken him two hours and a bottle of expensive champagne to get "what's her name" to drop her panties and give him what every man in America wanted. But for all her beauty and silicone, she was a complete bore in bed. The woman lay there just like a sack of flour and Solomon had never been more disappointed. He probably would've had more fun watching paint dry or grass grow.

The red numbers on the alarm clock next to the bed read four-thirty. *Hell, the room is paid for,* he thought as he rose from the bed. Solomon didn't even try to be gentle or quiet as he reached for his discarded Armani slacks and Italian leather loafers.

"Where are you going?" she asked, her voice deepened by sleep.

"Home," he said.

"But, I thought we could . . ."

"Listen, we're done. And honestly, there's nothing you can say or do to make me want to spend another minute with you," Solomon said as he buttoned his shirt. "The room is paid for, but checkout is at noon."

"You're going to leave me here alone?" she asked incredulously. "How can you do this to me? Do you know who I am?"

Solomon shrugged as he picked his jacket up from the armchair near the door. "Just another piece and not a very good one," he said, then walked out the door. Solomon heard a crash as he headed down the hall to the elevator. Maybe if she'd shown that kind of passion in bed he would've stayed until at least five. Solomon chuckled as he stepped onto the elevator and rode to the W Hotel's parking garage. She, like so many before her, would get over it and have a great story to tell about her night in Solomon land.

Solomon Crawford was the kind of man that women couldn't help but get naked for. He had money, power, and model good looks. To the many women he'd bedded, he was an untamable stallion they had to ride at least once. And one ride was all they'd ever gotten. Solomon didn't believe in fidelity, love, or all that other bullshit that sold greeting cards and roses. He wanted sex and it was given to him freely. The only thing he'd ever worked for was building his family's hotel empire. The Crawford chain of hotels and resorts stretched across the United States and Canada.

Three years ago, Solomon had been handed the

reins to the business when Cynthia and Elliot Crawford retired from the hospitality business. His older brother, Richmond, was super pissed when he was passed over to run the business. Richmond was forty years old and thought he knew more about running a hotel business than "the little playboy."

But at age thirty-five, Solomon had been more than ready to take charge. Solomon knew the only way to shut Richmond up was to take the business to the next level and that he did with the help of his bright business partner Carmen De La Croix. Carmen talked him into investing in resorts and making the Crawford name synonymous with deluxe vacation resorts. Of course, Richmond thought this was a bad idea until they turned a million-dollar profit in the first quarter. And the money kept rolling in. Solomon knew he'd be lost without Carmen. She was the only woman he was able to talk to and trust. She didn't want anything from him and he liked that. Why couldn't the women he slept with be more like that? Solomon Crawford wasn't going to give anyone a diamond and a happily ever after—that wasn't the Crawford way.

Despite the hour, Solomon picked up his Black-Berry and dialed his business partner and best friend, Carmen De La Croix. She had to hear about his night.

Kandace Davis was tired of waking up in the cramped office of the restaurant she owned with her three best friends, Jade Christian-Goings, Serena

Jacobs, and Alicia Michaels. Glancing at the clock on her computer, she saw that it was nearly six A.M. "Damn," she muttered. "I did it again."

Kandace knew she had to get out of the restaurant before Jade came in, because she wasn't in the mood for another lecture. She picked up her leather bag and was about to stand up . . . too late.

"Kandace, you'd better not be in this office," Jade said as the door swung open.

"I just got here," Kandace lied.

"Umm-hmm, wearing yesterday's clothes?" Jade shook her head as she looked at her friend.

"I picked up these extra hours because you just had a baby. Why are you here?"

"Because James and Maurice are doing the 'daddy thing' today," she said referring to her husband, James and his brother. Kandace smiled remembering how Jade and James brought their son into the world just a few months after Maurice and his wife Kenya had welcomed their daughter into the family. Kandace was happy that despite the unconventional way Jade and James became husband and wife, hooking up in Las Vegas of all places, they seemed happy.

"So," Kandace asked, "since James and Maurice have the kids, what are you and Kenya going to do with yourselves?"

Jade clasped her hands together. "Kenya and I can actually do something other than lactate for a few hours. I've never worked the breakfast shift and . . . wait, this isn't about me. You need a break." Jade perched on the edge of Kandace's desk. "You've been in Charlotte for six months and I know you love

Atlanta. I've leaned on you so much, it's surprising that you haven't broken in half. This place is up and running, you've gotten us publicity all over the place. So, the girls and I decided . . ."

"Now you guys are making decisions about my life?" Kandace asked with a terse laugh.

"Yeah, because you won't," Jade shot back. "We're voting you off the island for two weeks. Go on vacation. You've got to relax. Everybody around here has noticed how tense you are. If you're trying to prove to Devon Harris that you're a capable businesswoman who no longer wants his cheating butt, mission accomplished."

Kandace stifled a yawn. "Since you chicks are making decisions, are y'all paying?"

Jade folded her arms underneath her full breasts. "Now you're just being ridiculous," she said. "I don't care where you go, but I don't want to see you for two weeks!"

Kandace knew Jade meant well and she rose to her feet and gave her friend a kiss on the cheek. "All right," she said. "But you guys are going to miss me. I'm leaving my cell phone, laptop, and everything right here."

"Good," Jade said. "Maybe while you're on vacation you'll have a little fun and get your feet wet."

"Whatever. All of us don't find Mr. Right on vacation like you did," Kandace said as she gathered her things.

Jade smiled and glanced down at her wedding band. "Yes, I was lucky in vacation love. I just hope you get lucky."

"I think I'm going to go somewhere and be pampered for two weeks. Then you all can eat your hearts out while you're here slaving away. And I don't need to get lucky, thank you very much."

Jade waved to her friend, "Kick rocks, chick," she joked.

As Kandace headed to her car, she thought about what Jade had said. Over the last six months, she had poured herself into her work because she had nothing else. Her life was all work because at home, Kandace had a big empty bed waiting for her and she was tired of it. Kandace hadn't been with a man in a year. Her last relationship ended when she decided that she'd wanted something serious. Robert Harrington was happy with the sex, the nice things that Kandace did for him, but he wasn't willing to take their relationship to the next level. After watching Jade get married, Kandace wanted her own marriage but Robert wanted no part of it.

"What's wrong with the way we are?" he'd asked when she'd broached the subject of marriage before she moved to Charlotte.

"I want to know that we're moving toward a future," she'd said. "Is that too much to ask?"

"This is just like a woman. Your girl gets married and then you think it's your turn to walk down the aisle. I don't want to get married."

"All right," Kandace had calmly replied. "If you don't want to get married, then I don't want to have sex with you. I don't want to do your damned laundry and I don't want to waste any more of my time."

Robert had promptly walked out of her penthouse. Kandace had packed for Charlotte and never looked back. If she'd been honest with herself, she would've admitted that Robert wasn't the man she needed to marry. He was selfish, he tried to be controlling, and he lacked passion in bed and in life. Of course Robert hadn't wanted things to change. He liked being in a rut, but Kandace had grown tired of it.

She knew for a while that her relationship had been a dead end, had actually realized it over a year ago. But because she had been comfortable with him, she stuck around until she saw what a real and passionate relationship looked like. Jade and James had inspired her to seek something better and real in her relationships. Maybe pressing Robert about marriage had been her way of ending the relationship.

Yeah, she needed a vacation. But more than anything else, she needed some sleep. Kandace drove to her uptown townhouse and for once, she was happy her bed was empty.

CHAPTER 2

Solomon woke up on Carmen's sofa to the smell of bacon, cheese eggs, and grits. When he'd called her the night before and started telling her about the boring model, Carmen invited him over for breakfast.

"Have you ever stayed with a woman and watched the sun rise?" she'd asked when he walked in the door before dawn.

"Nope. It gives y'all romantic notions," he said before plopping down on her plush sofa and kicking his feet up on the coffee table. "What are you doing up?"

"About to go for a run," she'd replied. "Got to keep the blood flowing. The renovations in Sugar Mountain are complete today and the Weather Channel is calling for three to four feet of snow this weekend."

"Maybe I should go to North Carolina and check on the latest resort," he'd said as he yawned. "And you shouldn't go jogging in Central Park while it's still kind of dark out there."

Carmen, who'd been dressed in an NYU sweatshirt

and a pair of skin-tight yoga pants that accented her ample curves, sauntered over to Solomon and tweaked his nose. "Be careful, you're going to make me think you care," she'd said.

Solomon was already asleep by the time Carmen had pulled her sweatshirt off.

"You sure know how to wake a brother up," Solomon said as he walked to the doorway of Carmen's kitchen. "What's cooking?"

"Since you're going to go to North Carolina, I pulled out some southern breakfast food," she said with a smile plastered on her comely face.

Solomon nodded at her. "That's what's up," he said. "I'm probably going to gain fifteen pounds down there. They say southern cooks are the best."

Carmen cocked her head to the side. "You know we have a state of the art workout facility at Carolina Serenity," she said. "The last thing you want to do is ruin that body."

Solomon flexed his sculpted muscles. "You're right. Can't bag models with flab."

Carmen laughed. "I'll fix your plate and you turn on the news. Maybe there's some good news about the stock market this morning."

"Carmen, you're the greatest," he said. "But I don't think any miracles happened overnight."

As Solomon headed back into the den, she beamed brightly.

Moments later, Carmen walked into the den with Solomon's plate and hers balanced on her arms. "Here you go."

Solomon took both plates and set them on the

table, then he pointed at the television. NY1 was reporting on President Barack Obama and First Lady Michelle Obama. "They broke the mold when that woman was created," he said before digging into his breakfast.

"I'm sure there are other women out there like her," Carmen said.

Solomon shook his head as he shoveled in a mouthful of grits. After swallowing, he said, "Nope. Most women don't have an identity of their own and don't know how to support a man. She could've easily told him, 'Hell no, I'm doing my thing and you run for president later.' Instead, she stood by him without losing herself in his dream."

"I would stand by my man, just like Michelle."

"I bet you would," he said. "You're going to make someone lucky one day." Solomon looked down at his watch. "Damn, I got to get into the office. Richmond wants an update on the resorts." *And I got to get some real food, because, Carmen, you are no southern cook.*

"Don't you want to finish your breakfast first?" she asked.

"Wish I could, but you know Richie Boy. He wants you when he wants you. Thanks for taking me in and for this," he said, pointing at the plate.

"Anytime. I have to keep my business partner happy," she said with a sweet smile.

When Solomon hit the street, he thought about calling a car. The winter air was biting, but he didn't mind walking. He wasn't exactly looking forward to sparring with Richmond this morning and Carmen lived only three blocks from the office. Leaving his car parked in the garage at Carmen's place would be one less headache for him to deal with when he reached headquarters. Richmond made a point of parking in Solomon's spot when he came to the office. It was his way of saying he should've been running the company. Solomon smiled sardonically as he turned down Fifth Avenue. It made sense that Solomon's headquarters would be located in the center of the city. He wasn't one to shy away from the spotlight, and everything he did, including business, was done for maximum attention.

Solomon entered the building, nodding to the security guard as he headed up to the top floor. Looking down at his watch, he realized that he wouldn't have much time to shower and change before his brother arrived.

When he got into his office, Solomon turned on the television and saw his bedmate from the previous night being led away from the W Hotel by police. Solomon turned the volume up.

"Model Kinsley Monroe may be one of *Maxim*'s hottest women, but the staff at the trendy W Hotel saw what else is hot about the sexy model—her temper. Monroe was arrested early this morning after trashing a suite at the boutique hotel. Sources at the Times Square hotel say Monroe entered the hotel after the *Maxim* party with hotel mogul Solomon Crawford. Crawford was not at the scene when the trouble started. Crawford's company is about to open a luxury resort in North Carolina, despite the troubling economic times. The Crawford chain of hotels has remained profitable this quarter, but insiders in the industry wonder if Solomon Crawford is stretching his company too thin by venturing into resorts when people are opting to stay at home rather than spending money for luxury vacations."

Solomon snapped the TV off and plopped down in his desk chair. Getting linked to Miss-Model-Gone-Wild wasn't the way he needed to launch the opening of the resort in the Carolinas. As he rose from his seat to take a shower, his office door burst open.

"Thanks for knocking, Richmond," he said, without looking at his brother.

"This is how you kick off the resort opening, by getting caught up in yet another scandal?" Richmond raged.

"What scandal?" Solomon asked flippantly. "There are no pictures and I didn't destroy a room. Whatever Ms. Monroe did is her sin, not mine."

Richmond shook his head. "When are you going to settle down and stop with the conquests of women? This is why Mom and Dad should've trusted me to run this company."

"Why, because Vivvy has your balls in her purse? Say what you want about what I do after-hours, but you would never have been able to expand this business the way I have. The only bad publicity is no publicity," he snapped.

Richmond shook his head. "My marriage has nothing to do with this. If I were the one sitting in that chair, I would've known better than to undertake a resort expansion in this economy. And the mountains down south? How profitable do you think this is going to be?"

Solomon reached into his desk and pulled out the research he and Carmen had done prior to purchasing the resort. "If you would stop reading Page Six and read the reports I send you, you'd know all of this."

Richmond flipped through the thick folder, not reading the research. "So, this was Carmen's idea? What do you really know about this woman?"

"That she's a hell of a business partner who has vision—something you lack."

Richmond narrowed his eyes at his brother. "Let me guess, you're sleeping with her too."

"Actually, big brother, I don't mix business with pleasure. Again, why are you so worried about my bedroom activities? Must be boring being with the same boring woman every night."

"Because they always seem to make front page news," Richmond said. "I'm stepping back. This resort is yours and Carmen's to ruin. Hopefully when you lose enough money, Mom and Dad will come to their senses and let me run the company and take the Crawford name off the gossip pages."

Solomon shook his head and fought the urge to punch his brother in the face. "You wouldn't know what to do with this company if it was handed to you. Ever think that's why the firstborn was passed over?"

Richmond's hazel eyes sparkled with anger. "You asshole. I can't wait to see you fail." He threw the folder across the room and stormed out of the office.

CHAPTER 3

It was noon before Kandace woke up, and her first impulse was to head into Hometown Delights. Instead, she got out of bed and headed for her laptop. She typed VACATION SPOTS into her Google search bar. An ad popped up for Carolina Serenity and its grand opening this week.

"Wow, the mountains . . . I never thought about going there," she said as she clicked on the colorful image.

Soft sounds of jazz played through her speakers as the Web site loaded. Kandace clicked on the details of the new resort and found plush suites with king-size beds in half of the rooms, marble fireplaces, wall to wall carpet, and garden tubs. There was a full service spa, which offered one complementary service with a week's stay. Ski lessons were available with professional skiers.

"I guess I could try the skiing lessons, but I don't know if I want to risk falling on the slopes," she said as she clicked on the reservation tab. Kandace was excited to get away as she entered her information into the computer. As she clicked the reserve button, her BlackBerry rang.

"Hello?" she said, without looking at the caller ID screen.

"Is it true? You're finally getting a life?" Serena joked.

"Whatever. Let's see how you heifers get along without me for two weeks."

"Just fine," Serena said. "Besides, I'm going back to Atlanta now that Jade has this place and motherhood under control."

"What about you and Antonio?" Kandace asked as she printed her reservation confirmation.

"You know, I don't want to talk about that," she said, but Kandace heard something in her voice that she'd never heard before—emotion. She wanted to ask Serena more questions about her "relationship" with Antonio, but Kandace let it go, knowing her friend would blow her off and keep whatever was wrong close to her chest.

"So," Serena said, "where are you going?"

"Sugar Mountain. Just made my reservation at Carolina Serenity. Doesn't that just sound heavenly?"

Serena laughed. "Yeah, if you like snow. I figured you'd go some place tropical or back to Las Vegas."

"No more Vegas trips for me—and who goes to Vegas to relax? Do you find gambling relaxing?"

"That's true. Well, have fun, be safe, and please leave the laptop at home. I'll call you when you get back," Serena said.

After hanging up with her friend, Kandace read more about the resort. It was a new property in the

Crawford Hotel chain. The Crawford family business was nationally known for its boutique hotels and customer service. Kandace was sure she was going to have the best and most relaxing two weeks. If she had as much fun as she thought she would, she might even stay until Thanksgiving.

After logging off the Internet, Kandace decided to treat herself to some vacation clothes, including a pair of Uggs. After all, she was going to be in the snow and that's just what those boots were for. She dialed Jade's number as she reached for her car keys.

"Yes, Kandace?" Jade said when she picked up.

"What do you say we do some shopping?" Kandace asked. "I've got to get some ski gear."

"Ski gear? You're taking your vacation in the snow? That's funny."

Kandace smacked her lips. "Look, I grew up in Guam. It doesn't snow there. Besides, the resort where I'm staying looks divine. I'll probably just watch the snow fall from the spa."

"Where are you going, Vail?"

"No, Sugar Mountain. It's not that far a drive from here and it's supposed to snow next week. The Web site said that it's cold enough to make snow anyway."

"I don't see the big deal about snow, but I'm glad to hear you excited about a vacation. Wish I could take this shopping trip with you, but James and Maurice are done playing super dads. I knew they wouldn't last all day. Kenya owes me a trip to Starbucks as soon as Jaden starts drinking a bottle."

Kandace laughed. "That's why women are the caregivers," she said. "Well, I'm going to get my

Uggs. Maybe I'll stop by the restaurant to make sure everything is okay."

"Don't you dare. Shop, then go home and get ready for your trip," Jade cautioned. "You're banned from work."

"Fine," Kandace said with a chuckle. When she and Jade said their good-byes, Kandace headed outside to her car and SouthPark Mall. Two hours later, she was all shopped out with enough winter gear for her trip, including a pair of chocolate brown Uggs.

Kandace unpacked her shopping bags, ready to hit the road. Morning couldn't come soon enough.

Sweat poured off Solomon's forehead as he ran on the treadmill. The day had started out horrible and gotten worse. First, his office was bombarded with calls from reporters about his dalliance with the *Maxim* girl. Then Richmond returned with a message from their parents. "Straighten up," he'd said his parents had warned. "Finally, they are tired of seeing our name dragged through the mud because you can't control your libido."

He was sure that Richmond had been leaning on his parents for months, despite the success of the business and the new direction he and Carmen were taking the company in.

"Thought I'd find you here," Danny Jones said as he climbed onto the treadmill beside his best friend. "You've been all over the news today."

"Yeah, I know," Solomon said as he slowed down to a brisk walk. "I have got to stop attracting crazy women."

"Crazy hot," Danny said. "Kinsley Monroe. Damn."

"Please, her looks are all that she has going for her. I guess I was supposed to be impressed by her cover. She didn't know who she was dealing with."

"And speaking of not knowing who you're dealing with, have you considered my random background check offer?"

Solomon stopped his machine just as Danny was getting his started. He smiled at his friend, who was more like a brother to him than his blood relative. Danny was a private detective who had spent five years on the force with the NYPD before he struck out on his own. Truthfully, if it wasn't for Solomon and so many of his indiscretions—tracking down false paternity claims and keeping scorned women quiet—Danny wouldn't have been in business over a year. Now, he was one of the most sought after PIs in the city.

"Yeah, you can get started on that while I'm down south," Solomon said.

"So, who's the Southern babe that's sending you down south? Or are you trying to get out of the media spotlight until the thing with Kinsley blows over?"

"I'm going to check out my new resort and make sure it meets Crawford standards. And who knows, I might run into a few hot snow bunnies."

"Somehow I knew women would come into play at some point. Are you ever going to settle down?"

Solomon ran his hand across his damp chest. "How about no? I'm having too much fun. And there is enough of me to go around."

"What happens when you meet a woman who knocks you off your feet?"

"Will never happen. I've come to this conclusion about New York women: they want my money and I want their bodies. Like the Rolling Stones said, 'You can't always get what you want,' unless your name is Solomon Crawford."

The men broke out laughing. "That's bullshit," Danny said. "Tell me something . . . You and Miss De La Croix, that's strictly business?"

"Yes."

Danny shook his head. "That woman is fine. And her body is sick. An ass you can sit a beer can on, and the way she fills out a top. I just want to lick her."

"What's stopping you?" Solomon asked as he began lifting free weights. "She's a great girl. I'm making her rich, so you don't have to worry about her pulling out a shovel and digging for gold."

"All women aren't bad," Danny said. "You didn't get like this until . . ."

"Don't say it," Solomon cautioned. The last thing Solomon wanted to think about was his broken marriage to Alyessa Cartwright. He'd loved her more than he wanted to admit. They'd met at a concert in Central Park during the summer of 2000, back when he was more carefree and studying filmmaking at NYU. Alyessa had the SoHo look down, from her wide afro to her platform-sandal clad feet. Her cocoa skin and shimmering brown eyes took his breath away. That night, they'd sat down and talked through the concert. By the end of the night, Solomon was falling in love. Over the next three years, he and Alyessa had fallen deeply in love and Solomon was about to premier his feature film at the New York Film Festival.

Beauty's Embrace had been the fictionalized account of his love affair with Alyessa. The crowd loved it, especially the ending, which Solomon had described as yet to be written. As the credits rolled, he'd dropped to one knee in the crowded theatre and asked her to marry him. When she'd said yes, Solomon had been ready to give Alyessa her happily ever after and lots of babies. His family had been slow to warm to Alyessa, however, feeling that she was too common to be a Crawford. But Alyessa had been anything but common. She was of British decent and had come to New York to escape her domineering family. Had it not been for the headlines of her engagement crossing the pond, Alyessa and Solomon would've been able to have the dream wedding that they'd planned.

But on the couple's wedding day, a man showed up at the church claiming to be Alyessa's husband.

"Husband?" Solomon had demanded. "How in the hell can you be married when we just took our vows?"

"Solomon, I'm sorry, I didn't think it would matter," she'd said as she attempted to close the space between them. "I don't love him."

He'd pushed her away from him. "Get the hell away from me, you lying bitch. So, was I just the means to an end for you? You wanted to get away from your terrible family life and I was your sucker? Hey, man," Solomon said, "take your wife and get the fuck out of here."

Right then, Solomon had sworn that he'd never trust another woman again. One of the first cases he'd given Danny had been to track down Alyessa. When Danny reported that Alyessa was living a life of luxury and was happily married to a duke, Solomon resolved that women weren't to be trusted and he'd never allow another one to get close to him. He'd switched his career focus from filmmaking to the family business, which shocked his family and the Los Angeles studio executives who'd been interested in putting his movie on the big screen.

At first, Solomon had allowed Richmond to take the lead at work. He'd watched his brother and learned everything he needed to learn about the industry. Looking back on it, Solomon was pretty sure Richmond hated the fact that he was such an excellent teacher now that he was taking orders from his little brother.

"You all right over there?" Danny asked as he stepped off the treadmill.

Solomon dropped his weights. "Yeah, I'm just thinking about what I need for this trip. I'm probably going to make a regular reservation and see how smoothly things run. My workers don't need to know I'm looking over their shoulder."

"That's a good idea. Maybe while you're gone, I can get Carmen to go out on a date with me," Danny said as he wiped his face with the bottom of his T-shirt.

"Good luck on that," Solomon said. "I don't think I've seen her go out on a date since she's been in New York. She needs a life."

Danny flexed his muscles. "And I'm just the man to give her one."

CHAPTER 4

When Kandace pulled up to the mountain resort, she thought she'd found the route to heaven. Snow quietly fell on the lush green grass, and in the background of the eight-story resort was Sugar Mountain in all of its snow-covered glory. Kandace couldn't tell if it was real snow or manufactured, and it didn't matter one bit. She turned her gaze to the classic building in front of her. It resembled a castle, with frosted windows, two towers, and what looked to be a giant snow globe over the entrance. Inside the globe was the Crawford crest, which adorned all of the hotels in the chain. This one was covered in snow. "Wow," Kandace said as she put her car in park. "I can't wait to see the inside." As she stepped out of the car, she was met by two porters dressed in gold and cream uniforms.

"Hello, ma'am," the taller man said. "We'll take your bags and Tony can check you in curbside if you'd like."

Impressed by their customer service, Kandace

smiled brightly and popped her trunk. "Thank you, Cal," she said, reading his name tag. "I don't have my reservation number handy, so I'll go inside."

"All right, ma'am. Enjoy your stay at Serenity," Cal said as he and Tony lifted her bags from the rear of her rented SUV. Kandace smoothed her ponytail and headed inside. Entering the lobby was another breathtaking experience. The lobby was decorated in lush earth tones. The plush carpet was a cocoa brown color, and in the corner, the fire inside the fireplace roared. Kandace wanted to snuggle up in the lavish love seat across from the fireplace and read a good book.

"Good afternoon, ma'am," the desk clerk said. "Are you checking in?"

"Yes. Kandace Davis."

The clerk pushed her blond hair behind her ears and began typing Kandace's name into the computer. "Yes, Ms. Davis, I have your reservation right here. You're going to be in our Wonderland Suite. It is a beautiful room with a private balcony and a fireplace."

"Great, Brandi," Kandace said, after reading the clerk's tag. "I have to say, this place is beautiful."

"Isn't it? You're going to love your room," Brandi said as she passed Kandace her key card. "It's on the fifth floor and three doors down on your right. Would you like me to schedule your spa appointment for you?"

"That's all right. I'll take care of it later, but thank you."

Cal and Tony approached the desk with Kandace's

bags and Brandi told them where to take them. Kandace had expected the porters to ride on the elevator with her, but they didn't. When she arrived on the fifth floor, she saw the porters leaving her room. *Did they run up the stairs?* she wondered as she entered the room. As soon as she stepped through the doors, any thoughts of the porters were replaced by the lavishness of the Wonderland Suite. Her feet sank into the white carpet as she made her way to the center of the room to take it all in. Her king-size bed looked as if it were three feet off the ground, and it was covered with a gold and cream goose down comforter. A twenty-seven-inch plasma TV hung on the wall. Kandace's gaze fell on the marble fireplace in the middle of the sitting room. It was already stocked with wood, and in front of it was a sofa similar to the one in the lobby. Turning back to the bedroom, she saw the cherrywood wardrobe was open and her luggage was resting on the shelves. Unable to resist the call of the bed any longer, Kandace plopped down on the comforter and closed her eyes. So far, her vacation was wonderful.

When Kandace woke up, the sun was setting. She rushed over to the large bay windows and watched the majesty of the setting sun in the Carolina sky. The blue sky was a royal purple with bursts of orange. She saw a few people skiing down the hill next to the resort. Kandace figured that it was a beginner's hill, but she wasn't going try it.

Stepping into the bathroom, Kandace ran her hand across the marble countertop, then she turned on the jets in the walk-in shower. She stripped her clothes off and stood underneath the warm spray. As the water poured over her, Kandace felt nearly orgasmic. Shaking her head, she realized that this was the closest thing to sex she'd experienced since her breakup with Robert. It wasn't that she hadn't had offers for meaningless sex or promises of one-night stands that would make her knees tremble. But Kandace wasn't a one-night stand, meaningless affair type of woman, and that seemed to be all men in Atlanta wanted. Charlotte hadn't offered many more choices.

She saw how those types of relationships had hurt her mother, beginning with her father. Kandace thought of him as more of a sperm donor since she'd seen him only once in her life. For years, Kandace had more uncles than she could count. They never stayed around long and her mother always cried for weeks until she met someone else. Maybe that's why Kandace had stayed with Robert for as long as she did. He allowed her to mask the heartache she continued to carry over Devon Harris.

Sure, she was able to work with him now, but back in college when she'd found out that he'd cheated on her with the one girl she couldn't stand, Jolisa Covington from Richmond, Virginia, she'd been devastated. Her family had money and Kandace's didn't. The only reason Kandace had been able to attend Spelman had been because her mother had joined the army when Kandace was six years old, after her latest relationship fizzled. Scholarships and financial aid had been Kandace's best friends until she found a plum work-study assignment. When she'd started dating Devon, son of NBA player and Atlanta god, Devon Harris Sr., Kandace was about to start believing in fairy tales. Then she'd met his father, who made it clear to the couple that Kandace wasn't the kind of woman he wanted to see his son with.

Then *she* had been brought into the picture. Devon Sr. had handpicked Jolisa to end Kandace's relationship with his son. Jolisa had been given carte blanche to make herself at home in the Harris household. At first, Devon had denied any attraction to Jolisa. He'd called her an annoying groupie. Then, she'd become just his homegirl. And finally, Kandace had walked in on the aftermath of Jolisa and Devon's lovemaking.

Kandace hadn't needed to hear Devon's excuses. She'd heard them all before when one of her mother's boyfriends had done the same thing to her. She pushed past him, leaving her dreams of moving to Paris with him crumpled like the sheets on his bed. One day, she'd vowed, Devon would be sorry he'd treated her this way. She had no idea that she would end up in business with him. Happily none of her old feelings returned. She was over Devon and no matter how Jade tried to tell her that she should give him another chance, she wasn't going to do it.

Kandace was not going to play the same fool twice.

As she turned the water off, Kandace grabbed one of the plush towels and wrapped herself in its warmth. She headed into the bedroom and sat on the edge of the bed with the hotel information booklet. There was a five-star restaurant on the property with dinner service, and also the option to order from the menu and have it delivered. What caught Kandace's attention was the fact that dinner could be delivered to the hot tub. She snapped the book shut, crossed over to her suitcase, and grabbed her lime green bathing suit. Once she put the bandeau suit on, she placed her dinner order, grabbed the hotel robe and her Uggs, then headed out the door.

Solomon was restless. He'd been at the resort for six hours and no one knew who he was. That was great and so was the service that the staff had been providing. They were living up to the Crawford standard and he was proud. Now that he had taken care of business, he needed something else to occupy his time. *Might as well check out the hot tub,* he thought as he pulled off his sweater and kicked out of his pants. Solomon grabbed his Ed Hardy board shorts from his suitcase and pulled them on, then headed out to the hot tub grotto. He and Carmen thought the grotto would be a good idea for guests who came to the resort without their families. At first, Solomon had thought it was a silly idea since their peak time would be in the winter, but the grotto was heated and could be cooled in the summer.

As he entered the grotto and saw the woman in the lime green bathing suit leaning back with her eyes closed, he knew Carmen had been right all along. He stood at the edge of the tub watching her. She was a chocolate beauty with at least a D cup. He wondered how her strapless suit held her breasts up.

As she stretched her legs, he noticed how shapely they were, and when she lifted her leg to her chest Solomon began to salivate. She had perfect toes, suckable toes. Looking down at his crotch, he saw how much of an effect this woman was having on him. Solomon climbed into the hot tub, happy that water hid his throbbing erection. At the sound of the splashing water, the woman opened her chocolate brown eyes and peered at him.

"My goodness, I didn't realize anyone else was out here," she said as she quickly lowered her leg.

"You don't have to get shy on my account," Solomon said.

The woman sighed and rolled her eyes. This was a reaction that he wasn't used to. Was he being ignored? He glanced at the woman again, and yes, he was being ignored. She'd leaned her head back and had her eyes closed as if he wasn't even there.

Solomon inched closer to her. "Since we're the only ones out here, you could at least introduce yourself to me."

"And why would I do that?" she asked. Her voice had a hint of a southern accent and a load of sensuality.

"Because it's the polite thing to do."

She smacked her lips and moved further from him. "I don't feel like being polite," she replied.

"Now, that's not nice," he said. "I thought women in the south believed in southern hospitality."

The woman stood up, and when Solomon saw how her wet suit clung to her ample ass, he inhaled sharply. "There's something else that southern women are known for," she said. "Not talking to jackasses."

As she strode over to the lounge chair where she'd placed her things, Solomon hopped out of the tub and crossed over to her.

"I guess I deserved that," he said.

The woman wrapped the hotel robe around her damp body and tossed her ponytail back. Solomon could not help but wonder how her hair would look tumbling down her shoulders. It was obvious that she wasn't wearing a weave because she didn't seem to mind getting her hair wet.

"Are you still here?" she snapped. "Listen, I don't know about you, but I'm here to relax, and these last few minutes around you have been anything but relaxing. So, I'm going to leave." Her face, though it was contorted by anger, was beautiful, especially her full lips. Solomon wanted to just reach out and take her bottom lip between his. He inched closer to her, thinking that one kiss would melt this beauty's resistance. But the threatening look she flashed him stopped Solomon from proceeding with his wanton desire.

"What in the hell is wrong with you?" she demanded.

"Let me just say, you're the most stunning woman I've seen in ages, and if I'm coming on too strong, I apologize," he said, his voice oozing with the Crawford charm that had caused countless thongs and panties to drop.

This woman wasn't buying it as she placed her tote bag on her shoulder. "I'd appreciate it if you moved out of my way," she said as she extended her hand and pushed him aside.

"I'd love to know your name," he said as he took her hand in his and held it.

"And people in hell would love ice water. Let me go." She didn't make much of an effort to free her hand from his, and Solomon smiled. After a moment, he let her go as she'd requested. He wasn't used to rejection and there was no way he planned to give up.

She silently moved away from him and didn't even glance back. As he watched his mystery lady walk away, Solomon knew he had to find her. Just as he was about to dry himself, he saw one of the waiters from the restaurant enter the grotto to remove the used dishes. Solomon smiled, knowing the woman's room number would be on her dinner slip. Before the waiter took the plates away, Solomon crossed over to him.

"Excuse me," he said. "How many people ordered dinner in here tonight?"

"I'm sorry?" the waiter asked.

"Were there a lot of people in here? A young lady just left and she forgot something. I want to make sure she gets it," Solomon bluffed.

"I'll be happy to return her lost item," the man replied as he'd been trained to do.

Solomon—the businessman—was happy, but the man trying to find the sexiness that had just walked out of the hot tub needed information. "It's a rather delicate item and I'm not sure she'd want a stranger returning it," he said.

"If you don't know her room number, I'm willing

to guess you're a stranger too," the waiter replied, struggling to keep his voice respectful.

Solomon sighed. It was time to unleash the big gun. "Do you know who I am?" he asked.

"Other than the fact that you're a valued guest at our resort, I'm going to say no."

Solomon chuckled again. This guy was trained very well. "Solomon Crawford. I own the resort."

The waiter raised his eyebrow and studied Solomon's face as if he was trying to recall the image he'd seen in his training manual. Of course Solomon was fully clothed and smiling in the Crawford Hotel Handbook.

"Mr. Crawford, I didn't recognize you," the man said.

"I noticed, and I think you handled things superbly, but I need that woman's room number."

"Of course, sir," he said, then handed him the food charge slip. Solomon looked up at the waiter.

"What's your name?"

"Matt, sir."

"All right, Matt, I'll ask one more thing of you. No one needs to know I'm here. So, if you can keep your mouth shut, expect a bonus at the end of my stay," Solomon said. "A big bonus."

Matt smiled brightly. "Yes, sir."

"Thanks. And you're doing a great job. Keep it up," Solomon complimented as he read the food slip. Kandace Davis was staying in the Wonderland Suite, and from the looks of her dinner order she was alone. *Ripe for the picking,* he thought as he left the grotto.

* * *

Kandace stormed into her room and thought about calling the front desk to complain about that jackass. That jackass with the sexy emerald eyes, hard body that seemed to be designed for pleasure, and hands that probably knew how to find every erogenous zone on any woman's body. When he held her hand, she felt a sizzle that spread from the tips of her fingers to the center of her womanly core. And there she was standing in a bathing suit that she was sure barely covered her ample assets. Inadvertently, Kandace ran her hand across her bottom. Yep, her suit was showing off her cheeks. No wonder he walked over to her and tried to run that weak game. She rolled her eyes. No matter how cute he was, she would not succumb to his smooth voice and killer body. At least she didn't give him her name. Now, she wished she'd brought her phone so that she could tell Alicia and Serena about the jerk. They knew how to handle men like that. Serena probably would've pushed him into the hot tub and Alicia would've made him feel worthless with her biting sarcasm.

Well, if I see him again, I'm just going to ignore the horn dog, she thought as she peeled off her wet suit and headed for the shower.

Still, as she stood in the shower, her mind wandered back to his haunting eyes, and despite herself, when she felt the lick of the water against her neck, she thought of his lips and tongue being there. Kandace quickly shut off the water.

"Get it together," she admonished. "He's just trying to score, and you were the only one in the hot tub."

Just as Kandace finished drying off and rubbing lotion on her skin, there was a knock at the door.

"Yes," she said as she wrapped herself in the robe and looked through the peephole.

"Delivery for Kandace Davis," the hotel messenger said. Kandace opened the door and accepted the large white box.

"Wait, let me get you a tip," she said.

"No need, ma'am. It's been taken care of," the delivery man said. "Have a good evening."

Kandace looked at the box, wondering who sent her a gift. She was sure it wasn't any of her friends, but no one else knew she was staying there. She looked down at the ivory box and saw that it had come from the resort's gift shop. There was no card on the outside of the box, so Kandace opened it. Inside, she found a red fur bikini. Kandace lifted the barely-there garment from the box and a card fell to the floor. She dropped the box on the bed and picked up the card.

I want to see you in this and then I want to see it on the floor. It was signed, *The Jackass.*

"He has some damned nerve," she muttered as she grabbed the box and then stuffed the bikini back inside. Kandace grabbed a pair of lounge pants and a tank top, then she stuffed her feet inside her Uggs and headed downstairs to the gift shop. The message on the card echoed in her head. *I want to see you in this and then I want to see it on the floor.*

What in the world made him think she'd wear

that bikini, and more importantly, what in the hell gave him the balls to think she'd take it off for him? Kandace stormed inside the shop and walked up to the counter.

"Yes, ma'am, how may I help you?" the clerk asked with a cheery smile on her face.

"I received this," Kandace said as she dropped the box on the counter. "Could you return it to the sender?"

The clerk lifted the outfit and inspected it. "Oh, it hasn't been worn."

"And that is a pity," a velvet smooth voice said from behind her. "You would've made that suit look good."

Kandace whirled around and faced him. "Just who in the hell do you think you are?" she asked. "And how did you find my room?"

"I'm a man who gets just what I want and right now, I want you," he said boldly.

Kandace rolled her eyes and attempted to walk past him, but he pulled her against his hard torso and her breath caught in her chest as he brought his lips to hers. Kandace's body tingled from her scalp to the tip of her toes as he leaned closer and took her mouth with a searing passion that she thought was reserved for Hollywood movies and romance novels. For a brief moment, Kandace lost herself in the kiss, awakened by his tongue dancing against hers. But her common sense took over and she pulled back from him and slapped him with all her might.

"Stay away from me!" she snapped. "Don't send me any gifts and don't you ever touch me again."

He stepped back and studied her body, reading the flashes of anger in her eyes, and the pout of her lips. "Are you sure that's what you want?" he asked. "Because your body is saying something else."

"It's saying get the hell away from me," she said as she pushed him, then stormed out of the shop. Much to her dismay, he followed her.

"Hey, Kandace, wait," he called out.

She turned around and glared at him. "What you need to do is stop talking to me as if you know me," she said.

"You don't know who I am, do you?"

"And I don't give a damn."

"You will. What do you say we have dinner tomorrow night? In the grotto."

Kandace shook her head in disbelief. "Are you mental? I wouldn't have dinner with you if you were the last person on earth and had the final piece of meat in the world." Kandace stomped off and headed for the elevator.

Solomon fought the urge to follow Kandace onto the elevator. The things he could've done and the buttons he could've pushed with her in that enclosed space. But Solomon knew he had to bide his time carefully. Smiling, he was happy that she wasn't aware of his reputation or his true identity. Now he'd try something different with a woman—being himself.

CHAPTER 5

Kandace slammed into her room and flung herself across the bed. The kiss played in her mind as she rolled over on her back. His lips were soft, his technique was skillful, and had he not been the most arrogant and pompous jerk she'd ever met, that kiss would've affected her core.

Who was she trying to fool? That kiss stirred a dormant part of her that she wanted him to explore, slowly and thoroughly. *Stop it,* she thought as she picked up the hotel phone and dialed Serena's number. She knew this call was going to cost her a pretty penny, but she needed to tell someone about this jerk.

"Hello?" Serena said. Kandace could tell she didn't recognize the number on her caller ID.

"Serena, it's me."

"You couldn't go one day without calling? I'm not telling you anything about the restaurant," she said.

"That's not why I'm calling. I need your brand of advice," Kandace said.

"My advice?" Serena asked. "Are you sure, because I'm not going to be sugary sweet like Jade and Alicia."

"That's why I didn't call them. We need to make this quick. I'm on the hotel's phone." Kandace launched into her story about the mystery man, their encounter at the grotto, his gift, and the kiss.

"He kissed you? Just like that, no provocation or anything?"

"That's what I just said. Now, what should I do?"

"I would cuss him out and . . . No," Serena said. "You're on vacation and you could use a bit of sex in your life. What's a vacation fling going to hurt?"

"Did you not hear anything I said about this man? He's arrogant, self-righteous, and I don't care how good he looks. Besides, I don't even know his name."

"How did he find out yours and your room number?"

"Haven't a clue. Maybe he paid off one of the hotel staffers. I'm tempted to complain to management about this jackass. I came here to relax, not to get stalked."

"Tell him in no uncertain terms, or better yet, find out who he is and turn the tables on him. If he's a high roller who can pay people for information, he must be somebody important."

"That sounds like a lot of work and I'm not feeling it. Besides, I left my computer at home."

"Then just wait and see what he sends you next," Serena said. "Look, I have to go. Someone's at my door."

"Antonio?"

Serena hung up without responding. Kandace

would've called her back, but she decided to watch a movie instead. As she flipped though the channels, her mind wandered back to that man—the touch of his lips and the feel of his body pressed against hers.

Get a grip! What has lust ever gotten anybody? Kandace stopped flipping the channels when she looked up and saw *him* on the screen. He was dressed in a tuxedo, looking the epitome of class and culture. He was accompanied by an A-list actress whose movie had just premiered, but this shot was an older one.

"It looks as if Solomon Crawford has struck again," the announcer said. "Despite rumors that his relationship with Heather Williams, star of *Just That Kind of Girl,* was getting serious, Crawford wasn't on the red carpet last night and Williams declined to answer any questions about the hotel mogul."

Kandace shook her head as everything started to come together. No wonder he found out her name and which room she was staying in. He owned the place.

You don't know who I am, do you? Now that statement made even more sense. He was used to models, actresses, and singers throwing themselves at him. Kandace wasn't going to fall for it. She grabbed the remote and switched the channel, at the same time stating firmly, *I am not going to be another one of Crawford's conquests.*

Solomon headed in to his room and stretched out on his bed. More than anything he wanted

Kandace and that killer body lying next to him. He wanted to peel her clothes from her body and kiss every tantalizing inch of skin he'd exposed. Of course, he would pay close attention to her nipples, licking and sucking them until she begged for more. Just thinking about it made him hard. Maybe he needed a cold shower until he convinced her that she needed to take a ride on him. As Solomon stripped out of his clothes, his cell phone rang.

"Crawford," he growled.

"What's wrong with you?" Carmen asked. "Is everything all right down there?"

"Yeah, it's fine. And let me tell you, the grotto was a great idea. Our guests are looking lovely in it," he said.

"Sounds like you've already met someone," Carmen said quietly. "That's fast, even for you."

"Something like that. I will say this, being here is heavenly. No one knows who I am. That's going to make it even better with Kandace."

"Kandace? What is she, twelve?"

"Definitely not. So, have you heard from Danny?"

"Why do you ask that? He's your friend."

Solomon laughed; his friend had apparently chickened out. "He wants to take you out. He thought there was something going on with us, so I gave him the green light. He's a good guy and you know, Carmen, you work too hard."

She sighed into the phone. "I'd rather work hard until I get what I want."

"Let me guess. You want the fairy tale and the house with the white picket fence. That's cool, but you don't have to limit yourself while you're holding out for Mr. Right."

"I already met Mr. Right. He's just not ready to commit yet," she admitted.

"If he doesn't want you now, why should you wait for him?"

"He's worth it," Carmen said.

"Does he know how special you are? Because if he doesn't, he's not worth a damn."

"He'll know soon enough that he can't live without me and we'll be together. But enough about me. What's up with your latest piece?" Carmen asked.

"Nothing yet. She's different, not the typical woman. She doesn't seem that impressed with me, but that's going to change soon enough," Solomon said confidently.

"Hmm," Carmen said. "Be careful. I heard southern women can get pretty clingy."

"I'm not worried about that. But if you go out with Danny, make him take you to the Blue Water Grill."

"You don't have a problem with your friend going out with me?" she asked. "What if I find him to be a jerk?"

"You guys are adults and anything that happens between the two of you is between you two," Solomon said.

"All right. Well, if he calls, I might go out with him. By the way, Richmond called me. He's very upset about your name being linked to Heather Williams and her recent depression."

"Tell him that he has other things to worry about

and this latest news story isn't going to do anything but put more bodies in our hotels."

"I tried to tell him that, but he's not happy at all," Carmen said.

"If he calls you again, tell him to take it up with me when I return," he said. "Don't let me hold you up. We'll talk later."

"All right," she said. Solomon hung up the phone and decided to head back to the grotto in case Kandace was there to relax. If he saw her again tonight, he'd get more than a kiss.

Carmen knew something was different. Something was going on with Solomon and this woman, Kandace. First of all, Solomon didn't work for any woman and he seemed to be willing to chase after her. *Why can't he chase after me? How can he not see that I'm the woman for him? He needs someone who can match him on every level, not some country bumpkin.*

Carmen called the front desk manager at the hotel. "Good evening, Frances," she said. "This is Carmen De La Croix from Crawford Hotels."

"Yes, ma'am, is there a problem?"

"No, I just need to check our guest registry. Please e-mail it to me. I hear that things are going really well in North Carolina."

"Yes, they are. We're at ninety percent occupancy and all of our themed suites have been rented."

"That's good. I'm really proud of the hard work that the staff has put in down there," Carmen said.

"Thank you, ma'am," Frances said. "You should have the guest registry in your in-box by now."

"All right, Frances. Thank you for your help." Carmen hung up the phone and checked her e-mail. She scanned the list for Kandace's name and Solomon's. She smiled when she found his alias, Steven Carter. *I should've known he was using this name. I guess he didn't want the staff to know he's staying there. Kandace Davis . . . who is this woman who can afford the Wonderland Suite for two weeks?*

Just as Carmen was about to type her name into Google, her cell phone rang. "What?" she snapped.

"Is this Carmen?" a smooth male voice, which wasn't Solomon's, asked.

"Who is this?"

"This is Danny Jones, Solomon's friend."

Carmen rolled her eyes. "Oh, hi. Solomon told me that you might call. I wish I could talk, but I'm in the middle of something."

"Then let's meet for lunch," he said.

"I'll call you back," she said, then snapped her phone shut. There was no way she would go out with Danny. He wasn't Solomon and she wasn't going to settle for second best.

If Kandace had been honest with herself, she would've admitted that the only reason she'd headed out to the grotto again had been because she wanted to see if Solomon was there. Now that she knew who he was, she knew how to handle him. But the truth of the matter was, she was curious about him and wanted to see what the fuss was all about. Granted, she didn't follow celebrity news closely, but she'd heard a few stories about Solomon Crawford and his exploits with some of Hollywood's finest. That kind of news wasn't the sort of thing Kandace and her friends paid attention to. His kiss, though, had gotten her attention, and the wanton part of her wanted more. She knew Solomon Crawford wasn't going to be satisfied with just a kiss. And if she was honest with herself, she'd be able to admit she wasn't either.

Kandace pulled on her freshly laundered bathing suit, grabbed her Uggs and robe, then headed out to the grotto. As soon as she made it to the entrance of the hot tub, Kandace thought about turning around. What was she doing? It was starting to snow, a sign that she should be sitting in front of her fireplace reading rather than trying to accidentally on purpose run into Solomon. Kandace dropped her hand from the doorknob and turned to head back inside.

"You're not leaving already, are you?" Solomon asked. She hadn't noticed that he'd crept up behind her.

"If I wasn't, I am now, Solomon," Kandace said.

"Oh, so you do know who I am," he said.

She shook her head. "Don't flatter yourself. It just so happens that your mug was all over the television this afternoon. Once I found out who you were, it put your attitude into perspective."

"And what perspective do you have now?"

"Obviously, you're bored and you think I'm

an airhead actress or model you can impress with your money."

"Something tells me you got your own money. And besides, I'm not interested in your bank book."

Kandace folded her arms across her chest. "And I'm not interested in you," she said as she opened the door to the grotto. Solomon walked in behind her, keeping his eyes on her shapely figure. When Kandace stopped, he ran smack into her backside. Solomon snaked his hands down her sides and cupped her bottom. Kandace gasped as he pulled her against his thick erection. Then he teased her neck with his lips. "You know you want me," he breathed, causing goose bumps to form on Kandace's arms.

"Get your hands off me," she said breathlessly, but she didn't move. She couldn't move because her feet had taken root and her body wanted his touch more than she was willing to admit. Solomon twirled Kandace around and forced her to face him. Though her face was contorted with anger, Solomon knew it was a mask. Masking her desire and passion. Anyone as angry as she was had to be passionate, and he was damned sure going to find out.

He brought his face level with hers. His lips were dangerously close to hers and he could feel her trembling. But instead of a kiss, Solomon got a swift knee to his midsection.

Doubling over in pain, he dropped to one knee. "The next time I tell you to take your hands off me, listen," Kandace hissed. "That pretty boy look may work on Heather Williams, but I'm not her."

Solomon looked up at her, his lips curled into a

smile as he wrapped his hand around her leg. "Smooth as silk and feisty. I like you, and you can deny it all you want, but you wanted me to kiss you."

Kandace tried to step back, but Solomon tightened his grip. "I'm still touching you," he teased.

"Are you dense?" she asked.

"No," he said as he released her leg. "I'm focused, and right now, I'm focused on you. Those legs are amazing."

"Solomon," she said, "I don't want you."

"But I want you, and nothing else is going to make me happier than having those legs wrapped around me."

"Then prepare to be sad."

He rose to his feet and stood inches away from her. "I don't think so," he replied. "You owe me, now."

"I don't owe you a damned thing."

He folded his arms across his chest. "Really? You assaulted me and I could easily press charges."

"Then do it."

"I'd rather do this," he said, then quickly pulled her against him and captured her lips with a passionate fury she couldn't escape.

Kandace melted against him and allowed him to press his body into hers. His arousal was evident as he deepened the kiss and his hands roamed up and down her body. She shivered as his kiss headed down her neck and across her collarbone. Then as quickly as the kiss began, Solomon ended it. "Now, lie to me and tell me you didn't like that."

She didn't answer him, couldn't because her tongue was thick and her mouth felt like it had been packed in cotton. Kandace shook her head and walked toward the edge of the hot tub. Solomon followed her and held his hand out to her. "What do you say we get out of here and go back to my suite?"

She took his hand and turned sideways to the hot tub. "Why don't you take a dip?" Kandace said, then pushed him into the hot tub. She sauntered out of the grotto, feeling as if she'd channeled her inner Serena. Still, she was bothered by how turned on she was by Solomon and his hot kisses.

He will not wear me down, she thought as she entered the lobby. Though in the back of her mind, she wondered what it would feel like to wrap her legs around him in the throes of passion.

Solomon kicked back in the hot tub and closed his eyes, Kandace's image appearing in his mind. She had definitely piqued his interest and he wasn't giving up on her. But he was going to have to change his game plan, he realized. Kandace didn't seem as if she was easily impressed. That made him wonder, who was she? He knew she was single, and from the cost of her room, she obviously had her own wealth. Leaping out of the tub, he dried off and headed to his room. He was going to find out what her story was, then shift his seduction into high gear.

When Solomon returned to his room, he opened his laptop and typed her name into the Google search box. He was surprised to see that Kandace was a businesswoman in her own right. She was co-owner of a successful restaurant in Charlotte with three other women, including the sister-in-law of Carolina Panthers' wide receiver Maurice Goings. Things were starting to click for him now. This woman was probably around men like him all the time and she didn't want or need a thing from them. Impressing her with money and gifts wasn't going to work. But he had something else she wanted, and that kiss in the grotto proved it.

CHAPTER 6

The next morning, Kandace awoke drenched in sweat. Her sleep had been plagued with heated dreams of Solomon Crawford's naked body. In her dream, he'd kissed every inch of her body, taking her to the brink of passion and beyond. Even as she sat up in the bed, her body throbbed with the phantom aftershocks of their lovemaking. Shaking her head, she grabbed the phone and dialed the front desk.

"Yes, Ms. Davis," the desk clerk said.

"I'd like to book my spa treatment," Kandace said.

"May I place you on hold while I check what times are available?"

"Sure," Kandace said as she kicked out of the blanket. While she waited for the clerk to return to the phone, her mind wandered back to Solomon. Why was she allowing him to get under her skin? He was just trying to make her another conquest and she was no one's belt notch. *He could be yours. Why not love him and then leave him alone? He'd never see it coming.*

"Ms. Davis, we have two times open. There's a nine A.M. spot and a noon spot."

"I'll take the noon appointment."

"Great. Is there anything else I can assist you with?"

"Umm, could you transfer me to the restaurant? I'd like to make a breakfast order."

"Yes, ma'am. Enjoy your day," the clerk said before transferring the call.

After ordering breakfast, Kandace looked out the bay window to check the weather. She smiled as she saw the gentle snowfall, then realized that she hadn't ventured out in to the snow since she arrived. Maybe before her spa appointment she would take a short walk in the snow. After all, she'd traveled to the mountains because she wanted to see snow and feel the coolness of it on her face like people in the Christmas movies. She stepped back from the window and sat on the sofa across from the fireplace. The snow could wait, she thought as she walked over to the fireplace and placed two logs inside, on top of the kindling already laid. As she struck a match to light the fire, there was a knock at the door.

"Wow," she said as she walked to the door. "That was quick."

Looking out the peephole, she saw a man standing there holding a large bouquet of roses. Placing the chain on the door, she opened it just a crack. "Yes?"

"Kandace Davis?" the man asked. "I have a delivery for you."

"Just a second," she said. Kandace dashed into

the bedroom and grabbed her robe, then opened the door. "Who are these from?"

"There's a card," he said.

"Let me get you a tip."

The man lifted his hand. "It's been taken care of. Have a wonderful day," he said.

Kandace took the spectacular bouquet of red, white, and pink roses from his hands and sniffed them before reaching for the card.

It's a shame that I was assaulted, yet you get the flowers. Why don't we start over? Hi, I'm Solomon, and I'd love to have you for dinner.

Though she read the double meaning in his card, Kandace couldn't help but smile. His intentions were clear. He wanted her in his bed for dinner, but it was not going to happen. She set the roses on the coffee table in the sitting room, admiring their beauty as she grabbed her book. *All I have to do is ignore him,* she thought as she settled on the sofa.

Solomon had sent roses to women before, but he never found himself wondering what any of them thought about the arrangements. He wished he knew what Kandace's thoughts had been when she got the flowers and read the card. He wanted her for dinner in every way; first he'd feed her, then he'd feed off her. She had to be sweet, from those luscious lips to the tips of her toes, and he intended to find out. It was slowly becoming an obsession with him to get inside her. As fiery as she'd been last night, he knew she would be wild in bed. She would probably make him call her name over and over again, after he'd made her scream his.

Knowing that Kandace probably wouldn't be sending him a thank you note, he decided to find out what she planned to do with her day. He headed down the back stairway, which was marked "employees only," and headed for the front desk manager's office. He figured he owned the place, he might as well use that to his advantage.

Carmen walked into her Manhattan office with a venti cup of Starbucks in her hand and a pair of Jackie O–style sunglasses covering her puffy eyes. She'd spent the night scouring the Internet trying to find every piece of information that she could about Kandace Davis. What she'd found out about the woman scared her because Kandace wasn't the typical woman Solomon sexed and left. She had more substance than the models and actresses that he normally bedded just to have something to talk about later. Kandace was everything that Carmen presented herself as, a businesswoman and a smart one at that. Though Kandace was running a successful restaurant in Charlotte with three business partners, she had a public relations business as well, based in Atlanta. Carmen hated her. She knew Kandace was going to be a problem. Carmen wasn't going to have anyone stand between her and the man she loved. She dropped down in her seat and snatched her sunglasses off. How could Solomon not realize that she was everything he ever needed?

She was beautiful, smart, and all she wanted was to make him happy. How blind was he? She knew that he wanted a woman who wasn't blinded by the Crawford fortune, and she wasn't.

Carmen booted up the computer and pulled up the Crawford Hotel's Web site. She clicked on Solomon's picture and gazed at his smiling face. Closing her eyes, she imagined Solomon standing at the altar dressed in an Italian tuxedo as she marched toward him dressed in an ivory Vera Wang gown. Her hair would be curled in ringlets because Solomon had once told her that style looked good on her. She wouldn't cry on the outside because her makeup would be too flawless to mess up with tears. And tears were a sign of weakness anyway.

Solomon would take her hand and kiss it as he stared into her eyes. It would be a storybook wedding and she'd finally be the woman she knew she could be. A somebody with a husband everybody wanted.

"Carmen?"

She looked up from the computer and saw Richmond standing there. "What is it?" she asked.

"I guess congratulations are in order," he said reluctantly.

"Yes, and you thought opening a new resort was a bad move," Carmen said as she leaned back in her seat.

"I guess people still want to go to the mountains. The holidays are already booked at the resort."

"Then why are you here?"

"I wanted to talk to you about your alliance with

my brother. Solomon couldn't do half of what he does without you, but you're never going to advance in the company if you continue to be his fall girl."

Carmen narrowed her eyes into tiny slits. "I'm no one's fall girl. Solomon has promised me . . ."

"Solomon doesn't give a damn about you and he's only keeping you around because you make him look good. Where is he now? Not here, not working."

"Get out of my office, Richmond. You're just jealous of him. You'll never be half the man Solomon is. Solomon has moved this company to the top of the hospitality industry and you just hate that your little brother is showing you up. What do expect from me? Solomon gave me a chance that I know you would've never given me."

Richmond shook his head. "You're a bigger fool than I thought. I'm sure there are many things Solomon gives you that I never would. I have morals. I don't know what's going on with the two of you, but when it comes to light, I hope there is still a business for me to run."

Stalking over to Richmond as he walked out of her office, Carmen slammed the door shut behind him. Kicking the door with her Jimmy Choo clad foot, she silently wished Richmond would be the victim of a violent robbery. Then she and Solomon would have the whole company to themselves. If that idiot thought she would betray her man, he was sorely mistaken. She would never do anything to hurt Solomon, and if Richmond knew what was good for him, he'd stay out of her way.

* * *

"Mr. Crawford, I had no idea you were staying here with us." The front desk manager, Frances Honeycutt, stood when she saw Solomon walk into her office.

He smiled at her as he extended his hand to shake hers. "I like to keep a low profile to get a true feel of the property. I have to say, you and your staff have been excellent. All of our guests are happy and will surely come back for another visit."

"Well, we, uh, are living up to the Crawford standard."

"Frances," Solomon said as he took a seat across from her desk, "are you nervous?"

She ran her hand down her throat. "It's just been my experience that when the property owners show up, there's a problem."

Solomon smiled. "Frances, you have nothing to worry about. But there is a slight problem."

Frances inhaled sharply. "What can I do, Mr. Crawford?"

"The guest in the Wonderland Suite, I don't think she's very happy."

Frances shook her head. "We haven't had any complaints, but I will be more than . . ."

Solomon held up his hand, cutting Frances off. "It's not that sort of problem. I met her and it seems as if she's suffering from being overworked. I'm just trying to make sure she gets taken care of in a very special way."

Frances's face relaxed and the tension eased from

her shoulders as she typed information into the computer. "Kandace Davis? I guess she's working on relieving stress. She has a noon spa appointment."

"Really?" Solomon said. "That's good to know. Frances, I want you to keep me informed of her movements. I'm going to do everything in my power to make sure she doesn't forget this trip."

"Mr. Crawford, I'm a little uncomfortable with this. Our guests expect privacy in a hotel."

"And I will respect Miss Davis's privacy. Keep in mind, I own this place and I'm not just someone off the street looking to harm a guest. Kandace and I have a history." *No matter how recent it is,* he added silently.

Frances nodded. "I understand, sir."

"And just so you know, there's nothing I'd do at this resort to cause a scandal. We have too much money to make."

"All right, Mr. Crawford."

Solomon pulled out his wallet, withdrew five crisp one hundred dollar bills, and handed them to Frances. "This is for your trouble."

She accepted the money and smiled. "Thank you," she said. Solomon looked down at his watch as he headed out the door. It was a little after ten. He had plenty of time to go to the spa and prepare his special surprise for Kandace.

Kandace woke up from her impromptu nap just as the flames in the fireplace flickered out. The book she'd been reading had long fallen to the floor and she was sure that she'd lost her place in the Phillip Margolin novel. Kandace loved reading suspense novels and would've kept reading had she not become transfixed by the snowfall outside and the warmth from the fire. She couldn't remember the last time she'd been so relaxed—not with all the drama that had surrounded getting the restaurant off the ground and Jade going into labor at the ribbon-cutting ceremony.

Kandace knew she needed the rest and relaxation, but she was never one to sit still for long. Looking at the clock on the television, she saw she had time to take a walk in the snow before her spa treatment. She hoped that she would not run into Solomon because she just didn't know how to take him.

CHAPTER 7

Kandace pulled her coat tighter as she walked near the beginner's ski hill. The snow was beautiful, but it was freezing cold outside, despite the fact that she was dressed in three layers of clothes. She dashed into the resort café to warm herself with a latte before her spa treatment. After placing her order and receiving her cup of gourmet coffee, Kandace searched for a table. When she found one, she was thankful to rest her feet. That is until she saw who was seated at the table next to hers.

"Kandace," Solomon said. "Did you like the flowers?"

"Actually, I did," she said as she took her seat. Solomon moved over to her table as if he'd been invited. She shook her head and sucked her teeth.

"Did I invite you to sit with me?" she asked.

"Not verbally, but I could see it in your eyes," he said.

Kandace took a sip of her latte, then looked at him. He was dressed in a pair of chocolate brown corduroy pants and a cream turtleneck that hugged his chest like a second skin. The heat she was feeling between her thighs had nothing to do with the beverage she was sipping as her gaze fell to his big hands. Flashes of her erotic dream jumped to the forefront of her mind. "You need to get your eyes checked," Kandace said as she took another sip of her latte.

"I have perfect twenty-twenty vision. What are you sipping on?"

"You own the place. Shouldn't you know the menu?"

Solomon smiled, revealing a dimple in his left cheek. She turned her head away and drained the rest of her drink. "I have to go," she said.

"You don't have to," he said. "You never gave me an answer either."

"An answer to what?" Kandace asked as she glanced at her watch.

"Can I have you for dinner?"

Kandace rolled her eyes and walked out of the café. She was tempted to answer his question with a yes, thinking about the arrogance of that man and the sheer sexiness of him. The angel on her right shoulder was whispering say no and walk away, but the voice coming from her left shoulder was much louder. "Let him have you for dinner. You only live once," Kandace heard the little devil on her shoulder cry out. Sighing, she wasn't sure how to answer Solomon's intriguing question.

* * *

Solomon kicked back at the table and watched Kandace sashay out the door. Her hips moved like palm trees swaying in a tropical breeze and he got hard just watching her walk. Since he knew she was going to the spa, he didn't make a sudden move to follow her. He was going to wait until she had no choice but to acknowledge the fire between them. When she was naked on the massage table, he'd make his move. Just as he was about to leave the café, his cell phone rang. He glanced down at the caller ID and saw that it was Carmen.

"What's going on, Carmen?" he asked.

"Guess who was singing your praises this morning?" she said happily.

"I'm kind of in a rush right now. I don't have time for guessing games," he replied as he walked out the door.

"Richmond came in my office this morning saying that Carolina Serenity is doing great," she said. "And that he was wrong to think opening our resort was a mistake."

"That's Captain Obvious for you. Look, I have to go." Solomon hung up the phone and headed for the spa. When he walked into the waiting area, the receptionist recognized him from his earlier visit.

"Mr. Crawford, hello," she said with a flirtatious lilt to her voice.

"Hi. Show me to the massage rooms again," he said, then offered her a wink.

"Down the hall and to the left. Only one is occupied right now," she said.

He nodded and headed to the room where he

knew Kandace was. He slowly opened the door and signaled to the masseuse to stay silent. Solomon stepped in and closed the door. On the table, he saw Kandace lying on her stomach with a towel covering her lower back. While some of her more interesting parts were hidden, what he saw lit a fire in his loins. Her legs were strong, thighs thick like a real woman and not someone who spent her life dieting for a movie role or a cover shot. Her skin looked like the finest milk chocolate and had him nearly drooling. Solomon handed the masseuse a hundred dollar bill and pointed to the door. The man took the money, nodded, and headed out the door. Solomon quickly took his place, massaging Kandace's shoulders and back with long deep strokes.

Kandace moaned in delight as his hands moved down her back. "That feels so good," she said.

Solomon leaned down and whispered in her ear, "I can make you feel even better."

Kandace opened her eyes and held her head up. "What in the hell are you doing here?" she demanded. Though she wanted to move, she wasn't dressed for running in her bandeau bra and barely there panties. Solomon looked down at her, seeing her bra with its clasp at her lower back for the first time, and shook his head.

"And here I thought you were naked," he said with a grin.

Kandace grabbed the towel and wrapped it around her waist as she slid off the table. "You're a stalker and this has to stop," she said. Solomon watched her lips move, but he couldn't process what she was saying. He'd known she was beautiful, but seeing her nearly naked, he couldn't hear past the crackling of desire in his heart and body.

"I'm not a stalker, but you're making a brother have to come on strong. You could end all of this if you'd simply cooperate," Solomon said.

"That's not what this is. You're just not used to someone refusing the great Solomon Crawford. Once again, I'm going to tell you no." Kandace followed Solomon's gaze to her breasts. "Pig!" she exclaimed as she covered her chest with her arms.

"Did you think I wouldn't look?" he asked as he shrugged his shoulders. Then he flashed her a wily smile. "You see them everyday. You know your breasts are amazing."

Kandace shook her head and reached for her robe. "Every time I start thinking you could be a decent guy, you go out of your way to remind me that I should stay far, far away from you."

Solomon rocked back on his heels. "What do you want, Kandace? What can or should I do to get you to admit you want me?"

"Try being sincere for once. I know you want to sleep with me, but give me a reason to sleep with you," she said bluntly.

He raised his right eyebrow. "I can give you several reasons. Multiple orgasms would be the first of many reasons."

Kandace sucked her bottom lip in and shook her head. "Any vibrator can give a woman multiple orgasms."

"But I'm far from a vibrator."

"Yeah," Kandace said. "You don't have an off switch."

Solomon poked out his lip like a sad little boy. "That was cold."

"And so was interrupting my massage. I came here to relax and because of you, I haven't gotten much of that done," she said, then poked him in his chest.

"Well, you've only been here for a day and the first few days of a vacation are never relaxing," he said. "And you have to admit, you like sparring with me."

Kandace shot him a cold look. "You're impossible," she said. "Let me guess. When you were a little boy Mommy and Daddy yielded to your every whim." Kandace gave him a slow once over. "Judging by your height, you played basketball and were the star of the team and that helped you get your way even more."

Solomon shook his head. "You don't know me, Kandace. I'd love for you to get to know me, but you can't seem to let yourself go enough to enjoy whatever happens."

He wrapped his arms around her waist and pulled her against him. "Go with the flow, baby."

Kandace stomped on his foot, though her blow made with a bare foot had little physical impact, and Solomon released her. "If you go out to dinner with me and have a horrible time, I'll take your no for an answer."

"And if I tell you no now?" she questioned. "What are you going to do then?"

"You know I own this place, right? So, unless

you plan on checking out, I'm going to show up everywhere you go until you say yes."

"And you don't think that's stalking?" she asked as she rolled her eyes.

He shook his head. "I call it being persistent. You can end this whenever you want. Agree to have dinner with me," Solomon said.

"Get out of here," Kandace said. "And maybe I'll consider it."

"I tell you what," he said as he backed away from her. "Since you say I ruined your spa treatment, have a deluxe one on me. That way you can't say you were too stressed out to have dinner with me."

"I said I'd consider having dinner with you, I didn't agree to anything," Kandace informed him.

Solomon opened the door. "But you will," he said, then winked at her before sending the masseuse back inside.

Kandace tried to think of something other than Solomon's hands as her real massage resumed. But she couldn't. His strokes felt so good and her body had been on fire as he touched her. She'd tingled from the roots of her hair to her toenails. Dinner with him would be dangerous, because she knew what his kisses did to her, and coupled with his touch, she was going to be in serious trouble.

"Miss Davis," the masseuse said, "we're done. If you put on your robe, I can take you to your facial."

"Thank you," she said as she rose from the table

and put on her robe. Kandace followed the man to another room and took a seat. Part of her wondered if Solomon was going to show up again. Once her facial got started, Kandace decided to relax and not worry about seeing Solomon again. At least not until she saw him at dinner.

Carmen slammed her phone into the cradle on her desk. She'd called Solomon five times in the last hour and her phone calls went directly to voice mail. She knew what that meant. Obviously that tramp Kandace had opened her legs to him. Carmen didn't know what it was about this woman that got under her skin so badly. Maybe it was the fact that she didn't know what was going on. When Solomon had his flings with models and actresses, he kept her in the loop, telling her how stupid they were and what a disappointment they'd turned out to be. This woman was different, because Carmen knew she wasn't stupid. And from the pictures she'd seen of her on the Internet, she wasn't ugly either. Still, she needed to know if Solomon had gotten what he wanted and was ready to move on. Better yet, to come back to New York. She picked up the phone and started dialing his number again.

"Knock, knock," Danny said from the door of her office. Carmen looked up and faked a smile as she hung up the phone.

"Danny, right?" Carmen said.

"You're killing my ego," he said. "I invite you to

lunch and you never call back, then struggle to re-member my name."

"I'm sorry, we just ran into some problems at the resort in North Carolina," Carmen lied.

"I thought Solomon was down there handling all of that," Danny said as he walked in. "You know that guy works you too hard. Does he realize how valu-able you are?"

"I knew what I was getting into when I signed up for the job," Carmen said with a hint of attitude in her voice.

Danny threw his hands up. "I was just kidding with you. No need to get so testy," he said. "Solomon is my boy."

Carmen raised her eyebrow and leaned back in her seat. "All right, why are you here?"

"At some point today, you're going to have to eat. I'm here to insure that you eat one of those meals with me."

While Carmen smiled at Danny, inside she was groaning and pushing him out of her office. Who did he think he was? Solomon Crawford? His line was stale and he didn't have half of the charm and charisma that Solomon had in his pinky finger.

"I'm sorry you wasted your time, but I can't go out to eat with you today. I have to put out this fire in North Carolina, head to my spin class, and then I have to brief Richmond on some other projects."

Danny perched on the edge of Carmen's desk and stared into her expressive hazel eyes. "Tell me something. Are we ever going to go out? If you're not interested, let me know and I can stop making a fool of myself."

Carmen patted his knee. "I'm sure you're a nice guy, but I just don't want to go out with you. Don't take it personal. I hope we can be friends, but nothing more."

Danny nodded. "I can live with that, especially since we're going to be seeing more of each other anyway."

"How so?" she asked.

"Solomon hired my company to run background checks on new employees and to do random background checks company wide."

Carmen tugged at her hair. "He didn't tell me about this."

Danny shrugged. "Probably slipped his mind. If you have any security issues or questions you want me to take a look at, I'm going to be right down the hall."

"Then I guess we should have lunch and talk about what you will be doing for us," she said as he stood up. "Is one-thirty good for you?"

"I'll check my calendar and get back to you," he said, then headed out of her office.

Carmen was going to have to make extra nice with Danny. The last thing she needed was for that chump to uncover what she had worked so hard to hide.

Three hours after she entered the spa, Kandace stepped out feeling like a brand new woman. She would have to thank Solomon for her deluxe treatment, which included a facial, pedicure, manicure, and an appointment with the hair stylist on duty. Kandace had decided to try something new with her hair and allowed the woman to take two inches off her brown tresses. She ended up with a sleek bob that highlighted her cheekbones and almond-shaped eyes. Though she'd have to give up her trademark ponytail now, she felt as if the sophistication of the cut was worth the sacrifice.

As she walked into the lobby, the front desk clerk stopped her. "Miss Davis, we have a package for you."

"Thank you," Kandace said as she walked over to the desk and took the box from the clerk. She knew it was from Solomon and a part of her couldn't wait to see what it was. Knowing him, she figured it was some skimpy piece of lingerie. And if it was, she was going to send it right back. *This man just isn't going to learn,* she thought as she tucked the box under her arm and headed for the elevator. When she arrived in her room, Kandace opened the box and instead of finding a tawdry piece of lingerie, she was treated to a beautiful red dress with a matching wrap. She pulled the dress from the box and held it against her skin. The silky material flowed as she spun around. "Good choice, Crawford," she said to herself. Kandace stripped out of her clothes and slipped into the dress. Solomon had gotten her size perfectly, and the strapless, tea-length dress complimented her new haircut.

"I'm not going to be able to wear Uggs with this," she said as she ran her hands down her sides. Just as she was about to take her dress off, there was a knock at the door. Expecting a delivery man, she dashed to the door and opened it.

Solomon expected Kandace to look good in red, he expected the dress to show off her shoulders and that phenomenal cleavage, but he didn't expect to be breathless when he saw her.

"What are you doing here?" she asked after a brief moment of silence.

"Shoes," he said. "I forgot to slip these in the box." Solomon handed her a shoe box. "Are you going to invite me in?"

"No," she said as she accepted the box. "I'll see you at dinner."

"Then why did you come to the door looking that damned good?" he asked as Kandace made an attempt to close the door. He wedged his boot-clad foot between the door and the jamb. "We could always have dinner inside."

"Move your foot before I change my mind about going out to dinner with you. You're supposed to be nicer."

"What can I say? I'm a work in progress."

"Good-bye, Solomon," Kandace said, then closed the door as he moved his foot.

Kandace was the kind of woman that Solomon realized he needed to meet. She didn't give him what he wanted right away and he had a feeling that she had many layers. The more he chased her, the more he wanted to get to know her. At some point, he wanted to have her between the sheets, but he'd be willing to wait, and Solomon Crawford never waited for anything—especially a woman.

Then again, it had been a long time since he'd had a reason to expect something special from a woman. Kandace seemed to be something special. As he walked toward the elevator, his cell phone rang again. He didn't have to look at the caller ID to know that it was Carmen. She'd been phoning all day and he couldn't figure out why she kept calling him. It was unlike her to be so annoying. Solomon knew if he didn't take her call now, she would interrupt his date with Kandace and he wasn't about to have that.

"Crawford," he said, when he answered the phone.

"Solomon, I've been trying to reach you all day," Carmen said.

"Is there a fire? What's wrong?" he asked as he headed for the stairs so that he could finish this call with her.

"When did you hire Danny? Are there some security issues that I'm not aware of?"

"Carmen," Solomon said, "is this why you've been calling me all day? I'm on vacation, all right? And when did you start questioning my decisions?"

"Well, I—I . . . It's just that I thought there was some sort of problem. I didn't mean to question you," she said. "Still, if there is a serious security issue, I should be made aware of it."

"Here's the thing," Solomon said. "We have to make sure everyone who works for us is on the up and up. We have to make sure everyone has the proper documentation and that we're not hiring illegal workers. We discussed this three months ago, remember?"

"Right. I'm sorry," she said.

"Do me a favor. Don't call me unless it's an emergency," he said.

"Of course. Sorry."

Solomon snapped his phone shut and headed to his room. He had a dinner to prepare for and nothing was going to stand in his way.

CHAPTER 8

As the day came to a close, Carmen felt horrible. Solomon had spoken to her as if she was just another common employee. He'd never talked to her in such a dismissive way and she knew it had more to do with that woman than his need for a vacation. Kandace Davis. Carmen knew she had to get rid of that bitch, but she wasn't sure how. She pulled up her Internet browser and started to type in Kandace's name again.

"You're still here?" Danny said from the doorway.

Carmen smiled at him. "Tying up some loose ends. What are you still doing here?"

"Settling in and tying up loose ends, like you. I didn't realize how many applications you guys got in. What do you say we get out of here and grab a hot dog and a pop?" Danny said.

Carmen pushed back in her chair and smiled. "I know we're going to be friends, but you can't expect me to eat street meat. Let's go to Jimmy Walker's and have a drink."

"Sounds good to me," Danny said.

Danny and Carmen walked to the bar in near silence. Danny tried to make small talk about the weather, but Carmen's mind was on getting to the bottom of why Solomon had brought the private investigator into the company. Arriving at the door of Jimmy Walker's, Danny opened it and held it for Carmen to walk into the dimly lit bar. She spotted two seats at the end of the bar and pointed them out to Danny. He nodded and followed her.

As soon as they sat down, the bartender crossed over to them and took their drink orders. When the bartender brought back Carmen's white wine and Danny's Corona, Carmen began peppering Danny with questions. "So, why did Solomon hire you?" she asked as she sipped on a glass of wine.

"He wanted to make sure all of the employees are documented workers. There are a bunch of new laws that are going into effect that fine businesses for hiring illegals. Solomon just wants to be on top of things. Why is this such an issue with you?"

"I guess it's just the newness of it," she said with a dismissive laugh. "Solomon didn't give me the details of your job description. I'm his right-hand woman, you know."

Danny eyed her suspiciously as he sipped his beer. Something was off about Carmen and it was more than her turning him down for a date. He had to find out what, if anything, she was hiding.

Solomon had never been very excitable. He didn't rush downstairs on Christmas morning, didn't get wide-eyed at surprise birthday parties, but tonight, he was a bundle of nerves. Seeing Kandace in the dress was an appetizer and now he was ready for the full course meal. The black Manolo Blahnik sandals would be the icing on the cake. "Calm down," he told himself. "How do I know that this isn't a colossal waste of time? Kandace could have a husband or a boyfriend in Charlotte. But if all it costs me is a six-hundred-dollar pair of shoes to find out, then so be it."

"Mr. Crawford," said the head chef, "dinner is ready if you'd like to taste it."

He nodded and followed the man to the stove. The chef had prepared pan-seared salmon, green beans with almonds, baby greens and fennel salad, and bananas foster for dessert. After tasting each dish, Solomon gave the man his stamp of approval. "This is going to be a great dinner," he said. "Make sure you don't let some other resort steal you away from us. I see your own restaurant in your future."

The chef smiled. "Thank you, sir."

Solomon shook hands with the chef, then headed into the dining area. The wait staff had made a booth private for him and Kandace. Fresh flowers adorned the table and two candles in the center of the table were ready to be lit. Looking down at his watch, he saw it was time for him to get Kandace. He couldn't help but picture the look of shock on her face when he ended up taking her to the restaurant and not his suite. At least, not right away.

* * *

Kandace slipped the strappy Manolos on her feet. They weren't her style—the heel was way too high and too *Sex and the City*—but they did make her legs look great and set off the dress. She knew how expensive the shoes and the dress were. The dress was Roberto Cavalli, a designer that Serena and Jade were crazy about. Kandace was content with clothes that just gave her a polished look. After assessing herself in the mirror one last time, she was certain she was sufficiently polished in her designer threads. "I bet he's going to try and have dinner in his suite and I'm not falling for it," she said as she adjusted her strap.

Just as she reached for her purse, there was a knock at the door. She opened the door and saw Solomon standing there dressed in a pair of black wool slacks, an olive turtleneck, and a vintage denim suit jacket. "Amazing," he said as he gave her a slow once-over.

"So, where are we going?"

"It's a surprise," he said as he extended his arm to her.

"It had better not be your suite, because I agreed to dinner and nothing else," she said with finality.

"The night is young," he replied as they headed to the elevator. "But for now, we're going to a private booth in the restaurant."

She nodded. "That sounds good. I'm almost impressed."

"Almost?" Solomon asked with a raised eyebrow.

"Yes," Kandace replied. "I figured you were going

to try and lure me up to your suite. But as you just said, the night is still young."

"That's right," he said as they stepped on the elevator. "You might be racing me to my suite before the night is over."

"I doubt that," she said as the doors closed. Solomon turned to her and pulled Kandace against his chest.

"You know why I picked out this dress?" he asked as he ran his finger across her shoulders.

Kandace tried to pretend she was unaffected, pretend that she didn't feel the press of his erection through his zipper, pretend that the touch of his finger wasn't making her tingle all over. "Why?" she found the voice to ask.

"Because it'll be so easy for me to take it off you," he said, then leaned in and brushed his lips against her neck. Kandace closed her eyes, shivering with anticipation for about three seconds before she pushed back from him.

"Let's do something different," she said. "You keep your hands and lips to yourself."

"Where's the fun in that?"

"Have you ever had a real conversation with a woman?"

The doors to the elevator opened and Solomon winked at her. "Maybe."

She shook her head as they walked into the restaurant. "I thought you were going to try and act like a real person," she said. "This is not attractive."

"But you are and you know it. If I didn't notice it,

then you would be upset," Solomon said. "That's how you women are."

"Maybe that's how the women you meet are, but I don't need you or any other man to tell me I look good. I already know that."

Solomon held his hands up. "Excuse me. Well, Miss Davis, I hope you will pardon me for underestimating you."

She rolled her eyes at him. "I'd love to meet Solomon Crawford."

"What do you mean?" he asked as he led her to the booth in the back of the restaurant.

Kandace looked into his eyes and shook her head. "Who are you? The real you, behind the money, the fancy clothes, and the slick attitude."

"All right, I'll tell you who I am if you do the same. Who's the woman inside you?"

Before Kandace could say anything, a waiter walked over and placed their salads on the table. "Please let me know if I can get you anything else," he said, then left the table.

"You go first," she said as she took a quick bite of her salad.

"Ladies first, my father always says," he replied.

Kandace fingered her hair. "Okay," she said. "I work too hard because I don't want to have to depend on anyone for anything."

"I know that. If you want to see the real me, it's only fair that I see the real you. Every tantalizing inch."

"See, there you go again," she said. "Can we have a conversation without the sexual innuendo?"

Solomon took her hand in his. "All right, I'm

going to be honest. This is new to me. I can't remember the last time I've been on a real date with a woman."

"Was this before or after you got your heart broken?"

Solomon tapped her hand. "You think you know me, huh?"

"I know your type. Men just don't deal with heart-break the way women do. You hide behind mean-ingless one-night stands and overinflated actresses."

He chuckled. "Been watching *Access Hollywood*, huh?"

Kandace shrugged. "Can't help but notice you on TV. You've been linked to every hot chick in the world. So, why me?"

Solomon smiled. "At first it was because your ass looked so great in that bathing suit."

"Pig," she said.

"Aren't we doing the honest thing here? You asked. I answered. You can't hold that against me."

Kandace looked down at her hand, noticing that he was still holding it, gently stroking the back of it with his thumb. She felt comfortable sitting there with him and she wondered if this was a part of his charm. Is this how he eased his way between the thighs of all the women he'd been linked to? Were those stories even true?

"Well, you saw me in the bathing suit and then what?" she asked.

"You challenge me, all right. I was really turned on when you didn't know who I was. I can't go any-where and not be recognized. It's really refreshing to know that you weren't blinded by my name and what I have."

"That's all it takes to get Solomon Crawford excited? I better alert the press," Kandace joked.

He brought her hand to his lips. "Your turn," he said. "Tell me why a beautiful and smart woman like you is still single."

"Because I don't believe in settling," she said, then toyed with her salad. "You know, some women still want real love. I'm willing to wait for it."

"Love? Yeah, right. No one believes in love anymore." Solomon jabbed at his salad. "Why don't we talk about something else?"

"Do you mean to tell me that you've been in love?" Kandace raised her eyebrows and broke into laughter. "That explains so much."

Solomon dropped his fork and folded his arms across his chest. "What's that supposed to mean?"

"I always heard that men couldn't handle heartbreak and you're proof of it," she said.

"Whatever."

She stroked his hand. "It's all right, we've all been there," she said. "I guess that's why you have to be with all of those women and pretend you're a playboy. Have you ever thought of telling her that you're sorry?"

Solomon pulled his hand away. "I have nothing to apologize for."

Before Kandace could say anything else, the waiter appeared with their salmon. They ate in an uncomfortable silence and Kandace couldn't help but wonder about the woman who'd broken Solomon's heart. After about ten minutes of silence, Kandace placed her fork on the edge of her plate and stared at Solomon's face. His handsome features were lined with annoyance as he ate. He held his head up and caught her eye. "Is something wrong with the food?"

"No, it's great. I think I offended you and I'm sorry," she said.

Solomon shook his head. "You made me think about something that I don't like to think about. And this is not how this date was supposed to go. I figured by now we'd be discussing going to my suite."

"Oh, I messed up your plan, huh?" she asked with a sly smile. "So tonight was supposed to be about seduction?"

Solomon cut into his salmon with his fork and winked at her as he brought the fish to his lips. "The night isn't over yet."

Kandace started eating again, savoring the taste of the salmon. Maybe she was wrong about Solomon. But then again, he was still a mystery. The only thing she knew for sure was that he wanted her and wasn't going to stop until he got her.

As Solomon ate, he thought about how close he'd come to telling her about his attempt at love. Not many people outside friends and family knew about that and it wasn't something that he was known to share. But he'd been tempted to open up to Kandace, tempted to let her see the real Solomon; yet he held back, kept his pain inside. Normally when he thought about *her*, he buried those thoughts between a woman's thighs. He'd cover the memories of the pain she caused with a meaningless romp and sprint from some woman's bed before sunrise. Kandace would not offer him that opportunity because over this one dinner, he realized that she was more than a temporary place holder. She wasn't the kind of woman he could just have sex with and leave. He didn't want to say it, didn't even want to admit to himself how special she could be.

"Why are you so quiet?" she asked as she finished the last of her dinner.

"It's not often that I watch a woman enjoy food."

Kandace laughed and dabbed at her mouth with her linen napkin. "What can I say? I own a restaurant."

He nodded. "So, how does this place rank?"

She dropped her napkin on the side of her plate. "It's very good. Be careful, I might send one of my partners up here to steal your chef."

"You wouldn't stand a chance," he said. "I pay well."

"Sometimes money isn't the answer to everything."

"Spoken like a woman who has her own," he said as he lifted his wineglass. "What do you say to dessert by the hot tub?"

Kandace took a sip of her wine. "I don't think so," she said. "I have something to do in the morning. But it was a lovely dinner."

"You can't leave yet," he said. "We haven't even had dessert."

Kandace folded her hands underneath her chin

and leaned over the table. Solomon focused on her lips. He felt as if he'd been a perfect gentleman all night and he wasn't going to let her go without giving her something to think about. He captured her face in his hands and brought her lips to his. Gently, he brushed his lips against her petal soft ones. Kandace moaned as his tongue entered her parted lips. He could taste a hint of chardonnay in her kiss and it made him want more.

"Excuse me," the waiter said, causing them to break their embrace. Solomon thought about firing the young man, but he was only doing his job. It wasn't his fault that his timing was off. "I—I have dessert."

He placed the flaming dishes on the table and scurried away. "Bananas foster?" Kandace said. "How could you possibly know this is my favorite dessert?"

"It was just a guess. It used to be my favorite dessert too," he said.

"Used to be?"

"The more I kiss you, the more your lips become the sweet treat I need," he said in a husky whisper.

"Solomon," she whispered, "I had a really nice time with you and the dress is lovely, but I can't give you what you want."

"What we both want," he said. "Kandace, I'm not trying to fall in love with you, but I know you feel the heat between us."

"And I told you, I don't settle. What happens after we have sex? I still don't know the real you and I'm not jumping into bed with you, no matter how much I want to," she said. Kandace rose to her feet and nodded toward Solomon. "I'm going on a nature hike in the morning. I guess I'll see you there."

"What?" he asked.

"You've showed up everywhere else I've been," she said. "Good night, Solomon."

He swore under his breath as he watched Kandace walk out of the restaurant. This was not the ending he'd planned for tonight. Had he been honest with himself, he would've realized Kandace was worth the work she was forcing him to do. Solomon leapt from the table and followed her. He touched her elbow when he caught up with her.

"Listen," he said. "You're right, I do want to sleep with you and we both know that's going to happen before you leave this resort, but it doesn't have to happen tonight. I don't want you to walk away because you think that I can't control my hormones. I'm willing to wait until you're ready to give yourself to me, without reservation."

"You certainly are full of yourself. What happens if I decide that I don't want to sleep with you?" Kandace asked.

Solomon stroked her cheek and smiled. "Then I guess you will end up in the *Guinness World Records*," he joked. "The woman who said no."

Kandace laughed. "So, I'd be the first?"

"In history. But it's a sad record to aspire to," he said. "Why don't we go skiing in the morning, instead of taking a hike?"

"No way! I don't ski and I have no desire to learn," she exclaimed.

"Come on, how can you come to the mountains

and not even try it? I tell you what, we'll stay on the kiddie slope and I won't let you fall unless I'm underneath you," he said.

"I don't think so."

Solomon leaned in and kissed her on the cheek. "We'll discuss it in the morning. Have a good night's sleep. Dream of me," he said before patting her gently on her bottom.

Kandace shook her head, then left. As Solomon watched her walk away, he couldn't remember the last time he'd had this much fun with a woman. Kandace Davis was definitely something special and worth the wait. But that wait had better not be a really long one.

CHAPTER 9

Kandace nearly floated to her room, her thoughts centered on Solomon and the brief look at the real man inside that she'd seen tonight. *So, the playboy has a soul,* she thought as she kicked off her shoes. *Tonight was really nice, but if he thinks I'm getting on some skis, he has lost his mind.*

Kandace stripped out of her dress and lay across the bed. As she closed her eyes, she thought about the kiss and how he made her feel when he touched her, the shivers that went up and down her spine when their lips met. How much longer would she torture herself? She knew she wanted him and she couldn't fool herself into thinking that anything that happened with Solomon would be more than a vacation fling. Sitting up in the bed, she thought about calling his room, but decided against it. If she was going to prove a point, then she had to see it through. But the more time she spent around Solomon, the harder it was going to be to keep her own desires under wraps.

* * *

It was after midnight when Carmen and Danny left Jimmy Walker's. While Carmen's mind had been filled with thoughts of Solomon and what he was doing in North Carolina, Danny couldn't wait to get away from her so that he could run a check on her. Their conversation over drinks had raised his suspicion level to high alert. She was cagey with details about her past, not telling him anything more than what was on the company's Web site about her. She wouldn't say anything about her family or where she was born.

"I had a wonderful time," Carmen said as they reached the subway entrance. "Are you sure you don't want to come over for a nightcap?"

"No, I have to get up early in the morning. We'll talk at the office tomorrow," he said.

Carmen grabbed his hand. "Are you sure you don't want one more drink?" she asked with a seductive lilt to her voice.

"Another night," he said, seeing right though her smoke screen. She nodded and headed into the subway. Danny turned up the street and headed back toward the office. He was determined to find out what she was hiding.

Solomon was nearly asleep when his cell phone rang. His first inclination was to ignore the ringing and roll over, but he figured if someone was calling him this late, then it must be an emergency.

"Yeah," he said when he picked up the phone.

"Solomon, it's Danny."

"What is it? Do you know what time it is?" he growled.

"Man, I wouldn't call you if it wasn't something serious. What do you really know about Carmen?"

"Look, I'm tired. Can we talk about this tomorrow?"

"Solomon, something isn't right about Carmen," Danny said.

"She turned you down or something? I cannot deal with this right now."

"All right. Listen to me. Carmen De La Croix is dead, has been dead for fifteen years."

Solomon sat up in the bed. "What?"

"I thought Carmen was too weird about me doing background checks on the employees, so I came back to the office tonight and ran her name and social security number though the system."

"Maybe you made a mistake," he said as he ran his hand across his face.

Danny sighed. "That's what I thought, but I ran it again. Same information came up. I think your girl assumed the identity of this dead woman."

"Why would she do that?" Solomon asked as he scratched his head. "This makes no sense."

"How do you want to handle this?" Danny asked. "Right now, I have her face running through a face recognition program to see who she really is."

"This is crazy," Solomon said. "Let me know what you find out and don't let anyone know what you're doing."

"There's one more thing," Danny said.

"What is it? Danny?" Solomon asked. He looked at his phone and saw that the call had been disconnected. He dialed Danny back. Solomon didn't like what was going on. He had a strange feeling about his friend and their disconnected call.

"Yeah," Danny said.

"What happened?"

"Ah, I was wrong," he said. "You were right, I made a mistake on that identification. Everything is all right, I'm sorry I disturbed you."

"D, are you sure? I mean, you sounded really . . ."

"I called the software manufacture and there was a bug in the software . . . and it's late. I think I typed her last name in wrong. You go back to sleep," Danny said.

"I'm turning the phone off," Solomon said. "So, if you have anything else to tell me, do it now."

"We're good, bro."

"All right," Solomon said, then disconnected the call. As he closed his eyes, Solomon had an uneasy feeling flow through his body. This wasn't like Danny. When he found out information, he was usually dead on with it. Solomon looked at his clock and saw it was after two. Maybe his friend was too tired to look at things properly. Deciding to push the call out of his mind, Solomon drifted to sleep with thoughts of Kandace dancing in his mind.

The gun was trained on Danny's chest and sweat beaded up on his brow. "I knew you were going to be trouble," she growled as she walked closer to his chair. "You are not going to stop me from getting what I want."

"Bitch, you're crazy, and if you kill me, you're not going to get away with it," Danny said.

"This is New York. People die every day."

"Carmen! You think Solomon is going to love the woman who killed his best friend?"

"He'll never know." She pointed the gun at Danny's computer and shot the monitor. He jerked at the sound of gunshot. "See, Solomon has a lot of enemies. He'll never know who did this to his friend." Carmen closed the space between them and placed the barrel of the gun in the center of Danny's chest. "Besides, I've never liked you. You wanted to be Solomon, but you couldn't. You don't have what it takes."

"You need help," he said. "There's something seriously wrong with you."

"All I need is Solomon, and you will not stand in my way. Bye-bye Danny." She squeezed the trigger. Blood splattered on her cheek and Carmen calmly wiped it away. "Stupid bastard."

After she watched the last gasps of air flow from Danny's body, Carmen began ransacking his office, trying to make the scene look like a robbery. She removed Danny's wallet from his pocket, took his briefcase and his laptop. Then she went into her own office and kicked over furniture and turned her desk over. Next, Carmen headed out of the office building through the fire escape. Her plan was to come in early and pretend to be shocked that Danny was dead. Maybe his death would bring

Solomon back to New York so that he could protect her from the killer on the loose. Then he'd realize that she was the woman he'd been looking for and they would be able to begin their life together. Out of this tragedy, Solomon would find his true love. Carmen smiled as she headed into the subway tunnel. When no one was looking she tossed the gun on the tracks. Then she set Danny's things on a bench and walked away. Now, she and someone else could benefit from his death.

There is no one who can come in between Solomon and me now. He's going to need help getting over the tragic death of his best friend and I'm going to be there for him and show him how much he needs me, she thought as she got on the train. *Yes, he's going to come back and that's when I'm going to tell him how I feel about him.*

The next morning, Kandace woke up with a smile on her face. She was looking forward to her hike with Solomon. Their dinner last night had been more revealing than she'd expected it to be, though she'd been surprised that Solomon hadn't done more than kiss her. Part of her expected to wake up in his suite with no panties on and a throbbing between her legs, but she wasn't disappointed that he didn't press the issue of them sleeping together immediately. Still, she yearned for him and that gave her pause. Other than the physical, what was it that she knew about him that sparked such desire and yearning inside her? Could it be that Solomon was unlike any other man she'd ever dealt with? He didn't intimidate easily. Kandace knew she was the kind of woman that men didn't know how to take. She was focused on her career and she demanded to be respected. When she had been with Robert, she'd been willing to settle because she'd been lonely, but her relationship with him was just like being alone. Though she doubted she'd ever have a serious relationship with Solomon Crawford, she could let go and have fun. Then she thought back to the trip she and her friends had taken to Las Vegas.

Jade had been lucky enough to turn a vacation fling into a lifetime of the real thing, but there was no way lightning would strike twice. Besides, James Goings was no Solomon Crawford. He wanted love and didn't have the baggage or the list of broken hearts that Solomon had. Kandace hopped out of bed and decided that today was about fun and she didn't have to think about a future or anything beyond the end of her vacation.

What's stopping you from letting go and giving him what both of you want? she asked herself as she picked out a form-fitting snow suit to wear on her hike.

"Yeah, what is stopping me?" Kandace said aloud.

After hopping in the shower, Kandace decided to stop fighting what she was feeling about sleeping with Solomon and to let it happen if the opportunity presented itself to her again.

As Solomon pulled his skull cap down on his head, he tossed his cell phone on the bed, deciding that he wasn't dealing with any phone calls today.

Since Danny had reassured him that everything was all right last night, he could spend the day focused on Kandace.

Little did she know, he was going to get her on a pair of skis if it killed him. There was no way that she could come to the mountains and not even try to ski. Solomon was a master skier, having spent time in Vail at several celebrity events. The last time he'd been skiing, he and Richmond raced down a hill and his brother was left with a broken leg while Solomon zoomed off with two snow bunnies. At the time, he hadn't known that his brother was seriously hurt, but Richmond had never allowed him to forget it. Sometimes, Solomon wondered if his brother had secret wishes to get rid of him permanently. Pushing thoughts of his brother out of his mind, Solomon laced his boots and headed to the lobby to wait for Kandace.

When he stepped off the elevator, he saw her standing there dressed in a form-fitting black and pink snow suit. Very cute and chic, but Solomon didn't know how warm she'd be once they got on the slope.

"Good morning, beautiful," he said as he crossed over to her. "I hope you have layers on underneath that."

"I do," she replied with a smile. "Are you ready for this hike?"

Solomon placed his hand on the small of Kandace's back. "I have another idea, and if you're up for the hike afterward, then sure."

She turned and looked up at him. "What other ideas do you have, Crawford?" she asked suspiciously.

"You'll see. For right now, you're going to need those layers," he said as he led her out the front door.

Kandace smiled as he draped his arm around her shoulder. "It's been really good weather these last few days," Solomon said. "Mother Nature has been making all the snow and saving us millions."

"Always the businessman, huh?" Kandace asked.

"I have to be," he said. "Let's stop right here."

She looked up and saw they were at the ski lift. "Why?"

"Because, I'm teaching you a lesson today. You can't come to Sugar Mountain and not go down the slopes. That's like going to Vegas and skipping the slot machines."

"I am not skiing," she said adamantly.

"It's just a lesson. If you don't like it, then we will take the hike," he said as he hopped on to the lift. "Why are you afraid to try something new?"

"Because I'm not a risk taker," she said. "And I don't plan on spending my vacation in a cast."

"I'm not going to let anything happen to those legs or any other part of your gorgeous body," he said as he brushed his lips against her cheek. Kandace playfully swatted him away.

"Solomon, you're going to make me hurt you," Kandace said. "And you better make sure nothing happens to me."

"Don't worry, if any part of you gets bruised or scratched, I'll kiss every injury you get."

Solomon walked over to the ski rental unit and grabbed a pair of skies for himself and Kandace.

She frowned at him as he walked over to the lift with the skis.

"Then you don't plan on kissing me at all because I'm not falling or skiing," Kandace said as the lift dropped them on the top of the mountain.

"Stop complaining," he said as he dropped the skis at her feet. "You have to at least try it before deciding that you hate it."

"Right now I'm hating you and I didn't have to try anything to figure that one out," she muttered as he fastened the skis to her feet.

Solomon nudged her with his elbow. "So beautiful, yet so evil."

As they approached the ski guide, Kandace picked up a handful of snow and made a ball. "Solomon," she called out.

He turned around and Kandace tossed the snowball in his face. Kandace broke out into laughter as Solomon wiped the snow from his face. "Oh, it is on now," he said as he scooped up his own handful of snow. Kandace tried to avoid him, but Solomon caught her on the hip with his snowball.

"You're in for it now," she shot back as she made another snowball. Solomon grabbed her around the waist and swung her around until she dropped the snowball.

"Oh, you're cheating," Kandace exclaimed as she pressed her hands against his chest.

"I never said I played fair," he quipped.

A resort employee walked over to them with a stern look on her face. "Excuse me," she said. "There is no horseplay on the mountain."

Solomon put Kandace down. "I apologize, Jean," he said after reading the woman's name tag. She looked up at him and her eyes widened as she realized who he was.

"Mr. Crawford, I had no idea that you were here today and I . . ."

Solomon held his hands up. "It's not a problem, we were out of line. Thanks for doing your job," he said with a smile.

"Would you like to sign up for our cross-country lessons?" Jean asked.

Kandace shook her head furiously. "Not at all," she said.

Solomon pulled Kandace against his hip. "She's a beginner," he said.

Jean nodded. "All right, if you two follow me, I can get you set up on the bunny hill."

Solomon and Kandace followed Jean to the beginner's slope where the instructors were fitting two ten-year-olds with skis. "Maybe this isn't a good idea," Kandace said to Solomon. "We could still go on the hike."

"Are you afraid you're going to get showed up by the kids?" Solomon asked. Kandace pinched his forearm. "Obviously, I'm not going to shut you up unless I ski down this mountain," she said.

"Actually, this is a hill," Solomon said. "And I'm going to be right beside you and the smile on my face won't be me laughing at you, I swear."

"Jerk!"

* * *

Carmen watched as Richmond talked to the homicide detectives from the NYPD. So far they'd deduced that whoever shot and killed Danny didn't enter the building through force and didn't steal anything. The detectives thought the killer made his or her escape through the fire escape. There were no fingerprints in the office other than Danny's. The crime scene technicians were processing the fire escape for fingerprints.

"Do you think he was killed by someone he knew?" Richmond asked.

What a stupid question, Carmen thought as she fought the urge to roll her eyes.

Detective Dave Myer nodded. "How long had Mr. Jones been with the company?"

Richmond shook his head. "Not long. My brother hired him to do background checks on our employees and I wasn't aware of his actual duties or anything like that."

"The computer was shot and the hard drive is missing," Detective Joel Cohen said. "Any idea what was on the hard drive?"

Richmond looked to Carmen. "Do you know what he was working on?"

"No, I don't. Other than what Solomon told me about the background checks, I have no idea what he was doing."

"Know of any possible criminal ties he may have had?" Detective Cohen asked, looking from Richmond to Carmen.

"As I said," Richmond said, "my brother hired him and he's out of town."

"We're going to need to contact your brother to ask him some questions," Myer said. "Does he have a number where he can be reached?"

Richmond nodded. "I'll give you his cell phone number."

"Where was he last night?" Cohen asked.

"In Sugar Mountain, North Carolina," Carmen said. "He went to check out our new resort."

"When did he leave?" Cohen asked.

"Two days ago," Carmen said. "He wasn't involved in this."

"Crawford Hotels isn't involved in this at all," Richmond added.

"It doesn't look that way," Cohen said. "From the looks of things, it seems as if this may have been a personal crime. I think Danny Jones brought his killer in the building with him."

"But just to be sure," Myer said, "we need to know if there were any employees in the building between midnight and two A.M."

Richmond walked the detectives to the door, telling them that he would take them down to the security desk to see if anyone had checked in the building after hours. Carmen headed for her office, hiding the smirk on her face from the shell-shocked employees she passed in the hallway. She was going to get away with murder—again. Now, she just had to get Solomon to come back to New York.

CHAPTER 10

After what had been a horribly funny skiing lesson that had seen Kandace hitting the ground more than once, Solomon and Kandace sat in front of the fireplace in the café sipping hot chocolate.

"Will you stop smirking at me?" Kandace said as she glanced at him.

"No," he said, then broke out in laughter. "I have never seen someone fall up a hill. You really can't ski."

Kandace tossed the plastic swizzle stick from her mug at him. "I told you that I didn't want to ski."

Solomon ducked out of the way and smiled. "You know you really had fun."

"No, *you* had fun laughing at me," she said as she poked her bottom lip out like a petulant child. "You and those damned kids."

"I think it was all the screaming that made everyone laugh so much."

Kandace rolled her eyes as Solomon leaned over,

kissed her on the cheek, and said, "At least it's only your pride that's bruised."

"And since you can't kiss that, keep your lips to yourself," she joked as he wrapped his arms around her shoulders.

"Why are you acting like that?" Solomon asked as he tweaked her nose. "Because I have more plans for you."

"I don't even think I want to know."

He pulled her face to his. Their lips were inches apart and Kandace knew he was going to kiss her. She wanted him to kiss her.

"First," he said, "we have to get you out of these clothes." He ran his hand down her arm. "Then into the hot tub to relax those tense muscles. Then I'm going to give you a massage so that you can relax even more and I can have my way with you."

Kandace brushed her lips against his. "What if I want to have my way with you?"

Solomon nearly dropped his mug of cocoa. "Did I hear you correctly?"

Kandace took the mug from his hand and placed it on the table. "Yes, you did."

He chuckled softly. "So, how do you want to have your way with me?"

She stood up and stroked his cheek. "I'd rather show you than tell you and I'm not showing you a thing until I get my massage."

Solomon rose from his seat and pulled Kandace against his chest. "Sounds like someone has been thinking about me stroking them since the spa."

"I'll meet you at the hot tub," she said as she pushed out of his arms.

"Umm, too bad you didn't keep that suit I bought you," he said as he watched her walk away.

Carmen's head was throbbing as she listened to Solomon's outgoing voice mail message for the tenth time in an hour. Where in the hell was he? With that bitch, no doubt. She slammed her cell phone against the desk. *I'm going to have to go down there and stake my claim on him,* she thought as she rose from her chair and stood at the window. "I'm not going to lose him," she mumbled.

"Carmen," Richmond said from the doorway, "are you all right?"

She turned around and frowned at him. "I'm just a little shaken up by everything that happened today. I wish Solomon was here."

"So do I. He got us involved with Jones. I have a bad feeling about this. We don't need this kind of publicity. It's bad enough that Solomon's exploits with women make the papers, but a murder in our headquarters," Richmond said as he shook with anger.

"Danny was Solomon's friend. If he was involved in something shady, I'm willing to bet that Solomon knew nothing about it," Carmen said.

"What did you know about Danny? Or about Solomon hiring him?"

She folded her arms across her chest and glared at him. "I told you that I didn't know anything about Danny's hiring, and Solomon said that it was for security."

"Some damned security. He's dead now. How the hell is he going to protect us? This is a scandal that we don't need." Richmond ran his hand across his face in a frustrated motion. "Have you gotten in touch with him?"

"He's not answering his cell phone nor his hotel room phone."

Richmond shook his head. "He wants to run this company, but when we need him, he's not here. I'd better get out in front of this."

"Wait," Carmen said. "When Solomon finds out what's going on, he's going to come back."

"With the twenty-four-hour news cycle, we don't have time to wait for Solomon to stop his vacation and come handle business." Richmond stormed out of the office and Carmen slammed the door behind him. Solomon would take care of everything, but he had to come back to New York.

Maybe I should go to North Carolina and get him, she thought. *I will if he doesn't answer the phone.* Carmen picked up the phone and dialed Solomon's number again.

"This is Solomon Crawford. I'm unavailable at the moment. Please leave a message and I'll return your call at my earliest convenience."

Carmen hung up before the beep and made another call to her travel agent. "I need a flight to Charlotte, North Carolina," she said when the agent answered the phone.

* * *

Solomon smiled as he watched Kandace enter the grotto. He'd told the staff not to let anyone but Kandace in the grotto tonight. An OUT OF ORDER sign had been placed on the door after the massage table and oils had been set up.

"Wow," Kandace said. "Massage table and everything, huh?"

"Yes," he said as he crossed over to her. Solomon gave her a slow once-over. She had on the hotel robe and a pair of Uggs and still she looked phenomenal. He tugged at the belt, which she had loosely tied around her waist. "Let's see what's underneath here." The robe fluttered open and Solomon grinned when he saw that Kandace was wearing the fur bikini that he'd sent her the night he found her in the hot tub.

"Aww, damn. I knew that would look good on you."

Kandace smiled as she did her Tyra Banks runway imitation. "It does look good on me, doesn't it?"

"But I still want to see it on the floor."

Kandace gave him another model pose over her shoulder and blew him a kiss. "If you're a good boy."

"A good boy? It's so much more fun being bad," he said. Then he captured her in his arms and kissed her with a scorching passion that made Kandace swoon. She wrapped her arms around his neck and pressed her hips into his. He was immediately aroused by her bold move. This was the side of Kandace that he'd been yearning to see. And so far, he'd been right about her. She was full of passion. As she slipped her hand down his neck, slowly snaking across his chest and down into his swimming trunks, she proved that she wasn't afraid to go after what she wanted. Solomon's knees buckled as Kandace stroked him while her tongue explored his mouth. She had the perfect combination of tongue and lip in her kiss. Solomon knew this was a feeling he wouldn't soon forget. Kandace pulled back from him and licked those swollen, well-kissed lips.

"So, do I have to take this off or are you going to do it?" she asked as she tugged at the string on her bikini. Solomon ran his hand across his face.

"Why don't you let me watch you take it all off?" he said in a deep voice that resembled a moan.

Kandace slowly untied her bikini top and then, like a Las Vegas showgirl, she covered her breasts as the top fell to the floor. Sensually, she twisted her hips, moving as if she heard her own bass line. Solomon stood there mesmerized by her dance as she dropped her arm and revealed a set of perfect breasts, creamy like the best chocolate, topped with a dark chocolate nipple. He couldn't wait a moment longer, he had to taste the luscious beauty that was Kandace. He reached out and pulled her against his chest by the top of her bikini bottoms. First he kissed her neck, slowly licking her until soft moans escaped her throat. With one hand, he eased her skimpy fur bottoms down. As Kandace lifted her leg to step out of her suit, Solomon slipped his hand between her thighs. Her wetness thrilled him, making the throbbing hardness between his thighs spring forward.

Kandace shivered as his finger dipped into her wet folds of flesh. But when he found her pleasure point and smoothly stroked it, every nerve in her body stood on end. "Ooh," she said as he moved his finger back and forth, making her wetter and hotter.

"You like that?" he asked as he continued his exploration. "I want to find every spot that makes you moan like that. You're so damned sexy." Solomon closed his lips around her nipple, flicking the hardened pebble with his tongue. Kandace dug her nails into his shoulders as waves of ecstasy washed over her body.

"I need you, Solomon," she cried out. "Need you inside me."

"And I need to be inside you," he replied. "But not until I taste you." He removed his finger from her pulsating mound and licked her womanly juices from it. "And that isn't enough."

Solomon scooped her up and rushed over to the massage table. He placed her on the table, and then lifted her legs as he marveled at the beauty of her long legs and thick thighs. Spreading them apart, he quickly dove in between and kissed her inner thigh before heading for her luscious core. He could feel her trembling as his lips touched her wet ones.

Kandace closed her eyes as she felt the warmth of Solomon's breath against her throbbing bud. When his tongue lashed her womanhood, she screamed out in pleasure. It had been so long since she was tasted this passionately. Solomon licked and sucked the most neglected part of her body until she was dizzy with desire. There was no vibrator in the world that could make her feel this good and make her climax over and over again.

"Open your eyes," Solomon commanded softly. "I want you to see how I'm making you feel so good."

Kandace moaned and watched Solomon as he continued to taste her and make her body quiver with pleasure. She lost count of the number of times he'd made her come after four and she struggled not to close her eyes and lose herself in the waves of pleasure. Solomon pulled back from her and shed his swimming trunks. The size of his erection caused her to gasp. He was big, bigger than any man she'd ever been with. No wonder he'd brought so many women to tears.

"I'll be gentle, at first," he said as he winked at her. Solomon walked over to the cart where the massage oils were and retrieved a condom. Kandace watched as he rolled the sheath in place. "Now, we're ready."

Kandace released a breath as he strode over to her and wrapped his arms around her waist. "I'm going to need more room than this table and you're going to thank me for it," he said as he lifted her from the massage table and walked over to the oversized sofa in the corner.

"I'm glad you have more than just a big ego, but you've done enough talking," Kandace said, then brushed her lips against his. Solomon sat down on the sofa with Kandace wrapped around him. As he attempted to lean back, Kandace placed her hand on his chest.

"No, like this," she said as she opened her thighs and guided Solomon into her valley. She threw her head back as he filled her. Solomon clutched her buttocks as she ground against his hardness. At first, their passion burned slowly, then everything around them exploded as Kandace rocked him harder and faster.

"Yes," he moaned. "Damn, baby, you feel so good."

"So do you," she cried as she felt an orgasm tugging at her senses. Kandace felt as if she was going to explode and Solomon wanted to take her over the edge as he pressed deeper and deeper into her. Kandace released a satisfied groan as she reached her release. Collapsing against his chest, she closed her eyes with a smile on her lips.

Solomon's body tingled as he held Kandace against his chest. He couldn't remember the last time he'd been so satisfied after sex. Thank God he'd been right about Kandace's passion. The way she took control of their encounter was damned erotic and something he hadn't experienced in a long time. He thought he was going to break the condom when he'd reached his climax. He released a cleansing sigh, then stroked her hair back from her forehead. She was beautiful in the afterglow of their lovemaking, he thought as she ran her hand across his chest.

"Kandace," he said, "I have one word to describe you."

"What's that?" she asked.

"Incredible."

Chuckling softly, she kissed him in the center of his chest. "I guess you're not half bad," she joked.

"Half bad? Woman . . ."

"I'm joking," she sang. "So, was all your stalking worth it?"

"Ask me again in the morning, after I eat you for breakfast."

Kandace propped up on her elbows. "You mean after we eat breakfast?"

Solomon kissed her softly on her full lips. "I meant just what I said."

After a quick nap on the sofa, Solomon and Kandace woke up feeling extremely hungry. "Let's go to my suite and order room service," she said. "Then we can talk about your breakfast dish."

As she slipped her robe on, Solomon realized he wasn't going to wait until morning to have his breakfast.

Carmen wanted to sleep, but that was the last thing she had time for if she was going to pack and make her flight. She really hated the fact that she wasn't going to be able to stay at her resort. All of the rooms were still booked. As she haphazardly stuffed clothes into her suitcase, Carmen realized that checking into another hotel would give her an added advantage. Solomon wouldn't know she was there immediately and she could get a good look at the bitch he'd been spending time with. Then she smiled, knowing if Solomon had slept with Kandace, that she was history. One thing Carmen could count on was Solomon's way with women and how once he'd gotten what he wanted, he moved on. Kandace was nothing more than a speed bump. If he didn't stay with all the actresses and supermodels that he'd been with, what was going to make this woman any different?

Carmen almost changed her mind about taking the trip as a wave of satisfaction washed over her. There had only been one woman in his life with any kind of staying power and that had been her. Everyone else was a temporary fixation that he'd quickly gotten over. Maybe it was time for her to tell him the truth—that she was in love with him—so that Solomon would stop wasting time with women like Kandace Davis. Yes, that was it! She was going to meet up with Solomon and tell him that she was the woman he'd been looking for. Maybe she'd tell him everything. Carmen stopped packing and thought about the first time she'd met Solomon.

Solomon had been downing glass after glass of champagne. When he'd finished his final glass, he tossed it against the wall of the reception hall. The young waitress jumped as shards of glass flew through the air.

"That damned bitch!" Solomon had screamed as he turned over the table holding his wedding cake. "Make a fool of me when you're already married? Did she think she'd get away with it?" The white butter-cream icing splattered against the wall.

"Mr. Crawford," the waitress had said. "Do you want me to clean this up?"

"I want you to get out of here."

"But, sir," she'd said as she slowly walked over to him. Despite his drunken state, he looked so handsome in his black tuxedo. He'd nearly ripped the collar of his shirt as he

snatched his bow tie off. He attempted to walk away from her, but he stumbled and fell on top of her. She'd slipped on some of the icing and Solomon Crawford was on top of her. Though his hard body was crushing her, she liked this position. She wished they were both naked, though.

"Are you all right?" he'd asked. "Did I hurt you?"

"No, I'm okay," she'd replied. The heat of his breath against her lips made her body tingle. "But you are in no shape to go out there."

"It's a damned shame that you're more concerned about me than my so-called fiancée is. She left, didn't she? Left with that man."

"Yes, sir. She's gone."

Solomon swore under his breath, his curses burning her ears. "Sir," she said. "Let me make you some coffee."

"I don't want any damned coffee. But I guess I could let you up," he'd said as he had made an attempt to stand. He'd wobbled as he held on to the edge of the counter and then extended his hand to her. She rose to her feet without taking his hand, afraid that the effort to help her would've dropped him to his knees again. He'd smelled so good, like patchouli and cinnamon.

"You're a mess," she'd said as she used her apron to wipe icing from his lapels and cheeks.

Solomon had grabbed her hand and kissed it. He had the softest lips, not like the lips of the boys she'd kissed or that horrible man who'd taken her when her mother had been sleeping. But she'd showed him and her mother that she wasn't going to take their shit anymore when she burned the house down with them locked in the basement. Everyone had felt sorry for her, but no one in her hometown would take her in. It had been her Aunt Lucy in New York who'd given her a home. A home where she was treated like a slave. But her Aunt Lucy would pay too.

"I've got to get out of here. Are the people gone yet?" he'd asked her.

"No, but there is a back way out of here. I'll help you."

He'd taken her face in his hands and kissed her lips ever so gently. "You don't know it, but you saved my life."

She tingled again, feeling as if she had met Prince Charming. But he wouldn't want her the way she was, so plain and mousy. She'd seen the woman he'd wanted to marry and she was beautiful. She knew she had to beautiful too. So beautiful that Solomon Crawford wouldn't be able to resist her.

Now she was and it was time for him to realize the sacrifice that she'd made for him and how he was the only man she could ever want.

CHAPTER 11

Kandace stretched her arms above her head as the first rays of the sun trickled through the white drapes. Her body ached in the best way—she ached like a woman who had been completely loved. Turning on her side, she saw Solomon smiling at her.

"Good morning, beautiful," he said, then kissed her on the forehead.

"Morning."

"I was just about to order room service. What can I get for you?"

"Anything is fine," she said. "Maybe some pancakes and strawberries and a lot of coffee."

Solomon stroked her cheek and smiled. "How hungry are you?"

She shrugged. "I don't have to eat right this moment."

He pulled the covers off her and smiled slyly. "Good, because I do." Solomon rolled over on top of her and slid down the length of her body until he reached the crest of her thighs. Dipping his head down, Solomon blazed a trail to her womanly core with his tongue. Kandace trembled with anticipation as she felt his hand roaming her thighs. He kissed her tender folds of flesh until she was dripping wet.

"Umm," she moaned as she pushed her hips into his lips. Solomon's tongue flicked across her throbbing bud and Kandace gasped as he palmed her bottom. With every lick, kiss, and suck, Kandace felt a small explosion between her thighs that was just a prelude to the nuclear meltdown Solomon was seeking to cause.

He dropped her hips and darted his tongue in and out of her, lapping up her juices.

"Solomon," she cried as she reached the point of no return. Her legs quivered and every nerve in her body stood on end.

He inched up her body, raining kisses on her stomach, her breasts, and finally her lips. Kandace moaned in satisfaction as Solomon wrapped his arms around her. "Enjoy your breakfast?" she asked.

"Oh yes," he said. "But you'd better let me order yours so that I can have seconds."

She smiled and kissed his cheek. "Please do."

After Solomon ordered Kandace's breakfast, she headed to the bathroom to take a shower. When she looked in the mirror, she saw the red passion marks across her chest and smiled. *Turnabout is fair play,* she thought. *I'm going to give Solomon some marks of his own.* Kandace took a quick shower, wrapped herself in a towel, and headed back into the bedroom. From the doorway, she watched Solomon arrange her breakfast tray. That man was too sexy for words as he stood next to the bed in nothing but boxer briefs. She dropped her towel and then crossed over to him. Kandace wrapped her arms around his waist and pressed her body against his back.

"That food can wait, but I can't. I want you," she whispered.

Slowly, Solomon turned around, eyeing Kandace's naked body with silent appreciation. "And you can have me."

Kandace slipped her hand inside his boxer briefs and stroked his rigid hardness. Solomon moaned and clutched her bottom as her hands glided across his manhood until he nearly exploded. She knew where and how to touch him. "Where's the protection?" she asked.

Solomon nodded toward the pillows as Kandace pushed him back onto the bed. Kandace reached underneath the pillow and grabbed the gold condom package. Before she opened it, she started kissing his neck, moving down to his chest, across his six-pack abs and stopping right at his thick erection. Flicking her tongue across the tip of him, Kandace felt a rush of desire and power. She'd never felt such a need to give pleasure to another person. Locking eyes with Solomon, Kandace took the length of him into her mouth.

"Umm," he moaned as she sucked him. Solomon stretched his arms above his head as she took him deeper inside. "Oh, Kandace." Shivering on the brink of an explosion, Solomon pulled her mouth off him. "Damn."

She smiled as she rolled the condom down his throbbing erection. He was powerless to move as she straddled his body and guided him into her hot, wet valley. Kandace rotated her hips as Solomon clutched her bottom in ecstasy. She felt so good, so hot and wet that he couldn't hold back his climax. He wrapped his arms around her and pulled her against his chest. "Don't do that," he groaned as she ran her tongue across his sweaty chest.

"What if I just do this?" she asked as she ground her hips against him. Solomon howled as every nerve in his body stood on end. He was immediately aroused again. Holding Kandace's waist tight, Solomon sat up and pumped into her body, making her scream in delight. He could feel Kandace's orgasm building as he went limp with his own. Solomon rested his head on her breasts and closed his eyes. "Oh, baby," he whispered.

"Umm," Kandace said as she shifted her body underneath him. "I'm guessing my breakfast is cold now."

Solomon propped up on his elbows. "And you don't care either," he said. Kandace shook her head and laughed. He stroked her cheek and just stared into her eyes.

"What?" she asked.

"I'm speechless and that doesn't happen often."

"Tell me something," Kandace said. "Now that you've gotten what you wanted, are we done?"

"Not by a long shot," he said. Words he'd never uttered to a woman before. Solomon knew he wasn't going to walk away from Kandace, he wasn't even sure if he could still walk. "Because I haven't gotten everything that I want."

"What else do you want, Crawford?"

Solomon smiled and kissed her chin. "I'll let you know when I think of it."

"I know what I want," Kandace said.

"What's that?"

"My hike!"

"And I thought you were going to opt for another ski lesson," he joked.

She shook her head furiously. "I will never get on another pair of skis. Tried it, hated it."

"All right, all right. We can go on your hike after lunch, if that's all right."

"Works for me. Now, I guess it's time for me to eat that cold breakfast over there," she said as she eased off the bed.

"I know the owner, I can get you something hot," he said as he reached for the phone and called room service.

After a fresh breakfast plate of pancakes, eggs, turkey bacon, and fruit had been delivered, Kandace and Solomon sat in front of the fireplace eating.

"Did you always want to go into the family business?" she asked as she picked up a strawberry from the bowl.

"Honestly, I had no intentions of getting into the business," he said.

Kandace eyed him suspiciously. "Really? But you're so successful at it. What was your first option?"

Solomon took a swig of orange juice to wash

down the bitter taste that was building in his mouth. "Filmmaking."

"Filmmaking? I would've never guessed that. Why did you give it up?"

"I just did," he said with finality in his voice.

Kandace knew she'd struck a nerve, but she was intrigued.

"What about you?" Solomon asked. "You always wanted to work in food service? Cooked on an Easy-Bake Oven as a kid?"

"Ha. No. I'm actually into marketing and public relations. I ended up co-owner of a restaurant as a business venture with my best friends."

"So, you ladies just woke up one day and decided that you wanted to own a restaurant?"

"Of course not," she said. "That doesn't make good business sense, does it?"

Solomon shook his head and Kandace continued. "My friend Jade was dealing with this asshole who duped her into investing in his crappy restaurant in Atlanta. When he became successful because of Jade, he thought he could just push her out of the way and replace her."

"Cold blooded," Solomon interjected.

"Well, we weren't standing for it," Kandace said. "And we decided to beat him at his own game. He was looking to expand his bland chain into North Carolina and we bought the property from underneath him."

Solomon nearly choked on a piece of strawberry. "Now, that is a hell of a business plan. I was wrong about the cold-blooded part. I think that describes you and your friends."

Kandace shook her head. "That's why love and business don't mix," she said. "But I'm sure you know that."

"Yeah," he said. "Besides, love is just another four-letter word."

"Ooh, spoken like a very bitter man. So how did she break your heart?"

Solomon narrowed his eyes at Kandace. Part of him wanted to keep up his playboy facade, but for whatever reason, he felt as if he needed to share with her.

"She was my muse. I loved her and was ready to marry her. I was at the altar, about to say 'I do,' when her husband showed up."

Kandace reached out and stroked his arm. "Solomon," she whispered.

"We met in Central Park. She had this bohemian vibe going on. At the time, that's what I was into. When she started speaking with this English accent, I think I fell for her right there on the grass. It helped that my parents were totally against us being together. Then, I wrote my first script, which was all about love, showed it at the Tribeca Film Festival. I had studios begging me to come to Hollywood and be the next Spike Lee. But that movie was all about her and when things fell apart, I didn't want to make any more movies."

"Solomon," she said again. He waved his hands as if to tell her that he didn't want to say anything else about it.

"What about you?" he asked. "How many hearts have you broken?"

"I don't break hearts," Kandace said. "I've gotten my heart broken, though."

"By what fool?" Solomon asked.

Kandace picked up a strawberry and bit the tip of it off. "The executive chef at my restaurant," she said after swallowing the fruit. "Devon Harris and I were supposed to be married right after college. But his father didn't think I was right for his son."

"So, why are you working with him?"

"He's famous and a good chef. Great publicity for the restaurant, and I don't see him that much anyway," she said.

Solomon couldn't explain what he was feeling. Okay, Kandace worked with her ex. He didn't have a claim on her, so he had no cause to feel jealous. Yet, he did. What if the old feelings returned when she went back to Charlotte?

Stay cool, he told himself. *This is what it is.*

"That's good business, right?" Kandace asked.

"What?"

"Putting the hottest Food Network star in our kitchen. We've been full every night since we've opened."

"Has he tried to rekindle the flame with you?"

Kandace laughed. "That ship has sailed, sunk, and is now home to a school of fish and coral reef."

"Are you sure about that?"

She folded her arms across her chest and cocked her head to the side. "Why does it matter? Would you give your ex fiancée another chance?"

"Hell no. It's one and done with me."

"And a leopard never changes its spots," Kandace said. "I guess we're both bitter. Maybe that's why the sex was so good."

"Maybe," he said. "Let's try it again to make sure it wasn't a fluke."

Kandace placed her hand on his chest and shook her head. "You owe me a hike, so I suggest you go to your suite, put on some warm clothes, and meet me in the lobby. Then, we can test your theory."

Solomon rose to his feet and winked at Kandace. "Yeah, we're going to test the hell out of that theory," he said as he headed for the door.

Carmen pulled up at the resort just in time to see Solomon and that woman walking out the main entrance. Ducking in the driver's seat of her rented SUV, she watched them walking as if they were close friends. Solomon lazily draped his arm across her shoulder and she looped her arm around Solomon's waist. "Where are they going?" she mumbled as she watched them disappear beyond the hill. Carmen jumped out of the car and stormed into the lobby.

"Hello, ma'am, welcome to . . ."

Carmen held up her hand and stopped the front desk clerk from speaking. "I'm Carmen De La Croix. I need to see Frances right now."

"Yes, ma'am," the clerk said as she picked up the phone and dialed the manager's office. "She will be right out."

Carmen folded her arms across her chest and rocked back and forth until Frances entered the lobby. "Miss De La Croix, is everything all right?"

"Can we talk in your office?" she asked.

Frances led Carmen into her office, her mind spinning with every worst-case scenario. Had something happened? Were they going to be shut down? Was she being replaced?

"Frances, something happened in New York and I've been trying to reach Mr. Crawford," Carmen said once she and Frances were in her office.

"Well, he's on the property, I'm just not sure where," she said.

"I need a key to his room so that I can wait for him."

"Is that a wise thing to do? I can have him paged," Frances said.

Carmen shook her head. "This is a sensitive matter and it's best that I see Mr. Crawford and tell him. Frances, we're partners. He won't be upset."

"I'll make you a key," Frances said as she headed to the front desk. Five minutes later Frances returned to her office and handed Carmen the key card. "Should I tell Mr. Crawford that you are here?" she asked.

"I called him," Carmen lied. "He knows that I'm waiting for him."

"All right. Well, is there anything else I can help you with? Do you need a room? We don't have any more suites available, but there is a single room left."

Carmen shook her head. "I'll be flying back to New York later. And I am thrilled that we don't have any suites left. Thanks for all of your help,

Frances." She left the office and headed to the top floor of the resort where Solomon's suite was. Carmen wished he was inside and waiting for her, but she knew he was with that woman. That bitch who had caused him to ignore her.

Carmen entered the room and was shocked to see that Solomon's cell phone was sitting on the table plugged into the charger. "He never leaves his phone," she muttered as she picked it up. There were nearly one hundred missed calls showing on his screen. She deleted each call since most of them had been from her. Carmen looked around the room for signs that Kandace had been spending time there. She ran her hand across the bed, which she could see had been made up by the maid staff because there was a square of chocolate on the pillow. Carmen inhaled deeply and smelled the faint scent of Solomon's cologne. She missed him so much and wanted to be with him in every way. Crossing over to his closet, she flipped through the clothes that were hanging there, stroking the material of a designer suit. She was wishing that Solomon would walk through the door and take her into his arms and make love to her. She didn't like the way he had looked at Kandace. He'd looked at her as if she were special, much like the way he looked at Carmen on the fateful day after his wedding. She'd known at that moment that she and Solomon would be together. The time was now and somehow, she had to make it happen.

But that woman. She was going to be a problem, Carmen could feel it. Dropping her hand from the sleeve of Solomon's jacket, she walked over to the bed and plopped down on it. Carmen closed her eyes, imagining that Solomon was there. How would she feel if he kissed her and removed her clothes slowly, massaging her tender breasts until her nipples stood on end? How would it feel to have him buried deep inside her wetness? Carmen slipped her hand between her legs, imagining that it was Solomon. Moaning, she nearly brought herself to the brink thinking about Solomon doing that to her. It was time for her to have him, and anyone in her way would have to suffer.

CHAPTER 12

"Look," Kandace said as she pointed to a deer in the distance munching on dried grass. "Isn't it beautiful?"

Solomon laughed quietly. "Yeah, until it hops out on the road and hits your car."

She smacked him on the shoulder. "Can't you enjoy nature for a second? It's like Bambi," Kandace said.

"All right," he said as he shivered briefly. "Ooh, look at Bambi. What are you, some kind of nature buff?"

"No," she said. "But I grew up in an area where there was no snow, no lush woods, and no quiet deer."

"Really? And where was that?"

"Guam. My mother was in the military and we were stationed over there for a while. I think she joined the army after things went bad with my father to get over the heartbreak. She was a runner."

"A runner?"

"Didn't face her problems, just ran from them

only to make the same mistakes over and over again. I was so glad to go to college and have stability for four years. That's where I met Jade, Alicia, and Serena. We ended up getting close like real sisters. We didn't have to join a sorority because we had each other."

"That's good. Women don't keep close relationships very long," he said.

"You know the wrong kind of women," Kandace replied. "Look." She pointed to a blue jay resting on a snow-covered branch. "I wish I had my camera or my BlackBerry."

"You have a subscription to *National Geographic,* don't you?"

"No, I don't," she said. "But National Geographic is one of my favorite channels on DirecTV."

"And when you were a little girl you knew all the bird calls, didn't you?" he ribbed.

"All the ones in Guam," Kandace replied with a laugh. "What about little Solomon? What did you do when you were a boy?"

"Hmm, besides terrorize my nanny? I was into Tinkertoys, building cities to tear them down."

"So destructive."

"I was a boy with too much freedom. My parents were busy building the hotel business. My brother, Richmond, was too into comic books to be much fun. I had to do my thing."

"Playing Godzilla?"

Solomon laughed and nodded. "There was this little bakery about three blocks from our apartment. I'd give Gabby the slip and go there."

"And what did you do at said bakery?"

"Eat and flirt with the owner's daughter. She would always give me the best day-old éclairs."

"Always been a ladies man, huh?" she asked as she moved toward the tree where the blue jay was perched.

"She was six and I was nine. It made her day."

"And so modest," she laughed. "Look, more deer."

Solomon wrapped his arms around her waist and pulled her against his hip. "This is beautiful," he said, looking at her.

"It sure is."

Solomon cupped her chin and tilted her head upward. "I wasn't talking about the snow and the deer. I was talking about you." Before Kandace could respond, Solomon had captured her lips in a searing kiss that was sure to melt the snow underneath their feet. When they broke the kiss, she was breathless. "Solomon," she said, "we're supposed to be . . ."

"Doing whatever we want," he said as he caressed her cheek. "And I want you so bad right now."

"Then let's go back to my suite," she moaned as he slipped his hand underneath her jacket and stroked her back.

"You don't have to tell me twice," he said.

They left the path and headed back to the hotel. When they arrived at her suite, Solomon pressed her against the door and peeled each layer of her clothes off until she was wearing nothing but her black lace thong and matching bra.

"Damn," he intoned as he drank in her body. "You are so sexy."

Kandace smiled and reached for the zipper on his jacket. "No," Solomon said. "Let me just look at you."

Her face burned underneath his gaze. "It's not fair that I'm standing here like this and you have all of your clothes on," she said.

Solomon ran his index finger down the center of her chest and smiled. "On the bed—wait for me on the bed."

Kandace sauntered over to the bed, transfixing him with the sway of her hips. Once she made it to the bed, Solomon stripped down to his boxers and crossed over to her. She was lying in the middle of the bed looking more seductive than any super-model, and Solomon's erection made a tent in his shorts as he looked at her and slid her legs apart.

"It took you long enough," she said.

"Well, don't let me make you wait a second longer," he said as he hopped on the bed beside her. Kandace straddled his body and felt the throbbing evidence of his desire against her thighs as she kissed his neck. He grabbed her buttocks as her lips inched down to his collarbone. He held on tighter as her tongue danced across his chest and circled his nipples. Kandace arched her back as Solomon thrust his hips into hers. She needed him inside her, she needed him to take her to the brink of passion. But she had to make sure they were protected first.

"Solomon," she said breathlessly. "Protection."

"Yes, yes," he said as he lifted her off him. He dashed out of the bed and grabbed his pants from the floor near the door. Solomon quickly grabbed the gold condom packet from his wallet, then rushed over to the bed. Kandace had taken her panties off and was in the process of removing her bra, but he stopped her. "Let me take care of that," he said as he eased onto the bed and pulled her against his chest. He made short work of removing the lacy garment. He kissed her neck, then moved down to her smooth shoulder. "Mmm," she moaned as he massaged her breasts with the skill of a baker kneading tender dough. Solomon suckled her breasts, making her body hotter than a burning log in the fireplace. Easing her on to her back, Solomon nibbled every inch of her tantalizing body until he reached the crest of her feminine mound. Kandace trembled as she felt his breath at her wet folds of flesh, which craved his touch and his tongue. Solomon didn't disappoint as he dove between her thighs and kissed her until she released her passion.

"Solomon, Solomon," she called out as orgasms attacked her senses. He pulled back from her and tore the condom wrapper open, then rolled it in place. He had to feel her wetness wrapped around him. As he lowered himself on top of her, Kandace arched back and thrust her hips forward to meet his. Solomon melted inside her and groaned as she rocked with him. She was so wet, so hot, and felt so damned good. "Oh yeah," he moaned as Kandace tightened herself around him. "That's it, baby."

She called out his name again as their movements picked up speed and intensity. Solomon wrapped his arms around her and rolled to one side. Kandace wrapped her legs around him and ground against him. "Kandace," he called out. "Yes,

Kandace." Solomon quivered as he exploded. She collapsed against him and closed her eyes as her heart raced like a race car's engine.

Solomon kissed her forehead and held her tightly. Something inside him didn't want to let her go. "Hungry?" he asked.

"Starving," she replied. "We missed lunch, didn't we?"

"By a long shot, Miss Nature Hiker."

"Well, if you order us an early dinner, I'll get the fire going," she said as she stretched out against him.

"Sounds good to me," he said. "But we can wait a few minutes, because I don't think I can move right now."

Kandace kissed his cheek. "Me either," she said.

Carmen was tired of waiting for Solomon. There was no way he was still out with that woman. Slamming her hand against the bed, she picked up the phone and called the front desk.

"Front desk, this is Gia. How may I assist you today?"

"Gia, has Mr. Crawford returned to the property?" Carmen asked.

"I haven't seen him, ma'am," Gia said for the fifth time in the last hour.

Carmen slammed the phone down so hard that she cracked the receiver. Bouncing from the bed, she left the room and headed to the fifth floor where Kandace's suite was. There was no way he was with her. This wasn't Solomon's style. Carmen knew he'd gotten into her pants by now. *That dirty whore*

*was probably happy to strip down and get Solomon into
bed,* Carmen thought as she stepped on the elevator.
*He's going to tire of her soon, I know it. Solomon hasn't met
the kind of woman who can give him everything that I can.
I love him and I'm getting tired of waiting for him to realize that he doesn't have to go out and be with these airheads
when he can have me. We're going to be so good together
and no one is going to stand in my way.*

The elevator dinged when it reached the fifth
floor. Carmen saw a room service attendant heading to the Wonderland Suite. She ducked behind a
potted plant and watched a shirtless Solomon open
the door and take the food. Her knees nearly buckled when she saw the smile on his face. Carmen
couldn't remember the last time she'd seen him
that happy.

"The fire's going," she heard a woman's voice
call out.

"I'm coming, babe," Solomon replied, and Carmen's blood boiled. When he closed the door and
the room service attendant got on the service elevator, Carmen kicked the plant over and muttered a
string of curses under her breath.

"Babe? Babe? He called her babe? What does he
know about her and why is he in her room?" She
kicked the overturned flower pot again, then got
back on the elevator. As she rode down to the lobby,
Carmen formulated a plan to get rid of Kandace
Davis.

When she reached the lobby, she sought out
Frances. "I'm sorry, Ms. De La Croix, but Frances
has left for the day."

"Fine," she snapped. "I need a room."

"We're at full capacity," Gia said. "I apologize, but I can . . ."

"Don't worry about it," Carmen said with forced cheerfulness in her voice. "I'll check back tomorrow. If you see Mr. Crawford, I need you to call me. Can I leave my cell phone number with you?"

"Of course," Gia said as she handed Carmen a slip of paper.

Carmen wrote her number down. "It's important that you leave this up here for all of the desk clerks. I don't care how late it is, I need to talk to him immediately."

"Yes, ma'am," Gia said.

Carmen turned and walked out of the lobby. She didn't hear Gia tell the porter, "There is something strange about that one."

Kandace rubbed her stomach and leaned against Solomon's thigh after they finished their meal of grilled chicken, winter squash, corn bread, and chocolate cake.

"That was so good," she said.

"Better than your chef?"

"A little. You'd better watch that guy. I might pack him in my luggage when I leave next week," she said with a laugh.

"That's not going to happen," Solomon said. "I'm possessive of my employees and if any man is going to stow away in your suitcase, it's going to be me."

"Have you ever been to Charlotte?" she asked.

"I passed through there once. But I'm starting to feel as if I'm going to have a good reason to spend more time there."

"You know, you don't have to say that," she said. "We can have these two weeks and make memories and move on from there. I know that your life is in New York."

"Wait a minute," he said as he propped himself up on his elbows. "My life is wherever I want it to be. So, you're saying at the end of your vacation, you don't ever want to see me again?"

"Can we just be in the moment?" Kandace asked. "You don't have to make promises that you may not be able to keep."

"You're going to speak for me now?" he asked. "I do what I want. And when I make a promise, I keep it. And I don't make promises too often—ever, actually."

Kandace sucked her teeth and dipped her finger in the leftover icing from their dessert. Before she could lick the icing from her fingertip, Solomon beat her to the punch, slowly sucking the sweet chocolate from her finger.

"Hey. I wanted that," she said, then pretended to sulk.

"Well, if you're going to think for me, then I'm going to eat for you."

Kandace rolled her eyes and swiped the last bit of icing from the plate before Solomon could get to it. "I'm not listening to you," she said after eating the chocolate. "I'm living in the moment."

Solomon didn't say anything, he just held on to

her. A few days ago, he would've been happy to live in the moment, but after being with Kandace he knew no other lover would give him what she had given him. The passion was stronger than anything he'd ever felt and she didn't give a damn that he was Solomon Crawford. Maybe that was why he was so turned on by her. She was impressed with him as a man and not because he owned an empire or had money. Their conversations made him think, made him want to be honest, and he couldn't remember the last time he'd opened up to a woman because he felt comfortable with her.

"Solomon, did you hear me?" Kandace asked.

"What? I'm sorry, I was distracted."

"Cake . . . do you want to order another slice?"

"Yeah, but send it up to my suite. I want to show you something," he said.

"Show me what?" Kandace asked as she rose to her feet.

"Didn't I say 'show' and not 'tell'?" he quipped as he stood up and kissed her cheek. "Put some clothes on and get a move on, lady."

"You know what?" Kandace said as she slapped him across the chest. "There's not going to be too much more of that. I didn't join the military because I give orders, not take them."

"Ouch! Yes, ma'am," he said, giving her a mock salute. "You know, you're kind of violent. I bet you have a leather bustier and a whip under your bed in Charlotte."

"Wouldn't you like to know," Kandace replied with a sly grin.

"I intend to find out," he said as she sauntered into the bedroom.

Carmen sat in her car fuming about Solomon and that woman. They were so familiar with each other. In the past Solomon had only treated her like that and now he was all smiles with this temporary sex buddy. She had to end this and soon. One thing Carmen had to do was let Solomon know she was in town. *Maybe he'll return to his room and get his cell phone,* she hoped as she pulled out her phone and dialed his number again. *Please let him answer,* she thought as the phone rang.

"Crawford," he said when he answered the phone.

"Solomon," Carmen said with relief in her voice. "I've been trying to reach you. There is a problem in New York."

"Carmen, I'm sure you can handle it," Solomon said. "I'm on vacation."

"Business calls," Carmen heard Kandace say. "I guess the cake is mine."

Carmen pounded her fist into her thigh. That woman was still with him and in his suite. He never shared his space with anyone. What made this bitch so special?

"Actually, I can't handle it. Danny was murdered," she said.

"What? What did you say? Carmen, Danny was murdered? I just talked to him yesterday."

"That's when it happened, at the office. Richmond is making a lot of noise about not knowing why

Danny was hired or what he was doing at the office. Maybe you need to come back to New York."

"I'm going to call you back," he said, then hung up the phone. Carmen tossed her phone on the passenger seat and rubbed her throbbing thigh. *How am I going to get in his suite and get her away from him? What if he doesn't come back to New York because he's so hung up on her? She can't be that special. It's only been a few days. Other than sex, what does this tramp have?*

Knowing that Solomon was in his suite, Carmen figured it was time for her to get to know her enemy. She started her car and drove it to the back of the resort, where the employees parked. She noticed a group of housekeepers smoking near the employee entrance as she parked her car. *Great,* she thought bitterly. *Now I have to get past these women and find a uniform.*

Carmen exited the car and walked over to the women. "Hello," she said warmly.

"Hi, ma'am," the short woman holding a cigarette said. "The guest entrance is around the front."

"Oh, I know. I work here. I'm just going inside. How are things today?"

The other two women looked at Carmen and assumed she was one of the front desk clerks. "Fine," the short woman replied. "Except somebody kicked over a plant on the fifth floor."

"Some bad ass kid, probably," one of the other women chimed in. "Parents need to watch those little monsters. We have to keep this place looking like the brochures."

"Yeah," the other woman said. "Especially since Mr. Crawford himself is staying here."

The short woman puffed on her cigarette. "From what I heard, he isn't thinking about how clean anything is. He's with his girlfriend."

Carmen gritted her teeth and headed for the entrance. *She is not his damned girlfriend, you low class idiot.* Once she was inside, Carmen headed for the locker room, which was empty. She found a maid's uniform and put it on. Then she snatched a pass key card from one of the carts near the locker room door and headed up the service elevator. She hoped that Kandace wasn't back in her suite because she had work to do.

The tense look on Solomon's face as he dialed numbers on his cell phone worried Kandace. She wondered what was so intense that it had shifted his mood from carefree to melancholy.

"Damn it," he swore as he tossed his phone across the room. "How did this happen? How did this happen?"

"What's wrong?" Kandace asked timidly.

Solomon sighed and squeezed the bridge of his nose. "My best friend was murdered at my office last night."

"Oh no," Kandace said as she crossed over to him and wrapped her arms around his sagging shoulders. "How did it happen?"

"Police think it was a robbery gone wrong right now. But I don't understand how some punk robber got the jump on Danny. He is—was—a security expert. That's why he was working for me. We were doing background checks on the employees to make sure everyone was documented and that I didn't have any criminals on my payroll," Solomon said. "I talked to him and he said everything was fine. But he did say something about . . . No, when I called him back he'd said he made a mistake. This is crazy."

"Do you have to go back to New York and see how the investigation is going?" Kandace asked.

"I think I'm going to have to," he said. "I hired Danny and I want to know how a robber got past our security. I swear to God, I will fire everyone in that building if I don't get the answers I need."

"Solomon, you need to calm down before you go back to the city and fire your employees. You need to get the facts first," she said. "Going to New York half-cocked isn't going to change anything."

Solomon expelled a frustrated breath. "You're right. I still can't believe Danny's dead." He slapped his hand against his forehead. "He's always been closer to me than my own brother. Danny and I went through everything together and for some son of a bitch to just kill him . . . It's inconceivable that this happened to him."

"Crime is so random," Kandace said as she stroked his back. "Do you know if they caught the person who did it?"

"No. I'm sure the police are doing all they can since this is a high profile case. Damn it, I need to get with the publicity department to release a statement to the press. I should call his mother. Mrs. Jones is going to be devastated. He was her only son and . . ." Solomon's voice trailed off as he dropped his head in his hands. Kandace pulled him against her chest, not knowing what she could or should say to comfort him. Then she thought about how she'd feel if one of her friends had been murdered. She wouldn't know how to move, what to do, or be able to find comfort in anything. But she knew that she wouldn't want to be alone.

Solomon pulled back from Kandace and wiped his watery eyes. "I have to make some more phone calls and you're here on vacation, so if you want to go back to your suite, I understand."

"I'm not leaving you alone. What can I do to help? I can call the airlines and book you a flight while you make some more personal phone calls."

"Yeah, I didn't take the jet here," he said. "I'm going to need a car too."

"I can drive you to Charlotte Douglas International Airport," Kandace said as she picked up the hotel phone.

"No, no, you're not going to cut your vacation short because of me," he said. "Just have a car come and take me to the airport." Solomon walked over to Kandace and kissed her on the forehead. "Thank you for doing this."

"I can't imagine what you're going through," she said as she hugged him tightly.

"This is too much," he said as he started punching numbers into his cell phone. Kandace dialed the US Airways reservation line. Though she knew money wasn't a problem for Solomon, she negotiated a bereavement rate for his nonstop flight to New York. She hung up with the reservation agent just as Solomon was finishing up a call on his cell phone. "Is everything all right?" she asked.

"As well as can be expected," he said. "Mrs. Jones is beside herself with grief. I told her that I'm not going to rest until the person who did this to Danny is behind bars."

"Solomon, I hope you will allow yourself to grieve too," Kandace said as she sat on the edge of the bed beside him. "You're not going to be any help to anyone if you don't take care of yourself as well."

He laid his head on her shoulder and she stroked his cheek. "I'm not going to grieve until I find out why this had to happen to Danny. He didn't bother anyone."

"Do you think he may have known his killer?"

"Had to because there is no way anyone could have gotten the drop on Danny. Shit, I need to call Carmen back and find out what she knows."

CHAPTER 13

Carmen grabbed her cell phone as it rang and hit the IGNORE button before looking at the caller ID. The last thing she needed was to give away her position in the Wonderland Suite before going through all of Kandace's things. She was surprised that the woman didn't have a cell phone or a laptop in the room. *What kind of businesswoman leaves those things at home? She's just a poser. I bet she thinks she hit pay dirt with Solomon Crawford sniffing after her. Bitch! He is mine and you are not going to get in the way of what I have spent years building.*

Carmen moved across the room and grabbed Kandace's purse. She flipped through her wallet, taking note of the baby picture that was inside it. *A single mother? I guess she's trying to find a replacement for her child's father. She'd better keep looking because Solomon doesn't even want kids and he's not going to raise her bastard.* She dropped the wallet back in the purse and put it in the closet. Then she looked at Kandace's clothes, some of which still had the price tags.

I bet this low class tramp is going to return the clothes when she gets back to Charlotte, Carmen thought as she snatched one of the more expensive tags off a garment. She turned toward the bed and seethed as she saw the crumpled sheets. Closing her eyes, she imagined the things that Kandace and Solomon did on those sheets. "That should've been me!" Carmen shrieked as she threw herself on the bed and pounded the mattress. "Bitch!"

She rose from the bed and went into the bathroom to wash her face. Carmen knew she had to hold it together until she could come up with a plan to get Kandace out of the way. She'd been hoping that searching the suite would've given her a clue about what Kandace had done to bewitch Solomon, but there was no indication. Carmen gave the suite another once over before deciding to leave. If she couldn't find out anything about Kandace in her room, maybe she could find out something about her in Charlotte. She decided that she would drive to Kandace's restaurant and poke around.

Carmen dashed out of the room and rolled the housekeeping cart onto the service elevator. She hoped that no one was in the locker room when she arrived down there to change her clothes. Right now, she needed to be anonymous. The elevator doors opened and Carmen peeked around the corner to see if anyone was walking down the hall. She sighed with relief when she saw no one. Quietly, she rolled the cart to the locker room.

"Hey," someone called out as Carmen entered the locker room. "What are you doing in here?"

Carmen turned around and saw the shorter woman who had been outside smoking. "Yes?"

"You don't work in housekeeping. What are you doing in the uniform?"

"I do work in housekeeping," Carmen said calmly. "Why does it matter to you?"

"Because I'm the head of this department and I know I didn't hire you. I'm going to call security." The woman headed for the phone and Carmen pushed the cart at her, knocking the woman over.

"You're not calling anyone," she growled as she stood over her. "If you know what's good for you, you're going to pretend you didn't see me."

The woman coughed as she struggled to catch her breath. "Who are you?"

Carmen knelt down over her and grabbed her by the lapels. "I can be your worst nightmare. I'm going to change my clothes and you're going to keep your big fat mouth shut."

"You're crazy, I'm going to call security," the woman said.

Carmen knew that she couldn't allow the woman to call security but the look in the older lady's eyes told her that she was going to be a problem.

"You're not calling anyone," Carmen said then grabbed her hair and slammed her head into the concrete over and over again. It wasn't until she saw blood that she stopped.

"Oh my God!" Carmen whispered under her breath. "I didn't want to kill you. I didn't want to do this to you. You made me, you dumb bitch." She knew she had to act quickly. Carmen walked over to the locker room door and closed it. She rolled the cart against it to keep anyone from getting in. When Carmen returned to the woman's body, she looked down at her name tag for the first time. Her name was Anita. A small part of Carmen was sorry that she'd killed the woman. But that sympathetic voice in her heart was overruled by the loud voice in her head that told her Anita had to die. "She was in the way, and no one will stand between me and Solomon," she muttered as she dragged the woman's body from the middle of the floor into the bathroom.

Solomon lay back on the bed, unable to sleep. He envied Kandace, who was sleeping soundly. He'd been thankful for her and all the help she'd offered him. No matter what happened in New York, Solomon knew Kandace was going to be a part of his life for a long time. But he didn't want her to be just his friend. He wanted more. He wanted something real. Wanted to be the only man she offered comfort to, the only man she slept with and made love to. *Love? What in the hell am I thinking about? She's a good woman and I'd like to think anyone would've stayed and helped me through this. I am not going to fall in love with this woman.* As Solomon looked at her angelic face, he knew keeping his vow was going to be easier said than done. Kandace had already broken down a few of the walls he'd built up. He felt her stir slightly against him. Part of him wished that she would wake up so that he could talk to her about anything that would take his thoughts away from Danny's death.

Had one of the subjects of Danny's many investigations found him and exacted revenge? Over the years, he had cost cheating spouses millions of dollars. How many times had he told Solomon that he'd been threatened after testifying in court? What if one of those cheating husbands shot him?

That doesn't make sense, he thought. *It's not as if he'd investigated anyone with Mafia ties who could pull something like this off. But whoever killed him got past my security too easily. He'd said there was a problem with Carmen. I wonder if . . . No. Carmen wouldn't hurt anybody and least of all Danny. Maybe he'd found something on the computer about one of the employees. I should've taken his call more seriously. Danny wouldn't have called me that late for nothing. I should've known that.* Solomon eased out of the bed and grabbed his cell phone. Maybe Carmen could tell him what the police said the day after the murder.

"Hello?" she said breathlessly.

"Carmen, I've been calling you all night," he said.

"Sorry, I had the ringer off. Are you all right?"

"Not really. My best friend is dead, how do you think I feel?" he asked angrily. "Carmen, I'm sorry, you don't deserve that."

"It's all right," she said. "I know his death has come as a surprise to you."

"What did the police say about this case? Was anything missing?"

"They said it looked like a robbery. His wallet and laptop were gone and someone shot the computer on his desk. The police said it probably happened during a struggle for the gun," she said.

"Damn. I hate to think of him dying alone like that. Any idea how this person got inside? At night we have three security guards on duty and you have to have clearance to get up on the executive floors."

"Richmond has launched a full investigation to see if protocol was followed."

"Well, I'm flying back to New York in the morning to make sure Richmond doesn't make a mess of things," he said.

"You're going back to New York?"

"Of course. I won't rest until Danny's killer is caught."

"I was coming to North Carolina because I couldn't reach you by phone," she said. "I'm actually at the airport in Charlotte. Should I wait for you?"

"Carmen, you're too good to me. But you can head back to New York, or why don't you come to the resort and take my suite. I imagine this thing has you shook up as well. Who found the body?"

"Richmond did. But I came in right after and it was terrible," she said, her voice wavering. "I was so scared, Solomon. I really wished you had been there."

"We're going to find out who did this and you won't have to be afraid again."

"Thank you, Solomon. I guess I will come and check out the property," she said. "What suite are you staying in?"

"The Mountain Top on the eighth floor. I'll leave my key at the front desk for you. I'm going to try and make it back down here by the end of the week."

"Why?"

"I have some unfinished business. I'll talk to you later," he said as he saw Kandace get out of the bed and head to the bathroom.

Carmen slammed her hand against the steering wheel after hanging up with Solomon. She knew what—rather—who—his unfinished business was. Kandace Davis. She was going to put an end to all of that when she returned to the resort. All she had to do was figure out what buttons she needed to push to get rid of Kandace. Carmen checked the GPS system in her rental car for the location of Hometown Delights. Her plan was to camp out in the parking lot until the restaurant opened and then she'd make her move.

Maybe I should just burn this place down and then she'd have to cut her vacation short, she thought as she drove. The further she got down the road, Carmen decided against the arson. But one way or another, she would get rid of Kandace.

Kandace walked over to Solomon as he watched the snowfall from the window. It was a little after midnight. "Don't you think you should try and get some rest?" she asked. "You were tossing and turning so much before you got up."

"I can't sleep. I called Carmen to see if she could give me some more details about the investigation."

"Who is Carmen?"

"My business partner," he said. "She was in the office when Danny's body was discovered."

"Is she all right?" Kandace asked as she wrapped her arms around his waist.

"Shaken up, she said. My brother is allegedly running an investigation to find out how the killer got in."

"At least you know something is being done," Kandace said.

Solomon sucked his teeth. "You don't know my brother," he said as he turned around and faced her. "Richmond is doing whatever he can to make himself look good. He doesn't give a damn about Danny, and knowing him, he probably blames Danny for dying."

"You and your brother don't get along at all, huh?"

"He thinks he should be running the company. I wonder if he had something to do with Danny's death."

Kandace shook her head. "You can't be serious. Why would he do that? This thing is probably a nightmare for your public relations department, and if your brother wanted you to look bad, then he would've gone about it in a different way, don't you think?"

"I'm grasping at straws here," he said. "But everybody is a suspect until I find out the truth."

"Can I give you some totally unsolicited advice?" Kandace asked.

Solomon nodded. She rubbed his forearm gently, then said, "Don't go to New York hurling accusations. I'm sure everyone is upset about your friend's death. You're going to have to trust that the police will do their job."

"Yeah," he said unconvincingly. "I'm sure they are."

"Come on, let's go back to bed. Your flight leaves at eight and the car will be here at five-thirty."

"Thank you for being here and getting my flight and everything," he said, kissing her cheek.

"You're welcome," she said.

Solomon and Kandace snuggled against each other under the comforter, and this time, he drifted right off to sleep.

It seemed as if only a few minutes had passed when the blaring alarm of Solomon's BlackBerry woke the couple up at four A.M. Kandace rolled out of bed as Solomon padded toward the bathroom. Yawning, she reached for her yoga pants and pulled them on. She began to worry about Solomon and what he was going to do when he returned to New York. What if he did burst into his offices full of rage and accused everyone of being involved in the murder? That wouldn't solve a thing.

Why am I so worried about it? It's not my problem or my place to tell this man what to do. Solomon can handle this, I pray that he can, she thought while she put her shirt on and watched him walk out of the bathroom.

"You didn't have to get up," he said as he walked over to her and kissed her cheek.

"I wanted to see you off and make sure you're all right," she said. "Besides, I'm sure housekeeping is going to come and clean your room. I don't need to be asleep in your bed when the vacuuming starts."

"Take my number and use it. I've got the feeling that I'm going to need to hear your voice these next few days. In a perfect world, you'd be coming to New York with me so I could show you off," Solomon said.

"Maybe one day," she said.

"I'm going to hold you to that," he said. "And hopefully the circumstances will be a lot better."

She stood on her tiptoes and kissed him on the end of his nose. "Please be careful when you get there and don't go off half-cocked," Kandace said.

"I'm not going to tell you that I won't lose my temper when I get there, but I'm going to make an effort to control it," he said.

"That's all I can ask you to do," Kandace said. "Do you want me to walk down to the lobby with you?"

"You can if you don't want to go to your room and go back to sleep."

She stroked his cheek and offered him a small smile. "I can do that after you leave."

"All right, let me grab my overnight bag," he said.

Moments later, Kandace and Solomon were in the elevator heading to the lobby. As they rode downstairs, he held her against his chest. "I really enjoyed our time together," he said. "And as soon as this mess is cleared up, I expect to see you again."

"Solomon . . ."

"Don't make me send my jet to Charlotte and have a driver come find you," he said.

"All right, you won't have to do that," she said. The elevator doors opened and Solomon kissed Kandace on the lips.

"Please go to your room and get some rest," he said. "I can wait for the car alone and you look so tired."

"I want to wait with you. You'll be alone on the plane, you don't need a head start."

As they passed the front desk, the clerk waved in an attempt to get Solomon's attention, but he and Kandace passed her without looking in her direction. They headed for the sofa in front of the fireplace and the clerk started in their direction until the phone at the desk rang.

"I'm glad they keep the fire going all night," Solomon said. "Adds to the ambiance."

"Yeah. I'm amazed that you can still think about business," Kandace said.

He shrugged. "I can't help it. Besides, it keeps my mind off what's waiting for me in New York."

Kandace stroked his forearm gently. "Well, the car should be here soon and you'll be able to get back to New York and find out what's going on."

"I wonder if Danny's death had something to do with me."

"Why would you think that?"

Solomon shrugged. "Because this thing doesn't make any sense."

"What if it is a random crime?" Kandace asked.

"Too many layers of security for a robbery to happen in my building," he said. "Too many damned layers."

Kandace glanced at her watch. It was four-thirty. "I'm going to get us some coffee. Or maybe some tea for you. Solomon, you should really try and go home calm."

He didn't say anything as she headed to the drink kiosk in the corner where coffee and tea were available to guests twenty-four hours a day. Solomon dropped his head and prayed for strength.

Kandace returned with a steaming cup of tea for him and a cup of coffee for herself.

"Lemon and two sugars," she said as she handed him his drink.

"I don't even drink tea, so I'm guessing that's all right," he said with a slight smile.

Kandace took a quick sip of her coffee, noting the Seattle's Best Blend was great. As the caffeine began flowing through her system, she wondered how the killing of Solomon's friend was playing out in the New York media. With her work in marketing, she knew how tough reporters in the Big Apple could be. Since Solomon was used to making headlines for love gone wrong, she was sure they weren't being kind to him.

"How's the tea?" she asked.

"Pretty good, actually. I might have to start drinking it more often," he said as he took another sip.

"Well, think of me every time you do," she said. He smiled as he looked at her, knowing that he wouldn't need a cup of tea to think about Kandace.

The tapping on the window and the bright beams of the sun woke Carmen up. She rubbed her forehead and rolled the window down. "Ma'am," a

Charlotte-Mecklenburg police officer said. "Are you all right?"

Carmen blinked as she looked into the officer's face. "Yes, I'm fine. I guess I fell asleep."

"Is there someplace you need to be?" he asked.

"No. I was driving all night and I pulled into the restaurant and saw that it was closed, but I couldn't drive any further," she said.

"Well, you're going to have to move along. It's not safe for a woman to be out here sleeping in a car," he said.

Carmen smiled sweetly and said, "Yes, sir."

"There is a twenty-four-hour diner about two miles south of here. You should be able to get some coffee and a bite to eat there," he said.

"Thank you, sir," she replied. The officer nodded at Carmen and returned to his blue and white cruiser. She started her car and drove to the gas station close to the restaurant, parked near a gas pump, and filled the car's gas tank. Looking at her watch as she walked into the store to pay for the fuel, she realized that the restaurant would be opening in about an hour and then she could make her move.

It won't be long before Solomon and I are together, she thought as she walked up to the cashier.

CHAPTER 14

As soon as Solomon's flight touched down at JFK International Airport, his mood darkened. Being back in New York made everything real. Danny was dead and Solomon had no idea how he was going to deal with losing the best friend he ever had. He moved through the airport like a man possessed as he headed to the curbside to meet his driver. When Solomon spotted the driver holding a sign with his name on it, he hopped in the waiting Lincoln Town Car without giving the man a greeting.

"Where to, Mr. Crawford?" the driver asked once he was behind the wheel.

Solomon rattled off the address of his office building and eased back on the leather seats. For once, he didn't care how he looked when he arrived in the office. His pants were wrinkled, his shirt crumpled, and he didn't have on a tie. Normally, Solomon wouldn't dream of going into the office unless he was photo ready, since the paparazzi often waited for him.

Today, he didn't give a damn who was at the office or what conclusion people drew about him.

"Please be careful when you get there and don't go off half-cocked." Kandace's words echoed in his head as the car crawled along in traffic. Solomon pulled out his cell phone and called Richmond.

"Crawford," his brother barked when he answered the phone.

"It's Solomon."

"Great, you've decided to take a break from whatever woman you've been under or on top of to check on the mess you created, huh?" Richmond snapped. "Do you plan on coming back to New York and talking to the detectives about why you hired Danny Jones in the first place?"

"I'm in the city right now, stuck in traffic, and if I were you, I'd watch my damned tone," Solomon said icily. "I don't care how you feel about Danny, he was a Crawford employee. This is not just my mess, it is a company problem."

"A problem you created that I've been having to clean up while you play in the fucking mountains," Richmond barked.

"Just shut up, Richmond. This is something we've never dealt with and if I were you, I wouldn't be concerned with who hired Danny, but with who killed him and what effect this will have on our company. You always talk about my priorities, but what about yours? Don't you think you ought to put your childish rivalry with me on the back shelf until this crisis passes?"

Richmond groaned loudly into the phone. "I've

always put this company first. Unlike you. While you spend your nights getting photographed for Page Six, I'm working my ass off to keep our name as pure as possible."

"Why don't you tell me what, if anything, you know," Solomon said as he silently counted backward from ten.

"There isn't much to tell. Police think Danny brought his killer in with him. I've asked the security guards if they saw anyone with him and they said no."

"Have your reviewed the surveillance videos?"

"I turned them over to the police."

"What?" Solomon shouted as he squeezed the bridge of his nose. "How could you be so stupid? We should've allowed our security to go over them first."

"Excuse me? Why would I keep those videos? I'm not a detective."

"Obviously. Maybe I would've recognized the person who came in with him. Did you ever think of that?"

Richmond sighed into the phone, obviously tired of the conversation with his brother. "Then go to the police department and talk to the detectives. I'm done with this. And just so you know, I'm calling a press conference this afternoon to talk about this matter."

"Matter? My best friend is dead and you're calling it a *matter*. Go to hell, Richmond." Solomon pressed the END button, then tossed the phone on the seat beside him. "Driver," he said as he tapped on the window separating them, "take me to One Police Plaza."

Kandace woke up at ten-thirty from her nap. She was sorry to see Solomon go and she missed his arms around her. Now she had to find a way to fill her time without him being there. She rolled over on her side and pounded her pillow. There was no way she could sleep the day away when a fresh dusting of snow had fallen. Maybe she would take another hike or rent a snowmobile and go further into the woods. "That's a good idea," she mumbled as she tossed the covers back and sat up in the bed. But, before she headed outside, she picked up the phone and called Jade. She had to tell someone about her fling with Solomon.

"Hello?" Jade said when she answered the phone.

"What's up, Mrs. Goings?"

"Kandace, you'd better not be calling about work," her friend said. "I want to hear about snow."

"It is beautiful here," she said as she glanced out the window.

"Been skiing yet?"

"Once, and I will never do it again. But you will not believe who I met," she said.

"You met someone and you're telling me about snow? Details, please."

"Solomon Crawford."

"*The* Solomon Crawford? CEO of Crawford Hotels?"

"Yes," Kandace said. "We spent the last two days together and it has been amazing."

"Where is he now?"

"Have you been watching the news? I don't even know if it made headlines in Charlotte, but one of his employees was killed. He had to go back to New York. But, Jade, I'm starting to understand what went on with you and James when you two met in Vegas."

"You're falling for this guy after a few days?"

"No, not that. I'm talking the hot sex," Kandace said with a giggle.

"You know he has a reputation. He's like a super-model hunter," Jade said. "He's always on *Extra* or *Access Hollywood* with some beautiful woman on his arm."

"I'm not trying to become Mrs. Crawford and I'm under no illusions we're going to have a fairy tale Las Vegas wedding and start a family. But he's an incredible man," Kandace said.

"And a dog if you believe the press about him. I just hope you're not getting in too deep."

Well, it's too late for that because this man is like quicksand. I'm sinking into him, she thought. But she said, "No way. I've given up the canine. Speaking of dogs, how's Devon doing? Are we still getting customers because of his reputation and meals?"

"I knew that was coming, even when you pretended it was about business. He's wondering why you're avoiding him, but other than that, he's making our restaurant the hottest place in town. Hold on, Kandace."

"Why don't we talk later. This phone call is costing

me a lot since I was urged to leave my BlackBerry in Charlotte."

"All right. I'll call you later."

Kandace hung up the phone, then hopped in the shower. As she stood under the spray, she said a silent prayer that Solomon was all right.

"Miss Jade, over here," the waitress said.

Carmen smiled tensely. *Please don't let this woman ask me a bunch of questions,* she thought as Jade walked over to her.

"Is there a problem?" Jade asked as she looked from the waitress to Carmen.

"Oh, no, no," the waitress said. "She was asking about Miss Kandace. She said they were old friends, and since you and Miss Kandace are so close, I thought she should talk to you."

Jade gave Carmen a cautious once over. "Hello," she said.

"Hi, I'm April Martin. Kandace and I went to graduate school together and I heard about the restaurant and wanted to come check out the place and see if she was around," Carmen lied as she extended her hand to Jade.

Jade shook her hand limply and said, "Oh, well, that was nice of you to come all the way here to see her. But Kandace is on vacation."

"Darn. Did she ever get married? We lost touch after we graduated, but I remember there was this one guy who she was always talking about," Carmen said.

Jade laughed. "And you thought they were going to get married?"

"Well, I assumed they would."

"Maybe you have her mixed up with another classmate," Jade said. "What did you say your name was again?"

"April," Carmen said. "Why don't I just give her a call?"

"Yes. You should do that."

"One more thing. Is it true that you all have Devon Harris from the Food Network as your chef? How did you pull that off?"

"Are you sure you and Kandace were close?" Jade asked, raising her eyebrow suspiciously.

"I said we knew each other. I read about the restaurant on the Internet. I had business in Charlotte and decided to stop in," Carmen said.

"But you told Lynette you guys were old friends," Jade said.

Get out of my face, you nosy bitch! "No, she misspoke. If you talk to Kandace, tell her I said hello," Carmen said as she grabbed her purse and pulled out enough money to pay for her meal.

"I will," Jade said, eyeing Carmen with suspicion dancing across her face. "Do you have a card?"

"No, I don't. I'll just call her," Carmen said, then dashed out of the restaurant.

"What was that all about?" Jade mumbled as the door closed.

I still don't know anything about that bitch, Carmen thought as she got into her rental car. *Maybe I should wait this Jade person out and come back when there is another set of workers here. No, I have to get back to the mountains and see what I can do to her while Solomon is away. That's what I'll do.* Carmen started the car and headed for the interstate. She figured the sooner she returned to Sugar Mountain, the sooner she could push Kandace out of the way, even if that meant pushing her down the mountain.

Kandace entered the lobby and was shocked to see a number of police officers wandering around. *What in the world is going on?* she thought. She walked over to a group of guests huddled by the drink kiosk.

"Excuse me," Kandace asked a woman who was pouring sugar into a cup of coffee. "Do you know what is happening? Why are all of these police officers here?"

"I heard there was a body found on the property," the woman said before placing the plastic lid on top of her coffee cup. "One of the officers said something about it being a hotel employee."

"Oh my God," Kandace said. *This is the last thing Solomon needs.*

"Just terrible. My husband wants to leave now, but I refuse to go to South Carolina and spend the rest of my vacation with his meddling mother."

Kandace nodded, but her mind had turned to Solomon. Should she call him and let him know what was going on? *Is someone stalking his employees?*

"Unfortunately, the ski lift and most of the other outdoor activities have been shut down until the police finish looking for clues. Oh well," the woman said. "I hope the spa is still open."

"Someone is dead and you're worrying about a spa treatment?" Kandace said before thinking.

The woman shrugged, then took a sip of her coffee. "I'm on vacation and it wasn't a guest. It was probably something personal. I doubt we guests are in any danger. It has nothing to do with the free spa treatment that I'm entitled to."

Kandace walked away from the woman before she said something that she'd later regret. She headed back to her suite and once she got inside, pulled out Solomon's phone number and called him.

"This is Solomon Crawford. I'm unavailable at the moment. Please leave a message and I'll return your call at my earliest convenience," his outgoing voice mail message played back.

"Solomon, it's Kandace. Give me a call when you get this message," she said after the tone. Kandace hung up the phone and headed into the sitting area. All she could do now was wait for him to call.

Solomon cocked his head to the side and looked at Detective Dave Myer as if he was the biggest idiot in America. "How did you get this job again?" Solomon asked hotly.

"It is a simple question," the detective said as he rocked back on his heels. "Do you know if Mr. Jones used prostitutes?"

"He didn't," Solomon said. "And I believe I asked

you if you had looked at the video you took from my building."

"It's being reviewed," Myer said, then folded his arms across his chest.

Solomon sighed and rose from the wooden table. "I don't have time to sit here and banter with you when you should be out looking for my friend's killer."

"We are looking for the killer, but there are some questions that we need your help with."

"Go ahead," Solomon said as he picked up his vibrating cell phone and pressed the IGNORE button. This was the third call he'd gotten from North Carolina. He figured that it was Kandace calling and he'd apologize when he called her back.

"Do you need to take that call?"

"Can we just get this over with?" Solomon asked.

Detective Myer sat on the edge of the table and nodded. "Why did you hire Danny Jones?"

"I wanted to make sure all of my workers are documented," he said. "And I wanted to be sure that we were in compliance with all employment rules and regulations mandated by the state of New York."

"Did you think someone was working for the company who shouldn't be?"

Solomon crossed his legs and shook his head. "The last time I talked to Danny, he said everything was fine. He thought he had found a problem, but then he said he was wrong."

"What was the problem?" Myer asked as he pulled out his notebook.

"He called me the night of his murder and said

he'd found some information that didn't add up about my partner, Carmen De La Croix. But he called right back and said that he was wrong."

"Miss De La Croix was one of the first people in the office the morning after the murder."

Solomon shrugged his shoulders. "She's always in early. That's not unusual."

"Do you think she could've been involved in the murder?"

"No. Why would Carmen kill Danny? Besides, he had a thing for her. They may have gone out on a date."

"Do you think something happened between the two of them?"

"I wasn't here, so I wouldn't know. But I doubt it," Solomon said as his phone rang again.

"Your phone is pretty busy," Myer said.

You're a regular Dick Tracy, he thought bitterly as he pressed the IGNORE button again. "I am the CEO of a multimillion dollar company."

"But you were on vacation until today. Why did you leave town?"

"Do I need a lawyer? I mean, you're asking me questions as if I'm a suspect."

Myer threw up his hands. "I'm not saying that, sir. But you hired Danny and your brother said you didn't tell him."

"Does the police chief tell you about every new cop on the street? I run Crawford Hotels and I don't have to tell Richmond why I hire anyone."

"Okay. Now, Jones ran his own private investigation

company before you hired him. Do you think anyone he previously investigated could've murdered him?"

"If we knew the answer to that, then I wouldn't be here," Solomon said. "Why don't you get a hold of Danny's files and talk to the people he'd been investigating?"

"All right, Mr. Crawford. I guess that's all we need."

Solomon rose to his feet and walked out of the interview room filled with disgust at the poor job he felt the NYPD was doing. Before he reached the elevator, his phone vibrated in his pocket again.

"What?" he snapped.

"Mr.—Mr. Crawford, it's Frances from Carolina Serenity."

"What's wrong, Frances?" he asked with a sigh.

"There is a problem. Anita Hopkins, our housekeeping supervisor, was found dead on the property."

"What?" Solomon asked. "How did it happen?"

"We don't know yet. This morning one of the housekeepers came in and found her body in the locker room's bathroom," she said in a shaky voice. "The police are still investigating."

"Shit," he swore. "This is the last thing we need right now."

"The press has been sniffing around too. There are news trucks in the parking lot and police have shut down all of our outdoor activities until they clear the scene. We have no idea how much longer they're going to be here."

"Refer all press inquiries to the New York office.

Call our press office and tell them everything you know."

"Yes, sir."

"Are the guests all right?" he asked, though the only guest he was worried about was Kandace.

"Yes, they're fine, just full of questions. What should I tell them?"

"Let me get back to you. I'll have the press office fax you two statements, one to give to our guests and one for the media."

"All right," Frances said.

Solomon ended the call and stepped on the elevator. Now, he was wondering if someone was targeting his employees in an attempt to get to him.

CHAPTER 15

Kandace sat in her suite watching her telephone and willing it to ring. *Come on, Solomon. Call me back.*

She was sure that he knew what was going on by now, but she wanted to hear his voice and know that he was all right. Kandace threw another log on the fire and jostled it with the poker until the flames began to roar again.

Why do I care so much? Kandace thought as she took a seat near the fireplace. *Solomon is a big boy and he can take care of himself. Still, this has to be a lot for him to handle.*

She was about to pick up her book when the phone rang. "Hello?" she said.

"Kandace," Jade said. "I just had the strangest thing happen."

"Jade, can we talk about it later? I'm expecting a phone call. I'll call you as soon as I'm done," she said without giving her friend a chance to explain.

"All right, but make sure you call me back," Jade said. Kandace hung up the phone and chewed her bottom lip as she waited for Solomon's call. The longer she waited, the more doubt crept in about him. What if he wasn't going to call her? What if this whole thing made him focus more on his business and he forgot about her?

Kandace threw herself across the bed and pounded her pillow. "This is crazy," she muttered as the phone began to ring. She grabbed the receiver. "Hello?"

"Kandace, I got your message. Are you all right?" Solomon asked.

"Yes," she replied. "I'm fine, and I'm sure you know what's going on by now."

Solomon breathed heavily into the phone. "Yeah. I'm going to do a press conference and then I'm coming back down there," he said. "The cops up here are doing what they can to find Danny's killer and if I stay here, I might hinder the investigation because I'm sure they can do more. Besides, I've got to figure out what's going on. The last thing I need is a scandal at my new resort," he said.

"I was really worried about you," she said.

"Well, I spent most of the day at the police department giving a statement and trying to find out what information they had."

"Did you get anywhere?"

"No," he said. "It's times like this when I would turn to Danny to find whatever I felt the police couldn't. But he's not here now."

Kandace heard a catch in his voice and her heart skipped a beat. "Solomon, are you sure you want to come back down here?"

"I have to because if I stay in New York, there may

be another murder and I'm going to be responsible
for it. I'll call you after the press conference, all right?"

"Bye, Solomon," she said. When Kandace hung up
the phone, she was worried about how he was doing
and how he was going to deal with all the death going
on around him. She wondered if he had been fighting with his brother. Maybe that's why he wanted to
return to North Carolina, but he was walking from
one crisis into another.

Solomon wanted to fly back to North Carolina as
soon as he heard Kandace's voice on the phone.
Maybe she was afraid in the resort now that someone had been found dead. He wanted to hold her
and tell her that everything was going to be all
right, but that was something he couldn't tell her
because he thought there was something happening that was bigger than the police or anyone recognized. Was it possible that someone was after him
because of all the hearts that he'd broken?

"It's about time you got here," Richmond said as
he burst into Solomon's office.

"What time is the press conference?" Solomon
asked as he turned around and faced his brother.
"And what have I told you about coming in here
without knocking?"

"Sorry, King Solomon," Richmond sniped. "Is it
true that there was a body found at the resort in
North Carolina?"

"Yes, it is true, unfortunately. And I've called the
press office to write a statement and send it to the
Sugar Mountain resort and the guests. I don't think

we should talk about it in today's press conference. The two cases aren't connected and—"

"What are you trying to hide? It's not going to take long for the press to connect the dots, and if we're dodging questions at the press conference we're going to look bad," Richmond said.

"Look, I am in charge and I know what I'm doing here. North Carolina is a long way from New York and we don't know if this woman died of a heart attack or what. There is no point in making this a bigger deal than it needs to be," Solomon said.

"Fine. This is your mess to take care of. Are you going to North Carolina to deal with this situation, or do you want me to go?" Richmond asked.

Solomon furrowed his eyebrows. "What? You're offering to help me? What's going on?"

"I know you and Danny were close and I feel like I should give you a chance to grieve for your friend."

Solomon folded his arms across his chest. "That's bullshit and you know it," he snapped. "You don't give a damn about Danny or the maid who died at Sugar Mountain. You're doing what you can to make yourself look like a leader. It's not going to work, brother."

"You're a stupid, egotistical asshole," Richmond spat.

"And you're the one who said you wanted me to fail. So, why would I trust you to do anything?" Solomon snapped. "I wonder if you killed Danny."

Richmond slammed his fists into Solomon's desk, seemingly making the room vibrate. "Have you lost the little bit of mind you had left? Why would I kill Danny? Why would I put our company through all of this?"

"Because you want me to fail. Your words. And it makes sense that you could get in here without raising any questions. You would've been able to get close to Danny without him being suspicious about you or your motives."

"Idiot. Since you're playing Sherlock Home Boy now, why don't you ask yourself if I was seen in this area or on the video on that night? The answer is no because I was with my wife at a Broadway show. And if I was in here, why would I have turned those videos over to the police?"

"Get out of my office," Solomon snapped.

"I didn't kill your friend, but I'm sure whoever killed him was aiming for you. It's a damned shame that they missed," Richmond said before slamming out of his brother's office.

Solomon couldn't stop thinking about what Richmond said. How many times had he been threatened by women after he'd tossed them aside like yesterday's garbage? Maybe Kinsley Monroe did this. Or could it have been Heather Williams? Allegedly, Heather had family that had ties to the Mafia. She could've arranged a hit on him and it might have gone wrong. Danny could've been killed because they thought he was Solomon.

Now you are being ridiculous, he thought as he pushed away from his desk. *Kinsley and Heather wouldn't do anything like that. Women say stuff all the time, but I doubt any of them have the guts to try and come in here to kill me.* Solomon looked at his watch. It was fifteen minutes until the press conference was to begin. He needed to talk to his public relations staff and make sure they were on the same page. Once this thing was over, he was going to take the company jet to North Carolina and find out what was going on down there.

Carmen drove slowly into the parking lot of Carolina Serenity. The news truck and police cars reminded her of what she'd done the night before. The body had been found and now she was going to have to make sure she wasn't linked to the death. Carmen had been careful to clean the blood tracks she'd made when she dragged Anita's body into the bathroom. With all of the cleaning chemicals that had been at her fingertips, she would've been a fool to leave evidence. She'd washed everything that she touched and took the uniform that she'd worn that night and stuffed it in the bottom of her suitcase. She just hoped that the other women who saw her last night wouldn't recognized her if they saw her again.

She parked the car and headed inside. Carmen's heart beat faster as she walked past a group of officers.

"Excuse me, ma'am," one of the officers asked. "Are you a guest?"

"I am," Carmen said, then fished the key card Solomon had given her out of her purse. She flashed it to the officers and they allowed her to pass without asking any more questions.

She nearly ran to the elevator, hoping to avoid seeing anyone who might recognize her.

"Miss De La Croix," Frances called out. "Miss De La Croix."

Carmen turned around and faced the front desk manager. "Yes?"

"Did Mr. Crawford send you? He said they were going to fax statements to give to the guests and the media, but I haven't gotten anything and the phone will not stop ringing."

"Well, I'm going up to Mr. Crawford's suite and I will get back to you about the statements," Carmen said.

"Thank you. Can you believe this happened?"

Carmen folded her arms and asked Frances what the police had told her about the investigation into the death of Anita.

"Why don't we step in my office and look at the report they gave me?" Frances asked, not wanting to discuss the details of the death in the lobby where the guests could hear them.

"Sure," Carmen said as she followed her into the office. She took a seat across from Frances's desk. "So, what did the police tell you about the woman's death?" Carmen's heart thudded with fear. Did anyone suspect her?

"They think it may have been a domestic situation. One of the officers told me that Anita and her estranged husband have been going at it for a while. They've put out an all-points bulletin for Donald Brown. None of the housekeepers have seen him on the property. But he's under suspicion."

Carmen released a sigh of relief and quickly covered it up by shaking her head. "That's terrible," Carmen said.

"It is. We really need to boost our security around here," Frances said.

"I will bring that to Solomon's attention. Did the police say how she died?"

"Blunt force trauma to the head is the primary injury, but we won't know what caused her death until the autopsy," Frances said.

Carmen rose to her feet and headed for the door. "I'll call Solomon and make sure he faxes the statements to you."

"All right," Frances said.

Carmen got on the elevator and rode up to Solomon's suite feeling relieved that the police had a suspect and it wasn't her. Now, she could figure out how to get rid of Kandace without worrying about getting a murder charge added to her record and her secret identity revealed.

When she arrived in his room, she lay across the bed and fantasized about Solomon returning to join her and making love to him for the first time. Carmen slipped her hand between her thighs and rubbed herself as she imagined Solomon in bed with her. She couldn't wait until her dream became a reality. All she had to do to make that happen was get Kandace Davis out of the picture. She dropped her hand and rolled off the bed. Carmen grabbed her travel case and pulled out the nine-millimeter handgun with a silencer. She pointed the gun at the mirror. Part of her hoped that she could get rid of Kandace without using it, but she had no qualms about shooting the bitch if she continued to get in the way of her destiny.

The flashbulbs were nearly blinding to Solomon as he stood behind a podium with the Crawford Hotels logo on the front of it. He'd been used to the glare of the spotlight and at times he welcomed it, but today, it was too much.

"Mr. Crawford," a reporter called out, "what was your relationship with Danny Jones?"

"Danny and I were friends and Danny was one of the best private investigators in the city. As you know, hotels have a reputation for hiring undocumented workers. I wanted to make sure that was not going on at any Crawford hotel, so I brought Danny in to run background checks on our employees."

"Is it true that Danny Jones was involved in a Mafia investigation?" another reporter asked.

"No."

"Have police released any suspect descriptions?"

"You will have to ask the NYPD that question. I'm here to extend my heartfelt condolences to Danny's family and to offer a one-million dollar reward for the arrest and conviction of the coward who killed my friend," Solomon said. This caused a rush of questions from the reporters, which he ignored. "That's it," he said as he stepped off the stage. Richmond watched him from the corner and shook his head.

"A million dollars? Have you lost your mind?"

"Richmond, get out of my face. I have to go back to North Carolina."

"Is it the maid's death that's sending you back or the bitch whose bed you've been in?" Richmond asked with a smirk on his face.

Unable to control himself, Solomon hauled off and punched his brother. He didn't wait to watch him fall.

He darted up to his office and called the hangar where the Crawford jet was stored and arranged his trip to Charlotte Douglas International Airport. After he hung up, he picked up the phone again and started dialing Danny's number. When he realized what he was doing, Solomon dropped the phone into the cradle and shook his head. Normally he would've called Danny and put him on the case to find out who was targeting his employees, but that was a call he could no longer make. Solomon pounded his fist against the desk and dropped his head. Seconds later, his office door swung open and Richmond burst in holding an ice pack to his eye.

"I'm sick of your bar room shit," Richmond yelled as he approached his desk. "And this is the last time that you will put your hands on me."

Solomon rose to his feet. "What are you going to do, Richmond?"

"Bring you down to the gutter where you belong," Richmond spat, then threw his ice pack at Solomon, hitting him in the chest. "You'd better clean up this mess and I'm not going to help you."

Solomon glared at his brother. "I've never asked you for your damned help and if I had, you wouldn't have given it to me. I wouldn't be surprised if you're behind this."

"Here we go with this nonsense again. Why don't you just head over to Police Plaza and tell the cops your theory?"

"If I had proof, I would," Solomon said. "I'm going down to North Carolina and when I get back, maybe you should have your resignation on my desk."

"What?"

"I think I made myself clear. I want you out of this company. You're dead weight I'm tired of carrying," Solomon said as he tossed the ice pack in the trash can.

Richmond slammed out of the office muttering obscenities.

After his brother left, Solomon gathered his things and called Kandace's room. He needed to hear her voice.

"Hello?" she said when she answered the phone.

"Kandace, it's Solomon."

"Hi, how are you?" she asked, her voice brimmed with concern. Solomon smiled, despite the turmoil he'd been sinking in all day.

"I'm starting to feel a lot better," he said. "It's been crazy here, but I'm flying into Charlotte tonight so that I can see what's really going on at the resort."

"The front desk sent the guests a statement that said the police think this murder was a domestic situation," Kandace said. "Is that true?"

"As far as I know," Solomon said, not wanting to get into his theory over the phone. "We can talk about it further when I get back to Sugar Mountain. But the first thing I want to do when I get there is kiss you."

"Solomon, I'm sure you have more important things to worry about than kissing me," she said.

"Kissing you is the only thing I don't have to worry about. I'm actually looking forward to it."

"So am I," she said honestly. "But I've been so worried about you."

"I'm all right, I guess. When I booked the jet to go back down there, I hung up with the hangar and punched in Danny's number. I wanted to ask him to look into the death down there, and then I realized that he wasn't here anymore."

"Oh, Solomon."

"Yeah, I'm going to have to get used to that," he said as he closed his office door. "How was your day?"

"After the police left, I went out and rode a snowmobile," she said.

"Please tell me I didn't miss you falling in the snow again," he joked.

"Actually, I'm pretty nasty on the snowmobile. Maybe when you get back, I'll take you for a ride. I'll make sure you don't fall."

"I know what kind of ride I'm looking forward to tonight," he said seductively.

"If you're up for it, I'd be happy to strap up and give you what you want."

"Oh, I'm going to be up for it, believe that," he said as he waved his arm to hail a cab. "I'll give you a call from the plane. I've got to track down a cab. No matter how much money you have, a black man still can't get a cab in New York."

Kandace laughed and told him that she was going to have a snack in the café.

"Save some chocolate for me," he said as caught the attention of a Yellow Cab.

"Always," she said. "Be safe, Solomon."

"I will." They said good-bye as he climbed into the cab. Solomon knew that Kandace was just the calm he needed in the middle of this storm.

CHAPTER 16

Kandace looked up into the sky and held out her gloved hand to capture flakes as they fell. Then she laughed at herself because every time she saw the snow, she felt like a twelve-year-old out of school on a snow day. As she walked into the building, headed for the café, a woman bumped into her.

"Excuse me," she said. "I didn't see you there."

"That's all right," Kandace said.

The woman cocked her head to the side and gave Kandace a once-over. "Have we met before?" she asked.

"I don't think so," Kandace said as she attempted to sidestep the woman.

"I know who you are. You're Solomon's latest—um—friend," she said. "I'm Carmen De La Croix. Solomon and I are partners."

"That's nice," Kandace said.

"Partners in every way. I know you two have been spending some time together while you've been here, but that's over now."

"Excuse me?" Kandace asked, raising her right eyebrow. "What are you talking about?"

Carmen pushed her hair behind her ears and smiled at Kandace. "We had a fight before he came here and I know he was letting off some steam with you. He told me all about it, the hot tub and all of that."

"What are you saying? You're Solomon's girl-friend?" Kandace asked incredulously.

"Well, I'm the only woman in his life he's ever depended on. I'm here because of the current crisis at this resort and in New York. He told me to wait in his suite for him so that we could make up."

Kandace folded her arms across her chest. "Why are telling me this? Why don't you just traipse your ass up to his suite and wait for him then?"

Carmen smiled again. "Surely, you didn't think you and Solomon had a future. Yes, you're kind of cute, but his life is in New York, with me."

"Go to hell," Kandace sniped as she pushed past Carmen and stormed inside the café. Was she telling the truth? Was she Solomon's girlfriend? *What am I worried about it for? I knew this thing with Solomon was going to be a brief fling anyway. But I'll be damned if I'm going to be the other woman in his relationship. Maybe that's why all of his relationships with the models and the actresses fizzle, because of Carmen. Why can't men be honest?*

"Ma'am, do you need more time?" the barista asked Kandace.

"I'm sorry, I changed my mind. I don't want anything." Kandace tore out of the café and returned to her suite. She had a few choice words she planned to share with Solomon before she kicked him out of her life.

Kandace opened the door to her suite and shook her head for allowing herself to get caught up in this affair with Solomon. Honestly, she hadn't thought about having a future with him, but how could he be so dishonest? He should've told her that he had a girlfriend! And then he had the nerve to call her when he knew that woman was in his suite. "Son of a bitch," she muttered as she crossed the room and picked up the phone to call Jade. As the phone rang, Kandace considered packing her things and heading back to Charlotte. She never wanted to see Solomon Crawford's lying face again.

Solomon closed his eyes as the jet reached its cruising altitude. He was looking forward to seeing Kandace as soon as he returned to the resort. But he had to talk to Frances first and find out what was going on with the investigation of Anita's death. He shivered inadvertently. There was too much death around him and his work.

I hope Anita's death was simply related to her ex-husband and not something different. Maybe this is related to the way I've treated women. Should I settle down and just be with one woman and stop with all the games? Kandace is the kind of woman that I could see myself settling down with. . . . Wait a minute, I'm a long way from that. Danny would've loved this.

"Mr. Crawford, would you like a drink?" Rita, the flight attendant, asked.

"No, I'm fine. I'm going to make some phone calls and get some work done."

"Buzz me if you need anything," she said, then headed to the front of the cabin.

Solomon pulled out his BlackBerry and called Carmen.

"Solomon, hi," she said.

"Hey. I'm on my way back to the resort."

"Already? I thought you would've—"

"Well," Solomon said, cutting her off, "I want to see what's going on with the murder investigation and I wanted to see Kandace. I'll probably be staying with her, so you can keep the suite."

"Oh, all right," she said. "What time do you think you'll be getting here?"

"That's another reason why I called. What's the weather like? I'll be in Charlotte in an hour and a half, but I need to know what kind of car to rent."

"It's been snowing off and on all day. I'd get an SUV if I were you," she suggested.

"Thanks, Carmen. I'll talk with you tomorrow," he said. Solomon ended the call and then closed his eyes and slept for the rest of the flight.

When the plane began its decent, Rita tapped Solomon on the shoulder. "Mr. Crawford, you need to buckle your seat belt," she said.

"That was quick," he said as he lifted his seat and fastened his seat belt.

"You slept the entire flight," she said. "Would you like me to call and arrange a car for you?"

"I need a rental, something with four-wheel drive. I'm going into the mountains," he said as Rita took note.

Solomon couldn't wait to feel Kandace's arms around him and her lips pressed against his.

"Kandace, are you serious?" Jade asked as she listened to her friend tell her about the woman who had confronted her at the resort's café. "And Solomon didn't tell you that he and this Carmen woman were intimate?"

"No, but she made sure I knew all about it. Hell, she should've been talking to him and not me. I didn't make a comment to her," Kandace said as she paced back and forth.

"You sound kind of upset about all of it. I know you didn't think things were serious with this guy."

"No, I didn't. But I have never been and will never be someone's other woman," Kandace said. "I ought to pack up and come back to Charlotte."

"How about no? You should still enjoy your vacation," she said. "Don't let that dog steal your joy. And if you come back to Charlotte, you're still going to be banned from the restaurant. Speaking of the restaurant, do you know someone named April Martin?"

"I don't think so. Who is she?"

"She said you two went to graduate school together and she was stopping in to see you. I got a bad vibe from her."

"I don't remember any April Martin from graduate school. What did she look like?"

"Tall, light-brown skin, kind of Puerto Rican-looking."

"Long hair?"

"Yeah, you know her?"

"Umm-hmm. That was Carmen De La Croix. Something isn't right about that woman. I guess she Googled me after Solomon told her about us."

"She sounds like an unstable stalker. What if what she said about Solomon wasn't true?"

Kandace sighed and tugged at her hair. "Then why would she be staying in his suite?"

"Good point," Jade said just as Jaden began to cry. "My son is begging for attention or my breast. I'm going to call you back."

"Don't bother. I'm going to light a fire and finish reading *Wild Justice*. I'm sure Solomon and his girlfriend will have their reunion tonight and I won't have to look in his damned face."

"All right, but you know you're better off, right?"

"Yeah," Kandace said. But she sure didn't feel that way. As she hung up the phone, she wondered how she could've been so wrong about Solomon. No, she hadn't expected anything to happen beyond the end of her stay at Carolina Serenity, but he could've told her the truth, that he was in a relationship with that crazy woman.

"I can't believe she went to Charlotte looking for me when she knew I was here with *her man*. Crazy bitch," Kandace muttered as she crossed over to the fireplace and added fresh logs to it. Before lighting it, she decided that she was going back to the café to get that latte and brownie she'd wanted when

Carmen accosted her earlier. She grabbed her shoes, put them on, and headed out the door. She wasn't going to let anyone ruin her vacation. There were plenty of things she could do other than lay in Solomon's arms or kiss him.

To hell with him, she thought as she closed the door behind her.

Carmen watched Kandace from around the corner as she got on to the elevator. She knew that she'd gotten to her, but she wouldn't be satisfied until that woman left the resort. Carmen used her stolen pass key card and entered Kandace's suite. She quickly crossed over to the fireplace and smiled when she saw that it looked as if it had been used. Carmen figured that Kandace would probably use it again tonight since her bed was sure to be cold without Solomon in it. She knelt down and closed the damper on the fireplace.

"I wish I had some gas to pour on these logs. No, I can't do that because the fire would destroy this resort and Solomon loves this place. I don't want to do anything to hurt Solomon," she said as she headed for the door. The last thing she wanted to happen was to get caught in Kandace's room. Instead of taking the elevator, she dashed up the stairs to Solomon's suite. She couldn't wait until he arrived at the resort. She was going to be waiting to comfort him when Kandace kicked him out of her suite and her life. She could feel it in her soul that tonight was the night that things were going to change for her and Solomon. Tonight he was going to make love to her and they were going to be together.

Carmen smiled as she made it to the eighth floor. She had to hurry and get ready for Solomon's return. When she entered the suite, she called room service and ordered two steak dinners, a bottle of Dom Pérignon, chocolate covered strawberries, and a bowl of whipped cream.

"Make sure you bring candles," she told the operator.

"Yes, Miss De La Croix. Anything else?"

"No, just make sure after the meal is delivered that no one disturbs us. I want the phone placed on 'do not disturb' also," she said.

"Yes, ma'am."

Carmen hung up the phone, then headed into the bathroom and took a shower with honey lemon shower gel. She had to make sure she was smooth and silky when he touched her. She cursed as she realized that she'd left her razor in the bedroom. Hopping out of the shower, she dashed into the bedroom and grabbed her razor from her makeup kit. Glancing at the bed, she smiled as she thought of how Solomon would make love to her on top of the goose down comforter. *I'd better hurry before dinner and my man get here.*

On his drive to the resort, Solomon fought fatigue, but when he saw the shimmering lights of Carolina Serenity, his energy came back in spades.

As he pulled his rented Ford Explorer into a parking spot near the café, he caught a glimpse of Kandace sitting near the window sipping a drink. She looked beautiful in her pink sweat suit and her face scrubbed free of makeup. Solomon couldn't get out of the SUV fast enough to get to her. He needed her kiss and her touch more than anything else in the world.

He burst through the door and stood at Kandace's table. "Hello, beautiful," he said.

She looked up at him with a sour scowl on her face and quickly rose to her feet. "You son of a bitch," Kandace snapped, and tossed the contents of her cup at his chest.

"What did I do to deserve that?" he asked as he grabbed a napkin from the table and wiped the lukewarm liquid from his chest.

"Why don't you go to your suite and ask your damned girlfriend?" Kandace shrieked.

"My what?" Solomon asked as he furrowed his eyebrows in confusion. "I don't have a girlfriend."

"I'm not going to stand here and listen to your lies. She's in your suite. You just allow random women to wait in your bed for you?" Kandace glanced around the café and saw every eye in the place focused on her and Solomon. "I'm not doing this. But you'd better stay away from me."

He reached out and grabbed her arm, but Kandace snatched it away and tore out of the café. Solomon offered a terse smile to the patrons as he took off after Kandace.

He caught up to her as she stepped on the

elevator, despite the fact that she was furiously pressing the button to close the door. "Kandace," he said, "I don't understand this."

Kandace folded her arms and glared at him. "Why don't you go up to the eighth floor and ask Carmen what she said to me? Obviously, she knows what we've been doing and she felt the need to come all the way to North Carolina to stop it as she does with your other relationships. How dare you make me the other woman?" She pounded her fists against his chest.

Solomon held her wrists and forced her to look him in the eye. "You are not the other woman. Carmen is just my business partner."

"That's not what she said, and since she has free reign of your suite, I'm inclined to believe her," Kandace said as she pulled away from him. The doors opened to the fifth floor and Kandace bolted off the elevator with Solomon on her heels.

"Kandace," he said as she fumbled with her key card to open her door.

"I told you to stay away from me," she barked.

"No, I'm not," Solomon said. "You must have misunderstood what she said."

Kandace opened the door and Solomon stepped in before she could slam the door in his face. "Please talk to me, because all day I've been looking forward to seeing you and holding you."

"Save it," she said, throwing her hand up in his face. "Because you're a damned liar. Your girlfriend not only confronted me here, but she went to my restaurant in Charlotte. Something is wrong with her and I'm not getting in the middle of this bullshit."

"There is nothing to be in the middle of," he said with an exasperated groan. "Let's go upstairs right now and straighten this out."

"Are you dense?" she snapped.

"No, but I'm not going to let this misunderstanding come between us," he said.

Kandace rolled her eyes and pointed toward the door. "I want that door to come between us, because I'm done talking to you and being in your damned presence. Get out!"

"I'll be back," he said. "With Carmen. And we're getting to the bottom of this."

"Don't. Don't come back and don't bring that woman to my suite. Go, just go," she demanded. When Solomon saw the pained look on Kandace's face, he knew the best thing was for him to leave and deal with Carmen on his own.

What in the hell is Carmen doing? he thought as he exited the room and headed to the elevator.

CHAPTER 17

Carmen arranged the plates on the table and turned the lights off for the third time in the last hour. Looking down at her body, she was sure Solomon was going to love the black lace teddy she'd been waiting to show him since the day she bought it at Victoria's Secret two months ago. She adjusted her thigh-high stockings as she crossed over to the bed. Just as Carmen climbed into the bed, the door opened.

"What in the hell is all of this?" Solomon exclaimed.

"Solomon," Carmen cooed from the bed.

He stormed into the bedroom, ignoring the candles and soft music playing, and turned the light on.

"I've been waiting for you," Carmen said seductively as she lifted her leg.

"Carmen, what in the hell are you doing?" Solomon demanded. "Put some clothes on."

Carmen hopped off the bed and sauntered over to him. "I'd rather take your clothes off," she said as she tugged at his belt.

Solomon grabbed her hands and shook her. "What has gotten into you?"

"I'd like you to get into me," she said. "Solomon, I want you."

"Okay, you're a beautiful woman, but this isn't going to happen," he said as he dropped her hands.

"Why? Because of Kandace?" Carmen asked with her lip poked out.

"And because of our business together. Carmen, I'm not interested in you. I don't mix business with pleasure."

"Fine, I'll quit and we can just focus on the pleasure."

Solomon threw up his hands and shook his head. "Carmen, you can quit, but that isn't going to change a thing. I don't want to go there with you and I wish you hadn't lied to Kandace and told her that we're in a relationship."

She closed the space between them and stroked his cheek. "But I'm the only woman you will ever need. I have everything that you've always said you wanted. How can you not see that?"

Solomon pushed her hand away from his face and shook his head. "Carmen, I don't want you. I have never given you any hope of a relationship. This is unacceptable behavior. Put your clothes on and get out."

"But—but, Solomon, I love you," she stammered.

"And I feel sorry for you," he said. "Because I don't love you. Not in the way that you want me to." Solomon turned his back and headed out of the suite.

Carmen crumpled in a heap on the floor and

screamed. "No, no, no! He has to love me. He can't walk out on me! I saved his life, I saved his life." She scrambled to her feet and grabbed the bottle of champagne from the ice bucket on the nightstand next to the bed and threw it against the wall.

"I'm not going to lose him to that bitch!" she yelled as she pushed the night table over. "I'm not giving up on Solomon. I'm going to make him love me."

Kandace pounded the pillow on the sofa and tried to turn her mind off, but she kept thinking about Solomon and that woman. "Why am I doing this to myself?" she muttered as she picked up her book. As she attempted to start reading, Solomon popped into her mind again. She tossed the book across the room and then grabbed the phone. Kandace started to dial Serena's number, but she hung up. She didn't want to talk about this. She didn't want to explain why she was so vested in a man she knew she didn't have a future with.

"I've been a damn fool," she said as she walked over to the fireplace. Kandace struck a match and dropped it on the wood, then she headed for the bathroom and prepared the tub for a long bath. She poured the hotel-issued bath oil into the tub and headed into the bedroom to grab her robe. As soon as she stepped into the room, her eyes began to burn as smoke filled the room. "My God," she exclaimed as she ran into the sitting room, which was filled with smoke. Kandace ran into the bathroom and shut the water off, then she tore out of the suite, running smack into Solomon.

"Kandace, what's wrong?" he asked.

"Something's wrong with the fireplace. The room is full of smoke," she said in between coughs. Before Solomon could get inside the room, the smoke alarm began blaring. He pulled out his BlackBerry and called 911.

"I'm going inside," he said as he pushed Kandace aside.

"No, Solomon," she cried, but he didn't listen. She closed her eyes, thinking the room was on fire and he would be hurt. Moments later, two security officers and three firefighters bounded up the stairs and burst into the room.

"There's no fire," Kandace heard Solomon say. She walked into the room as one of the firefighters was leaving to get a fan to clear the smoke out of the room.

"What happened?" she asked as Solomon opened a window.

"The damper was closed," one of the firefighters said.

Kandace shook her head. "There's no way. I have been using the fireplace all day and . . ." She stopped talking when she realized that Carmen had as much access to the resort as Solomon did. It was totally possible that she got into her room and closed the damper on the fireplace. Was she really that unstable?

"It's possible that the wind blew it closed during the day," the firefighter said as he walked past Kandace to open another window.

"A wind named Carmen," she muttered as she covered her nose and headed to Solomon. She found him standing out on the balcony. "What are you doing out here?"

"I needed to talk to you about Carmen and what was going on with her. She did tell you that she's my girlfriend because she came here to make a move on me."

"Solomon."

He placed his hand on her shoulder as if he knew she was going to take off from him. "Listen to me, Kandace. She's gone. I told her to leave. Carmen thought she was the ideal woman for me. We were friends, at least I thought we were. When I was in New York, I'd tell her about the models and the actresses that I dealt with. It was like she was my business partner and my friend. I never knew she was harboring feelings for me," he said.

Kandace shook his arm off her shoulder. "So you told her about us and how I was a piece of vacation booty that you were enjoying while you were in North Carolina?" she asked incredulously.

"No, because you're more than that," he said. "I would never talk about you like that and I didn't share anything with her other than the fact that I met a wonderful woman."

Kandace glared at him. As much as she wanted to be angry with him and wanted to slap him for even mentioning what they had going on to Carmen, what he said made sense. She was obviously obsessed with him and seeing him with a woman whom he didn't toss aside made her angry. Angry enough to come to Sugar Mountain and try to get rid of Kandace and stake her claim on Solomon.

"Where is she now?" Kandace asked.

"I told her to get out," he said. "I don't want her and I don't understand how she could think that there was something between us."

Kandace shook her head, thinking of the times her mother had thought she'd met the one man who would love her forever and the heartbreak that resulted when she was smacked with the truth.

"Some women can't take no for an answer," she said.

"I'm sure she's embarrassed and on her way back to New York as we speak. I don't want to talk about her anymore, though. Are you all right?"

Kandace nodded. "Just a little shaken up. I thought this place was on fire," she said as she allowed Solomon to draw her into his arms. He kissed her on the top of her head.

"You probably don't want to stay in here tonight. The smell is going to be unbearable."

"I thought about that."

"And I'll take care of your clothes, have them steam cleaned to get the smell out of them," he offered.

"You don't have to do that," she said.

"I know, but it's what I'm going to do, so you can grab a few things and come upstairs with me until we find you another suite, which probably won't happen because we're completely booked."

Kandace smirked at him. "So what are you saying?"

"Basically, you're stuck with me, darling," he said as he tweaked her chin. "I'm sorry about all of this."

"Me being stuck with you or that crazy woman who tried to kill me?" Kandace joked.

"I'm definitely not sorry about you being stuck with me, because you owe me for that latte you made me wear and I intend to collect on that debt," he said with a lustful lilt to his voice.

"I guess I could throw myself at your mercy," she said. "At least I made sure it wasn't boiling hot."

"And for that, I might be merciful or maybe I want to hear you cry for mercy." Solomon thrust his pelvis into hers, showing her that he was ready to be inside her.

"There are still people in there," she whispered.

"Do you think I give a damn?" he quipped. "Let's get out of here. If you have something personal you want to grab before anyone sees it, I'll wait." Solomon pulled out his cell phone and called the house-keeping staff to come and clean her suite.

"What are you talking about?" she asked.

Solomon brought his lips to her ear. "That vibrator you compared me to."

Kandace slapped him on the shoulder and shook her head. "Lucky for you I don't have one, otherwise I really wouldn't have given you the time of day," she said.

Solomon folded his arms across his chest and gave her a look that read, "yeah, right."

Kandace raised her right eyebrow at him and asked, "What?"

"You're kidding, right?" he said as he wrapped his arms around her waist and pulled her against his chest. "No vibrator can do this." Solomon brushed his lips against hers, then ran his tongue across her bottom lip before devouring her mouth in a passionate kiss. Kandace swooned in Solomon's arms as his hands roamed up and down her back. Solomon's kiss lit her body on fire and sent any lingering thoughts of Carmen and her craziness flying from her mind.

"Then can we get out of here so you can show me all the things a vibrator can't do?" she asked when they broke off their kiss.

"Come on," he said as they headed back inside.

Kandace grabbed a black lace negligee and then followed Solomon to the elevator.

Carmen watched from the corner as Solomon and Kandace walked onto the elevator hand in hand. Her blood boiled in her veins as she saw the doors close. *He just needs time to realize that I'm the woman he's destined to be with. And that bitch needs to get out of the way.* Carmen stomped to the stairway and ran down the stairs with tears streaming down her cheeks. After everything she did, how could Solomon just toss her aside for that woman? A woman he didn't know and who didn't love him the way she did.

She doesn't know a thing about him and he doesn't know who she really is. Solomon knows me and knows that I only want to be with him. If he lost all of his money and everything I helped him build, I'd still love him. I know he loves me. He just needs to get away from that woman. I'm going to make that happen no matter what. Carmen slipped out of the building and got into her rental car. Her plan was to find a motel to check in to and then convince Solomon that he needed her in his life and not Kandace.

Solomon pressed Kandace against the door of his suite, happy that they were alone in the hallway. "What's that in your hand?" he asked as he took the sexy nighty from her. "Nice, but you won't need it."

"Really?" she asked as she tugged at his belt buckle.

"Yes. No need to cover that body with anything," he said as he brought his lips down on her neck. Kandace moaned as his tongue danced up the length of her neck.

"You'd better open this door before you start something," she said breathlessly.

"To open this door means I have to let you go and I don't want that to happen," he said. Kandace slipped her hand in his pants pocket and pulled out his key card.

"Then why don't I open the door?" she asked as she turned in his arms and unlocked the door. Kandace pushed the door open and gasped. "Oh my God."

"What in the hell?" Solomon exclaimed as he surveyed the damage in his suite. Broken glass littered the floor, the mirror in the bedroom had been smashed, and a night table had been turned over.

"I guess this is your parting gift," Kandace said as she and Solomon stepped over the glass and entered the suite.

"Why would she do this?" he asked as he checked

to make sure his clothes and computer weren't damaged.

"Because she's nuts," Kandace said as she surveyed the damage. "How long have you known her?"

"This was probably just her letting off steam. I'll call someone to clean this up," Solomon said.

"Are you sure she's gone and that she isn't dangerous?" Kandace asked as Solomon dialed the front desk. Kandace wrapped her arms around herself and shivered. "Solomon," she called out when she walked into the bathroom.

He rushed in behind her and looked up at the mirror.

I know you love me. We will be together, was written on the mirror in bright red lipstick.

"I don't think we should stay here," Kandace said. "She's clearly unstable."

"You're right. I'll get us another room and make sure Carmen is gone before we move back in here."

"What about my suite? She has a key here. But then again, she got into my room too."

"I'll alert the staff to keep her out of the guest area. Better yet, I'll have her banned from the property." Solomon walked over to Kandace and wrapped his arms around her. "We keep a spare room in the basement. We can stay there for the night."

Kandace rested her head on his chest and sighed. "All right," she said. "This is not how I envisioned this night ending. And are you sure she's gone? I bet no one would be able to hear us scream in the basement."

"Listen," Solomon said as he stroked her cheek, "I

know you didn't sign up for this. But it's as much of a shock to me as it is to you. I never thought Carmen would do this or that she was in love with me. So, if you feel like this is too much for you to handle and you want out, I understand. I'll even pay for you to finish your vacation wherever you want to go."

Kandace mulled over his offer. But she knew he wouldn't be there with her if she took him up on it, and that meant no more late night kisses, early morning lovemaking sessions, and everything else they'd been doing before Carmen showed up. Kandace enjoyed her time with Solomon and wasn't ready to give it up quite yet. Looking into Solomon's emerald eyes, she knew she couldn't leave. Instead of responding to him verbally, she stood on her tiptoes and kissed him ever so gently. "On top of everything that you have going on, I don't think I could leave you with a clear conscience," she said after breaking the kiss.

Solomon palmed her backside and smiled. "Just tell the truth. You'd miss me too much if you left."

"Whatever. You'd miss me so much that you would show up at my next vacation spot and start stalking me again."

"You're damned right," he said.

"I'm not going anywhere," she said. "But you owe me big time, Mr. Crawford."

"And how do you plan on collecting this debt?" he asked, bringing his lips inches from hers.

Before Kandace could reply, the housekeeping and maintenance staff entered the suite and started working to repair the damage. Solomon packed an overnight bag and then thanked the workers for coming so quickly to fix the suite.

One of the housekeepers stopped Solomon before he walked out the door. "Mr. Crawford, forgive me if I'm out of line, but there is evil afoot in this place," she said. "First Anita and now this. Something ain't right here, sir."

"I thought Anita's death was a result of domestic violence."

The older woman shook her head furiously. "Her ex-husband was already in jail when they found her. He'd been in the county lockup for two weeks because he'd been passing bad checks at the Piggly Wiggly."

"Is that so?" Solomon said. Though his mind wandered to whether or not Carmen had anything to do with Anita's murder, he quickly shook that thought out of his head. Why would she kill the housekeeper? Carmen couldn't be that violent, though she was the only connection to the deaths of Anita and Danny. But why would she kill them?

"Solomon?" Kandace said from the doorway. "Are you okay?"

"Yeah, yeah. Let's get out of here," he said as they headed for the elevator.

CHAPTER 18

Carmen walked up to the Wonderland Suite door and placed the master key card in the electronic lock. She'd seen the cleaning crew leave the suite and now she was going to lie in wait until Kandace returned. She knew that Solomon would probably keep her with him tonight, but she was going to have to come back at some point. And Carmen would be ready for her.

The faint smell of smoke hung in the air, but it wasn't unbearable. Still, if she had been smart, Kandace would've left town, because this was only the beginning. However, if she wanted to stay and fight, then she was going to have to suffer the consequences. Carmen pulled the gun from her waistband and cocked it as she stood in the middle of the suite. Closing her eyes, she felt the door open and saw Kandace walk in. Her lips were swollen from kissing Solomon and her neck had a bright passion mark on it. Carmen pointed the gun and shot her between the eyes before the tramp even saw it coming.

"Solomon is my man!" Carmen said as she opened her eyes, half expecting to see Kandace's dying body on the floor. "How am I going to make him see that he should be with me and no one else?"

She stood up and stalked back and forth in front of the fireplace. The only way she could make Solomon understand that he should be with her would be to get rid of Kandace. There was no other way around it. The bitch had to die.

Kandace smiled as Solomon led her to the lower level of the hotel. "What is this, the dungeon?" she asked as he opened the door to a basic room with a king-size bed and wall-mounted plasma TV.

"Yes," he said. "This is where unruly guests go."

"Then you should've been here a long time ago," she joked as she plopped down on the bed. "But really what is this room?"

"This is just an extra room where we put a guest that's waiting for a suite or is only going to be here for one night," Solomon said. "But notice how soft the bed is." He crossed over to her and jumped in the bed with her.

"I see," she said as he pulled her into his arms. "This place is just like you, full of surprises."

"And that's a good thing, right?" he asked as he brushed his lips across her collarbone.

Kandace took his face in her hands. "Let's say some surprises have been better than others."

"Good, because I have one that I'm sure you're going to like," he said as he slipped his hands underneath her shirt and stroked her stomach with his thumbs. Kandace closed her eyes, falling into the pleasure of Solomon's touch. He lifted her shirt above her head and replaced his fingers with his lips as he kissed her smooth belly, moving down to the center of her desire. Solomon pulled her pants and lacy panties down just enough to expose her wetness. Slowly, he slipped one finger between her wet folds of flesh, making her moan with delight and pleasure. Kandace arched her back as Solomon lowered his head and replaced his finger with his hungry mouth, licking and kissing her throbbing bud until her body shook like a trembling leaf in a windstorm. She gripped the back of his neck as her orgasm crashed down on her. "Solomon," she called out breathlessly while he showed no mercy, continuing to lap the sweetness of her juices. Kandace's body went limp by the time Solomon had gotten his fill of her. He inched up her sensitive body, stroking her and kissing her nipples until she cried out for him to stop.

"Baby," he growled in between licks, "I'm just getting started."

"I don't know how much more of this I can take," she said. Solomon slipped his hand between her thighs and stroked her until she was even wetter than before.

"You can take a lot more, I'm sure of it," he said as he brought his finger to his lips and sucked the wetness from it. "I know you're ready."

He captured her lips in a searing kiss that would've knocked her down had she been standing. Kandace wrapped her legs around Solomon's waist, pulling him closer to her. She could feel his hardness through the zipper of his jeans. She reached for his zipper, but Solomon held her wrists as he licked her neck, easing down to her collarbone and settling on her breasts. Kandace's body felt as if a thousand candles were burning underneath her skin as his tongue danced across her taut nipples. "Yes, yes, Solomon," she cried as he slipped his hand between her thighs and continued sucking her nipples.

Pulling back, Solomon looked into her eyes. "Are you ready for me?"

"No," she said. "Because I want to taste you now." Kandace pushed him on his back, then in a quick motion, lifted his shirt up and rained kisses down on his chest. She straddled his body and unbuckled his jeans, then stroked his erection up and down.

Solomon lifted his hips to help Kandace remove his jeans and boxers. When he was naked, she slid down the length of his body, allowing her tongue to blaze the path to his pulsating erection. He shivered when he felt the heat of her breath against the tip of his aching muscle. When she took the length of him into her mouth, his knees shook and his teeth chattered.

"Oh, Kandace," he groaned as she bobbed up and down. Solomon closed his eyes and threw his head back in sweet ecstasy. "Yes, baby, yes," he moaned as she brought him closer and closer to his release. Kandace pulled back, running her tongue up the length of his penis, sending chills up and down his spine. "I need to be inside you," he said as he gripped her hips.

She placed her hand on his chest. "Protection,"

Kandace whispered. She rolled to one side of him as he grabbed his discarded jeans and pulled a condom from his pocket. Solomon rolled the sheath in place in quick order, then returned to Kandace, easing behind her and pulling her against his chest. He slipped between her thighs, taking her from the back while nibbling on the side of her neck as she pressed against him. Her moans made him harder and he ground against her, eliciting the melodic tones of her pleasure that he yearned to hear. "Oh yes," he cried as he palmed her breasts, and Kandace threw her head back, expelling breathlessly, "So-Solomon."

He covered her mouth with his and kissed her, sucking on her full bottom lip as he released his desire.

Kandace turned around and faced him, resting against his chest and closing her eyes. "This has been a crazy day," she said.

"But a wonderful night," he replied as he kissed her on the cheek.

"So what happens next?" Kandace asked as she ran her hand across his chest.

"I've never gotten to this part before," Solomon admitted. "I've never wanted to know what came next with a woman. Never wanted to see another day with a woman that I'd gone to bed with. You've changed me and that's new to me."

"What makes me so special, Solomon?" Kandace asked, struck by his honesty. "How am I any different from those other women?"

He shrugged. "I don't know if it's one thing that I can pinpoint about you. Or if it is everything that makes you who you are, but you're a woman I want to know more about. I want to know what makes you smile, what makes you cry, and what turns you on—even though I have a good idea of what that is." Solomon took her hand and placed it on his flaccid penis.

"Whatever," she said with a sly smile. "It's not much of a turn-on right now."

"Let me catch my breath," he said. "And I know that it will be a huge turn-on for you again."

Kandace stroked his chest with her other hand. "Still, Solomon, I know your history and I'm not going to fool myself into thinking that we could possibly have a future here."

"Why not?" he asked. "I hope you know that I can do anything that I want. And since I want to be with you, I'm going to make it happen."

"And if I don't want it to happen?" she asked, then shifted in his arms.

"Since we both know that's not the case, I'm not even going to entertain that question," Solomon said as he pulled her closer to him. "Why don't you just live in this moment and we'll think about to-morrow in the morning."

"All right," she said as she reached to her left and picked the TV remote from the nightstand near the bed. Kandace turned the television on and flipped to The Weather Channel.

"If you're in the North Carolina mountains, get comfortable," Paul Goodloe said. "A cold front is pushing through and there will be ten to twelve inches of snow falling. People at the ski resorts should rejoice for the wonderful skiing conditions."

"Ugh, there's that word," Kandace said as she hit the mute button.

"What word would that be?" Solomon asked with a laugh.

"Skiing. I still, for the life of me, don't get what people see in sliding down a mountain with little control to stop yourself from falling," she said.

Solomon laughed and kissed her on the forehead. "With a little practice, you could shine on the mountain."

"Well, I'm not going to be here long enough to get that practice and I must say that my instructor sucked," she said, then pinched him on the arm.

Solomon rolled on top of Kandace and ran his tongue across her lips. "And you love it that your instructor sucks, licks, and kisses," he said as he ground his body against hers. Kandace responded by thrusting her hips into his and instantly felt that he was ready for more of her.

"Teach me something then," she moaned.

Solomon reached for another condom and proceeded to teach Kandace a sensual lesson in lovemaking for the rest of the night.

Carmen woke up from a restless slumber. Tonight she'd figured that she'd fall asleep in Solomon's arms, with his lips pressed against her cheek. Just like it had been so many years ago. The night that she'd fallen in love with him, Solomon had been so sexy as he slept, and despite how she tried to wake him up, he couldn't and wouldn't open his eyes. But that hadn't stopped her from roaming his body with her eyes, hands and lips. The feel of his skin, the smell of him, and the softness of his lips never left her mind. Carmen knew at that moment she had to re-create who she was to make Solomon care for her.

She sat up in the bed just as the phone began to ring. She picked it up and said, "Hello."

"You know, I'm so mad at you right now," the female voice on the other end said.

"Huh?"

"Kandace, are you in such la-la land that you couldn't call me? By the way, this is the friend you forgot to tell about Solomon Crawford—Alicia—just in case you have totally forgotten about me," she said with a laugh. "I think this was fate that you met him, and I know you're probably going to tell me no, but I need you to ask him if he will speak at the business conference I'm putting together. Of course James is going to speak, but we could get national coverage if Solomon Crawford would be our keynote speaker."

Carmen seethed as she listened to this woman rattle on. She should've known that bitch and her friends would seek to use Solomon. No, he wasn't going to speak at that conference and she wasn't going to allow these women to draw Solomon away from her.

"I'm sorry, Alicia. Kandace checked out and I don't think she's ever coming back," Carmen said in an eerily calm voice that belied the anger brewing in her very being.

"Who is this?" Alicia asked. "Where is Kandace?"

Carmen slammed the phone down and walked over to the window. She watched the steady snowfall and wished Solomon was standing beside her as she was sure he'd stood beside Kandace and witnessed the beauty of nature. Then she knew he'd turn to her and see her with new eyes. Eyes that saw how she had been the only woman there for him during his darkest day and that she was the woman he should be loving. Not all of those models, actresses, and definitely not Kandace Davis.

She's no better than anyone else and Solomon will see that I'm the only woman who has ever had his back. I'm the only woman who has ever given a damn about him, even when he was at his worst. The only thing I've ever wanted from you is your love, Solomon. And I don't care what else I have to do, I'm going to make you love me, she thought as she pounded her fist against the windowsill. "I'm going to make him love me," she muttered as her hand throbbed.

Morning came in with a foot of snow and Kandace crept out of Solomon's arms hoping to catch a glimpse of the falling snow, but the window in the room didn't look outside, just into the boiler room. She shivered as she glanced at the equipment, seeing how the metal and blinking lights of the monitors were a direct contrast to the plush luxury of the rest of the hotel. *This is a dungeon, I don't care what Solomon says.* She returned to the bed and crawled back in beside Solomon.

"I was wondering where you disappeared to," he whispered as she nestled against him.

"I'm surprised you even knew I was gone with all that snoring you had going on over there," she quipped as she kissed his cheek. "I was hoping I could see the snow this morning, but this room has no view."

"I told you, this is a temporary room where people just stay for a few hours or one night. Our suites should be ready today, but I have a better idea than you moving back into your Wonderland Suite."

"And what would that be?" she asked.

"Spend the rest of your vacation on the eighth floor with me. I have everything you want—a fireplace, excellent service, and me. You're here through Saturday, right?"

"Yes, but what about . . ."

"What about nothing," Solomon said. "When you leave here, I want you to be totally relaxed and completely satisfied. Let's just say it's the unofficial Crawford Hotels motto."

"Oh, so you make sure all of your guests take a ride on Solomon?"

He laughed and tweaked her nose. "Just the ones who fill out a lime green bathing suit like you did and are named Kandace Davis."

"Good answer," she said.

"And," Solomon said, "we might as well give another guest a chance to experience this place."

"So, this is a business move, huh? And here I was thinking that you liked me."

"Oh, I do like you, I like you a lot," he said seriously. Kandace raised her eyebrow at him.

"You don't have to say . . ."

"I know, and trust me, I wouldn't say it if I didn't believe it or mean it. Kandace, you're special, very special to me, and I want to see where we go in the future."

"With you in New York and me in Charlotte or Atlanta? Long distance relationships didn't work after summer camp when we were kids. What makes you think it will work now?"

Solomon propped up on his elbows. "Let's see," he said. "I have a jet and I can be wherever you are whenever I want. Don't make me build hotels in Charlotte or Atlanta just so I can see you every day."

"I really think you'd to that," she said with a laugh.

"Try me and find out," he said. Solomon stretched his arms above his head and yawned. "And as much as I hate to get out of this bed with you, I have to go check in with my front office manager and make sure Carmen's not on the property, and also find out what's going on with the murder investigation."

Kandace shivered at the mention of Carmen's name. "God, I hope she's gone," she said. "How long have you known her?"

"Nearly four years, and all that time I had no idea that she was crazy. When I walked into my suite last night, she was waiting for me as if we were involved in more than business. That was a side of her I had never seen and never want to see again."

"What are you going to do about her? I mean, she's so involved in your business and there's no way you can work with Carmen after all of this," Kandace said.

Solomon nodded in agreement. "I wish this never happened, you know. As crazy as she is, she was a great asset to the business, but she has to go." He reached for his BlackBerry and sighed. "I'm going to hate making this call."

"To who?"

Solomon dialed a number. "To my brother, Richmond."

"Do you need some privacy?" she asked.

Solomon shook his head, but Kandace went into the bathroom anyway. She needed a shower to wash away the feeling of dread that had settled on her shoulders as she thought about Carmen De La Croix.

"Richmond," Solomon said. "We need to talk."

"What? You have more accusations to hurl at me?" he snapped.

"Actually, no. First, let me apologize to you for the things I said when I was in New York. I know you didn't have anything to do with Danny's death and I have to tell you, you were right on another front," Solomon said as his stomach clenched. Apologizing wasn't his strong suit and apologizing to Richmond was akin to standing in front of a firing squad.

"Wait a minute. What are you admitting I was right about?" Richmond asked, and when Solomon heard the smugness in his voice, he wanted to hang up on him.

Instead, he decided to tell him why he called. Getting rid of Carmen was more important than worrying about his brother being a jerk. "Carmen De La Croix."

"What about her?"

"She's crazy and we need to let her go. Call the IT department and have them remove her access from the computer system. Then I need you to send an e-mail to all of our properties and have her banned from the locations."

"What happened?"

"That's not really important, but you were right about her. Who knows, she may have been . . ." Solomon's voice trailed off as he thought about the last phone call he had with Danny. "What is the detective's number who is handling Danny's murder investigation?"

"You don't think she had something to do with it?" Richmond asked.

"After what happened down here, I wouldn't be surprised," Solomon said. "But she's fired. She no longer works for us and we have to make sure she's far away from us."

"I can't say that I'm surprised that she's nuts. Since you've been gone, I've had some strange conversations with her. Any time I mentioned your name, she'd get this strange look on her face, as if I was making sacrilegious comments about Jesus."

"Really? I guess you were trying to enlist her for your coup d'état," Solomon observed.

"Maybe. I told you a long time ago that you were placing too much trust in this stranger."

"Okay, I don't need to hear 'I told you so' right

now," Solomon said. "Just give me the detective's number."

"All right," Richmond said with a hint of laughter in his voice. "Hold on and I'll find his card."

He makes me so damned sick, Solomon thought as he waited for his brother to return to the line. *It's too bad Carmen didn't develop a fixation on him.*

Richmond returned to the line and gave Solomon the detective's phone number. "I hope this woman has taught you a lesson," Richmond said.

"And what lesson would that be?" Solomon snapped. "According to you, it was going to be a woman I slept with that brought me down. I'm still on my feet and I never slept with Carmen. What is it that I should be learning?"

"Why do I even bother talking to you?" Richmond said. "Get this mess cleaned up or I swear, I'll have Mom and Dad remove you as CEO."

"You're not getting my job that easily," Solomon said, then pressed the END button on his phone.

CHAPTER 19

Even if Kandace thought the room was a dungeon, she couldn't deny how wonderful the six-speed showerhead felt as she stood underneath the warm spray. She hadn't been aware of how long she'd been in the shower until Solomon walked in to the bathroom and stepped in behind her.

"I figured that if I was going to get some hot water, I'd have to join you," he whispered against her ear.

Kandace turned around and smiled at him. "This shower feels so good. I've got to get one of these showerheads installed in my bathroom at home."

"Stop hogging the jets and let me see what all the fuss is about," he said as he lifted her into his arms. The water hit him in the face and he nearly dropped Kandace.

"Watch it," she said as she slapped her hand across his damp chest.

"You know I wouldn't drop you," he said. But he did put her down and blocked the shower spray from her. "Hot damn! What do you have the shower set on, boil?" Solomon turned more cold water on and Kandace laughed as she stepped out of the shower.

"That's just what you get for coming in between me and my showerhead," she said as she wrapped up in a plush towel. "How did the call with your brother go?"

"Ugh, if smug was a disease, he'd be fatal. I told him what happened here and I still got an 'I told you so.' But talking to him did make me think about something."

"What was that?" Kandace asked as she dried her face.

"The last time I talked to Danny, he said he'd found something out about Carmen that didn't add up. Then the line was disconnected. I called him back and he said he made a mistake. I didn't think anymore about it—then he turned up dead. If this hadn't happened with Carmen, I would've never put it together. I think she may have had something to do with his death."

"You think she killed him?" Kandace asked as she dropped her towel.

"I don't want to believe that. Maybe she let the killer in. I don't think Carmen is that dangerous, but just to be on the safe side, I locked her out of the company electronically," he said as he shut the water off.

"That's a good idea. How do you think she's going to react to that?" Kandace asked when he stepped out of the shower.

"Well, I hope the NYPD will keep her busy. After

I talk to Frances, I'm going to call the detective on Danny's case and see if he can find anything out about Carmen, and whether she was near Danny when he died."

"Are you sure she's back in New York? What if the police can't find her because she's still here?"

Solomon grabbed a towel and dried himself. "I don't think she'd stay here. Someone would see her and security would escort her off the property."

"This thing is starting to scare me," she said. Solomon crossed over to her and hugged her against his chest.

"I'm not going to let anything happen to you," he said. "If you don't want to stay down here alone, then come with me."

"But your meeting, that's about business and I shouldn't be there."

"And I'm not leaving you here when you just said you were afraid," he said. "So, get dressed and come with me."

Kandace decided not to argue and headed into the bedroom to get dressed.

The phone wouldn't stop ringing in Kandace's suite. Carmen wasn't going to answer it again, but she knew she had to get out of the Wonderland Suite in case Kandace's friends came looking for her. Looking out the window, she saw that the snow was falling fast and furiously, like a blizzard. She wouldn't be able to leave the mountain now, but she would have to find another place to go. Solomon had probably told everyone about what she did, which meant her access to the resort would be stripped away. Maybe she could stay in the basement room for a few days and then she would make her move. All was not lost with Solomon. Not yet.

The phone rang again, but this time it was her cell phone. "Hello?" she said in a whispered tone.

"Carmen De La Croix?" a male voice asked. It wasn't Solomon and that made her sad.

"Yes, who is this?" she asked.

"It's Detective Dave Myer, NYPD. I need you to come into the precinct and answer some questions about Danny Jones."

"I'd love to come in, but I'm not in the city right now," she said.

"Where are you?" he asked.

"Atlanta," she lied. "I was scouting a location for Solomon."

"Really? Are you not aware that he fired you?" he asked.

"Fired?" she asked with a terse laugh. "You're lying. Solomon couldn't run this business without me. He'd never fire me."

"Is that so? Because I spoke to him about a half hour ago and he told me that he did fire you and thought you might be in North Carolina at the resort where you trashed his room. The police are already investigating a murder there and we can ask the detectives to hold you until we get there."

"But I am not in North Carolina," she said. "I told you I am in Atlanta. Yes, Solomon and I had a misunderstanding, but that happens in all relationships."

"Am I hearing you correctly? You and Solomon Crawford were involved in a relationship? Miss De La Croix, I'm not an avid Page Six reader, but Mr. Crawford has been photographed with a number of women and you've never been one of them. Also, if you and Solomon are dating, why were you seen having drinks with Danny Jones the night he was murdered?"

Carmen felt cornered, just like the night the house burned. "Danny and I worked together," she said, after taking a clearing breath. "We had a drink, I went home, and he returned to the office. So, now that I've had an argument with my boyfriend, I'm a murder suspect?"

"Your boyfriend? Danny or Solomon?"

"Solomon of course," Carmen said. "I tell you what, I can come and talk to you next week."

"No, we need to talk to you now," Myer said. "And I'm willing to get on a plane and come right to North Carolina where your cell phone is pinging from."

Carmen hit the END button on the phone, then turned it off. She dashed out of the room and ran down the employee stairs, nearly knocking over two housekeepers on the third floor.

Carmen ran all the way to her rental car and climbed in the backseat so that she could clear her mind. The police were getting too close, and for Solomon to fire her, it was too much. *How can he do this to me? If it wasn't for me, this place wouldn't be open. Solomon can't do this without me and he's not going to. I know we can make up and we're going to be fine. She's behind this. Kandace told him to get rid of me, I know she did. She's threatened by me and how much Solomon and I mean to each other. I don't know why he's letting that piece of vacation ass tell him what to do with our business,* she thought as she crawled across the seat and started the car so that she could warm up. Carmen wanted to leave, but she couldn't be too far away from Solomon when he came to his senses. He would come around, and when he did he would beg her to forgive him and she would. Then they could get back to the way things used to be.

"I know you still love me, Solomon. I know it," she said as she turned the heat up higher. After a few moments, Carmen turned the car off because she didn't want to call attention to herself in the parking lot.

She would've driven to another hotel, but the parking lot was covered with snow and the plows hadn't come to clear a path for people to drive yet. Carmen wished that she'd taken a blanket from the resort so that she could cover up with more than the leather coat. All she had to do was wait until it was time for the shift change and she could sneak in and wait for Solomon. He would listen to her and he would get that woman out of their lives.

"If he doesn't, I will."

Kandace and Solomon walked into Frances's office and sat across from her desk.

"Mr. Crawford, I'm so sorry about what happened in your suite," she said. "I had no idea . . ."

"Frances, you need to make sure every staff

member knows that Carmen De La Croix is banned from this building. I think she could be dangerous and she may be involved in Anita's death," Solomon said.

"Why would you think that?" she asked. "Have you talked to the police?"

"No, but I think she's also involved in a murder in New York. I've called the detectives involved in that case and they will be sending someone down here to talk to the staff and work with the local police."

Frances tugged at her collar and expelled a long sigh. "She seemed so normal every time I talked to her," she said.

"What did you two talk about?" Solomon asked as Kandace squeezed his hand.

Frances rose to her feet. "Well, she called from New York right after we opened and asked for the guest registry."

"That's how she knew about me," Kandace whispered to Solomon.

"And you sent it to her?" he asked.

Frances nodded. "I mean, it didn't seem like an unusual request. I thought she wanted to monitor how many suites and rooms we'd booked. Everyone was talking about the fact that we were doing so well in this economy and how it was so remarkable. I thought maybe she needed the information for press or something. Then she came here looking for you, Mr. Crawford. She wanted a key to your room. She said she had a pressing matter to tell you and it was private."

Solomon shook his head in disbelief. "So you just gave her a key to my room?"

Frances widened her eyes as she looked at him. "She was my boss. What was I supposed to do? No one could locate you and your cell phone's voice mail was full."

Kandace patted the back of Solomon's hand. "Calm down," she said. "It's not as if you didn't use your role as owner to get what you wanted. Remember how you showed up every place I was?"

Frances's face relaxed for a minute and then she apologized to Solomon again. "I had no idea that she was a scorned woman trying . . ."

He held his hand up and cut her off. "No, you have the wrong idea. Carmen and I were business partners and she wanted more. But how did she get the key to Kandace's room?"

"I didn't give her a key to a guest's room. It is possible that she got a pass key card from a house-keeper cart," Frances said.

Kandace and Solomon looked at each other in disbelief. "Is it possible that she took a key from the housekeeper who was killed?" Kandace asked.

"Only housekeepers and the maintenance staff have those key cards," Frances said. "Oh my God, what if Anita tried to stop her and she killed her?"

Kandace shivered as terror froze Frances's face. "Mr. Crawford," Frances said, "we need to beef up security and . . ."

"I'll do it. I want to keep everyone safe. First thing we need to do is reprogram all of the locks so that the old pass key cards don't work."

Frances crossed over to her desk, picked up the phone and called the maintenance staff. "It will be done within the hour," she said.

Solomon and Kandace rose to their feet. "We're going up to my suite, and please make sure no one gets a key to the room other than me or Kandace," Solomon said as they headed out the door.

"Yes, sir," Frances replied.

When they entered the lobby, Kandace stopped and looked out of the glass front door. "Look at all of that snow."

"Wow," Solomon said. "And it is still coming down."

"You know, there is one thing that I want to do," she said.

Solomon wiggled his eyebrows. "Me too and as soon as we—"

She placed her hand on his chest and cut him off. "When it stops snowing, I want to make a snow angel."

"That's all?"

Kandace slapped him on his chest. "Remember, I grew up in Guam and there was never any snow. And snow in Atlanta is nothing but ice."

"All right, all right, snow angels it is. But you know you're going to be incredibly wet when you're done."

Kandace offered him a seductive smile. "I could be incredibly wet right now."

"So, why are we down here talking when I can take you up to my suite and find out?" he asked as he scooped her up into his arms and carried her to the elevator.

"Put me down," she laughed as he stepped into

the elevator car. Solomon stood her up against the wall and wrapped his arms around her waist.

"Incredibly wet?" he asked as he unbuttoned her pants.

"Solomon, what if those doors open and one of your guests gets on?" she asked as he slipped his hand inside her pants.

"Then you will have some explaining to do," he said as his finger reached the crotch of her panties. "Because you are incredibly wet."

"Solomon," she moaned as his finger found her throbbing bud, making her even wetter than she was before. Kandace looked up at the display and saw that they were on the fourth floor. "Are you going to do this all the way up to your suite?"

"Yes, unless you can't handle it."

Kandace gasped as his finger moved in circles inside her. "I don't think I can. There's no way I can stand here for another four floors."

With his free hand, Solomon pressed the button for the fifth floor and the doors opened instantly. "For the last time in Wonderland," he said as he removed his hand from her crotch.

Kandace pulled her key card from her pocket and unlocked the door. She barely closed the door and placed the external lock on the door before Solomon pressed her against the door, ripped her shirt off and pulled her pants down around her ankles. Kneeling down, Solomon's mouth found her hot opening and slipped his tongue in between her wet folds of flesh. Kandace threw her leg over his shoulder and held on to the doorknob as he licked and kissed her in the most intimate way. Her knees trembled, her heart beat like a conga drum as he sucked her clitoris until she felt her desire pouring from her body like rain. Solomon pulled back from her and lifted her into his arms and then he tossed her on the bed.

"I need you," she cried out as she unbuckled his belt and stroked his erection through his boxer briefs.

"I'm here baby, I'm here for you," he said as he started to kiss her heaving bosom. Kandace's nipples hardened in response to his tongue and the heat of his breath. She arched her body and Solomon wanted to dive in immediately, but he knew he couldn't do that. He couldn't risk an unplanned pregnancy or anything happening to her. He reached into his pocket for a condom and came up empty.

"Damn," he exclaimed.

"What's wrong?" Kandace asked.

"No protection," Solomon said as he rolled off the bed. "Wait right here and I'll be back with a condom. Unless you have one around here."

She shook her head. "We used all the ones you had here."

Solomon dashed to the door, then hollered out, "Don't move until I get back."

"All right," Kandace replied. But when she heard the door close, she got out of the bed and double locked the door. As she got back onto the bed, the phone rang.

"Solomon," she said as she answered the phone.

"I'm not moving, unless you count me answering the telephone. But you called, so it is your . . ."

"Kandace, it's Alicia. What is going on up there?" she asked, her tone peppered with worry. "I called you earlier and some woman answered the phone and said you'd checked out. Jade and Serena are getting chains put on the tires of James's SUV to come up there."

"A woman answered the phone? Oh my God, she was in here." Kandace bolted upright in the bed and looked around the room to see if anything was out of place.

"Who was in there?" Alicia asked. "She sounded strange and scary."

"I have to call you back. And there is no way you guys can get up here. There has to be at least two feet of snow on the ground."

"Please hurry and call me back," Alicia said. Kandace hung up the phone, hopped out of the bed, and dressed. Then she started looking through the room for signs of Carmen. She didn't find anything in the drawers or underneath the bed, but when Kandace opened the closet, she saw signs that the psychotic woman had been in her room.

Most of the clothes in her closet had been shredded. Shower gel had been squirted on all of her shoes, including her beloved Uggs.

"Damn it," she exclaimed. "This crazy bitch." Kandace dashed to the door and opened it just as Solomon was about to knock.

"What's going on? Why are you dressed?" he asked.

"She was here, in my room. She cut up my clothes and ruined my shoes."

Solomon swore under his breath as he walked in to the room and headed for the closet. "My goodness. All right, I'm going to call the police."

"I need to call Alicia back. She said she and Jade and Serena were going to try and come up here. Carmen answered my phone when Alicia called earlier."

"You can call her from my suite," he said as he dialed 9-1-1 from his cell phone.

Kandace leaned against the wall and dropped her head. *This is a nightmare. I could've gotten more relaxation working.*

Chapter 20

Carmen woke up when she saw the police cars pull into the resort. She smiled, thinking that Kandace must have found her parting gift. "I guess she did come up for air from underneath Solomon," she muttered as she turned the car on to warm herself from the cold. She was happy to see that the snow had stopped falling and the parking lot had been cleared. She knew she'd have to leave the property for now, since the police were there. Kandace would no doubt tell them that Carmen was the one who had ruined her clothes, and then they would come looking for her. She calmly drove off the property and headed to the only store that was open in the inclement weather. Carmen pulled her coat around her and headed inside. She needed coffee and something to eat. She hadn't had anything to eat in days and now she was starving.

"Are the roads bad?" the clerk asked when Carmen walked in the store. "I've been here since the snow started and I want to go home."

"They're pretty slick," Carmen said. "Do you have any coffee?"

"Sure do, just made a fresh pot. I hope you got more than that leather coat to keep you warm," the man said.

"Well," Carmen said as she poured herself a cup of coffee, "I need a blanket."

"I got some of those on the next aisle. Are you stranded here or something?"

Carmen picked up the blanket and sipped her coffee. "You could say that," she said as she walked over to the counter. "My boyfriend and I had a fight and I'm just trying to get away from him."

"Aww, a pretty girl like you shouldn't be out in the snow alone. I bet you don't even have chains on your tires. You're not from 'round here, are you?"

"No, I'm not," she said as she leaned across the counter and smiled in the old man's wrinkled face.

"Well, your boyfriend is a ding-dang fool for fighting with you and letting you drive in this snow. You're welcome to stay here until the snowplows clear the roads. I know that new fancy motel has some plows over there, but the state's plows should be along here directly. Then you make sure you leave that old boyfriend of yours out in the cold."

"It was just a misunderstanding," she said sweetly. "We'll make up and everything will be fine by the time we get back home."

"I sure hope you're right. Love is such a fickle thing," he said. "I tell you what, the coffee is on me and you go ahead and drink as much as you want as long as you keep me company for a while."

This is perfect, she thought. *The police won't come here looking for me because I'm sure Kandace thinks I'm lurking in every shadow in the resort. Not yet, but soon she will have to look in the shadows for me.*

"Well, thank you, Mr.—"

"Jansen, Rorie Jansen."

Carmen extended her hand to Rorie and smiled. "It's nice to meet you. My name is Sherry."

The police detective snapped pictures of Kandace's ruined clothes. "Now, tell me about this woman," he said as he looked at Kandace. "Why would she want to ruin your clothes, Miss Davis?"

"Because she's crazy," Kandace said. "She used to be one of the executives with this company and she thinks I'm a threat to her."

The detective sucked his teeth. "So, is this about a man or something?"

Solomon pounded his hand on the door. "This is about a disturbed woman who I fired. She's upset because she had romantic feelings for me that I didn't return. She's wanted in New York for questioning in a murder. I would suggest that you go out and find her."

"Don't tell me how to do my job," the detective spat. "All we have here are some ruined clothes and a woman who's angry. We don't have the manpower to waste on an investigation in to the matter of a scorned woman who is pissed off at her man."

Kandace grabbed Solomon's arm when she saw that he was about to grab the detective. "Calm down," she said. "Detective, this woman is dangerous and I don't feel safe."

"There's nothing we can do unless she threatens you physically. This is simple vandalism since both of you admit she had access to the rooms. It's a misdemeanor charge and she'd probably be able to bond out within an hour."

Solomon shook his head. "Well then, why don't you just get the hell out of here," he snapped.

The detective glared at Solomon and stomped out of the room.

"That was a colossal waste of time," Solomon said once they were alone.

"I know. But what am I going to do about clothes and shoes? Some of that stuff still had the price tags on," she lamented.

"It can be replaced without a problem," he said. "We can go to the gift shop right now. Then you can move all your replacement stuff into my suite. And the only place you're going alone is to the bathroom."

Kandace gave him a mock military salute. "Sir, yes, sir."

He leaned in and kissed her lips. "Funny. But I mean it. Carmen isn't going to mess with you anymore."

"I hope you're right and I hope she's really gone this time."

"If she isn't, I think the detectives from New York will be coming here to look for her in connection with Danny's murder," Solomon said. "I told Detective Myer all about her and what Danny said to me the last time we talked."

"Let's not even talk about her anymore. I just want to lie down," she said.

"All right," Solomon said as he placed his hand on the small of her back and led her to the elevator.

Once they made it up to the eighth floor, Solomon opened the door to his suite and Kandace crawled into bed. The suite looked totally different from the last time they'd been there. There was no broken glass, no notes written on mirrors, no overturned furniture.

"I'm going to order something from room service, some hot chocolate, or do you want something else?" Solomon asked as he sat on the edge of the bed beside Kandace.

"I don't want anything," she said.

"Are you all right?" he asked.

Kandace propped up on her elbow and looked him directly in the eye. "What do you think? This disturbed woman cut up my clothes. I know they can be replaced, but I feel terribly violated."

"I know, I know," he said as he wrapped his arms around her. "I'm sorry that I brought this into your life."

"As much as I'd love to blame you, I believe you when you said that there was nothing going on between you and that woman. But why is she so obsessed with you?"

Solomon shrugged his shoulders. "I thought Carmen and I were just friends. Maybe I told her too much about my personal life and she thought she could become what I was looking for."

"What are you looking for?" Kandace asked.

"She's right here in my arms," Solomon said.

Kandace shook her head. "I find that so hard to believe," she said. "We barely know each other."

"But I really dig what I know," he said, then kissed her on the cheek. "You get some rest and I'll check on getting you some clothes."

Kandace nodded, then closed her eyes. Before long she drifted off to a restless sleep.

While Kandace slept, Solomon talked to the manager of the gift shop and requested that she bring up a few racks of clothes and shoes for Kandace to try on when she woke up. He assured her that he would take care of the bill and that he would make sure the inventory was replenished once the roads were clear and planes could fly into Charlotte without a problem.

"Well, our sales have been down with all of the police activity that has been going on around here," she revealed. "So I wouldn't worry too much about restocking."

"I bet a number of guests have cut their vacations short," he said. He made a mental note to check with Frances to see how many people had left the property. Solomon found himself happy that the snowstorm had stranded the guests who remained at the resort.

"When do you want the things sent up?" she asked.

"Send them now," he said.

"Yes, Mr. Crawford." After hanging up with the gift shop, Solomon ordered hot chocolate and sweet croissants for him and Kandace to snack on after she finished picking out her clothes.

When he hung up the phone, he walked into the bedroom and found Kandace waking up.

"That was a quick nap," he said.

"I couldn't sleep much. I kept seeing her face," Kandace said. "I really hope this thing is over."

Solomon crossed the room to her and stroked her cheek. "I think it is," he said. "I really do. And I know what to do to take your mind off Carmen and her craziness."

Kandace narrowed her eyes at him. "I hope you don't mean sex," she said.

"Not right now. But I have a surprise for you," he said. Just then there was a knock at the door. "And it's here." Solomon opened the door and two gift shop workers wheeled in three racks of clothes and shoes.

"What is all of this?" Kandace asked as she sat up in the bed.

"You need clothes," he said as he handed crisp fifty-dollar bills to the workers. "And here you go."

Kandace hugged him tightly. "Thank you," she said.

"Well, this is sort of my fault, so I want you to pick anything you want," he said as he closed the door behind the workers. "And I want you to get your *America's Next Top Model* on."

Kandace pulled her pants and top off. "All right," she said as she walked over to the clothing racks in her lace panties and bra. "We'll start with the ski wear because I still want to make my snow angels and there is plenty of snow out there to make them in."

Solomon took a seat in the plush arm chair and smiled as Kandace pulled on a red and black one-piece ski suit that was waterproof. "This should keep me from getting incredibly wet when I make my snow angel," she said as she zipped up the suit.

"I like it. Especially the way it hugs your hips," he said. "Next outfit."

Kandace unzipped the outfit and shrugged out of it. "I guess I need something for dinner, since we do plan to get out of this suite before I leave at the end of the week." She flipped through the rack and found a black, yellow, and tan sweater dress. "I had a pair of shoes that would've gone great with this," she lamented.

"Try it on," Solomon said as Kandace held the dress against her body. "Because I can't wait to take that off you."

She winked at him as she pulled the dress on, which fit her perfectly. "I think we should definitely go to dinner tonight," she said as she looked at herself in the mirror.

Solomon walked over to her. "Let me show you where I think this dress would look best," he said as he lifted it up over her head and haphazardly tossed it on the floor. "Promise me that it's going there after dinner."

"It depends on how good the meal is," she joked as she shrugged out of his embrace. "So, are you ready for the fashion show to end already?"

"Not yet," he said as he picked a slip dress from the rack. "Try this on."

Kandace took the dress from him and kissed him gently on the lips. "You know this is too much."

"And I know that anyone else would've left me in the cold when Carmen showed up the first time. You're special, Kandace, very special. And I will do anything for you," he said as he held her against him.

She was about to kiss him again when there was another knock on the door. "What is it now?" she asked. "Macy's?"

"No, but you might want to cover up, and did you call your friends?"

"Shoot, I forgot," she said as she dashed into the bedroom.

Kandace dialed Alicia's number and smiled as she thought about what Solomon had done for her. He was sweet and special, but was she fooling herself to think that they would share anything beyond the end of the week?

"Hello?" Alicia said when she answered the phone.

"Alicia, it's Kandace."

"It's about time you called me back. What is going on up there?" Alicia asked. She heard Serena call out, "She's lucky the road conditions won't allow us to drive up there."

"Things have been kind of crazy," Kandace said. "Solomon's business partner was stalking him. She cut up my clothes and had been hiding out in my suite."

"What? That's crazy. Are you sure he wasn't sleeping with her?" Alicia asked.

"She is deeply disturbed, Alicia. When he tells me that their relationship was strictly business, I believe it, because she's acting like all she needs is a pot and a bunny."

"Michael Douglas slept with Glenn Close in *Fatal Attraction,* remember? Are you coming back to Charlotte when the road conditions improve?"

Kandace heard Jade yell, "She'd better. This is no relaxing vacation with some stalker tracking her every move. Solomon Crawford isn't worth it."

"Actually," Kandace said, "I think he is."

"All right," Alicia said, "I'm putting you on speaker."

"What in the hell are you doing?" Serena demanded. "Please don't tell me you think you and the player of the century have a future?"

"You know," Jade said, "I don't normally agree with Serena on matters of the heart, but she has a point."

"Okay," Kandace said, "I didn't say I was falling in love or getting married, but why should I let this crazy woman win? Solomon and I are having a great time. We're hanging out and getting to know each other."

"How dangerous is this woman?" Serena asked.

"More than likely she's gone. The police in New York are looking for her," Kandace said, deciding that she wasn't going to tell her friends that Carmen was wanted in connection with a murder.

"Maybe it was a bad idea for you to leave your BlackBerry in Charlotte," Alicia said. "And when you get home, I'll get on you about not telling me about your liaison with Solomon Crawford."

"Yeah, I'll tell you all about it," Kandace said as she looked up and saw Solomon standing in the doorway holding a tray of hot chocolate and flaky croissants. "Listen, ladies, I'm fine and being well taken care of. But I have to go right now."

"Oh my God," Serena said. "Do you two ever come up for air?"

"Shut up, Serena," Jade said. "Be careful, Kandace, and have fun."

"Says the woman who married the first man she met on vacation," Alicia quipped.

Kandace smiled as Solomon placed the tray on the night table beside the bed and then crawled onto the bed beside her. "All right, girls," Kandace said as Solomon's hand snaked up her thigh. "I'll call you tomorrow."

"Bye," the women said in concert.

Kandace hung up the phone and turned her attention to Solomon. "Did you come in here to rush me off the phone?" she asked.

"Come on, you're lying here in that and I'm supposed to stay in the room while you're in here?" Solomon asked as he kissed her collarbone. "Besides, I didn't want the chocolate to get cold."

"Sure you didn't," she said with a sly smile. Solomon handed her the mug of hot chocolate and laughed.

"All right, so, I came to rush you off the phone. I know how you women get. You probably could've stayed on the phone for hours, just talking about me," he said with a slight chuckle.

"And why do you assume my friends and I were

talking about you?" she asked. "Women can talk about things other than men."

"But you don't and we love it," Solomon said as he picked up his mug of hot chocolate.

Kandace sipped the rich drink and closed her eyes in satisfaction. "I'd better get dressed," she said as she set the mug on the nightstand.

"Now, why would you do a thing like that?" Solomon asked. "When I was just sitting here admiring the lovely view." He ran his index finger down the length of her arm.

Kandace swatted him away. "Because I want to try out my waterproof suit. And you can take it off me when I'm dripping wet."

Solomon inched his hand between her thighs. "And you're telling me that you aren't right now?"

Kandace clamped her legs shut on his hand. "That's for me to know and you to fantasize about. Put on your layers, Crawford. We're going to play in the snow."

He leaned in and kissed her on the forehead. "You are such a kid."

"That's right," she said. "And unless you want me to throw a fit like a five-year-old, you're going to hand me that ski suit."

"All right, all right," he said as he rose from the bed. "Whatever Kandace wants." Solomon headed into the sitting area and got the outfit she requested. When he returned to the bedroom, Kandace was leaning against the doorjamb with her panties in her hand.

"I changed my mind," she said. "I want to play with you instead."

He tossed the suit over his shoulder and pulled Kandace against his chest. "Let the playing begin," he said.

After two hours in the store with Rorie, Carmen was ready to leave. She wanted to get as far away from the loquacious man as possible. He'd told her about his dead wife, who'd passed away three years ago after a bout with cancer. Then he told her about his thirteen grandchildren who lived all over the country. His oldest grandson, Trey, was in the navy in Greece and always e-mailed pictures, but he could never view them unless his younger granddaughter came over and pulled up the Internet for him.

Carmen looked out the window as he launched into a story about the family reunion last summer when it was more than ninety degrees every day and the state was in a horrible drought. "They couldn't turn the water hose on and—"

"Look," Carmen said, "the plows are clearing the roads. We can get out of here."

"I was having such a good time talking to you, Sherry, that I didn't even pay attention to what was going on out there. You're going to leave now?"

"I think I made my boyfriend suffer enough. I bet he's worried about me since we don't know anyone around here," she said as she hugged her blanket against her chest.

"Well, you be careful out there, little lady. You want

a cup of coffee to go? Take one of those travel mugs and fill it up. And you can come back anytime for a visit," Rorie said as Carmen took a dusty travel mug from the shelf and filled it with coffee. She knew she'd need the warmth when she got back to the resort—unless she could use her pass key card to get in the room in the basement. There, she could hide out and catch Kandace off guard. Then she would get rid of her, and Solomon would have no choice but to turn to her and finally fall in love with her.

I know he loves me and when he understands how long I've loved him and how I will do anything for him, he will give me the chance I deserve, she thought as she put the top on her coffee mug and waved to Rorie. She shivered as she stepped outside in the cold air and rushed to her car. Before leaving, she filled the car with gas just in case she had to sleep in the car. Arriving at the resort, she was happy to see that the police cars were gone. Did that mean they thought she was gone?

Carmen smiled. Kandace wouldn't know what hit her.

CHAPTER 21

The sun was starting to set when Kandace and Solomon woke up naked and satisfied. He stroked her forehead and smiled at her. "Tell me that you had more fun in this bed with me than you would have had rolling around in the snow," he said.

"Of course I had fun with you," she replied with a smile on her face. "But I hope you don't think this gets you out of playing in the snow."

"Not at all," he said as he nestled against her.

"Good, then let's go outside and play before it gets too dark and the streetlights come on," she joked.

"They had streetlights in Guam?" Solomon asked with a laugh.

"On the army base where we lived, yes, and my mom didn't play with me getting in the house late. She had rules and regulations," Kandace said. "But she didn't apply those rules to her own life all the time."

"Was it hard growing up on an army base?"

Kandace nodded. "It seemed like as soon as you

made friends, they left. That's why Alicia, Serena, and Jade are so important to me. A lot of friendships don't last past college, but we all needed different things and found it all in each other."

Solomon nodded and got a far-off look in his eye. "Yeah, I know what it means to have someone who has your back."

"You're thinking about your friend?" she asked.

Solomon nodded. "Danny would've loved you," he said. "He wouldn't have believed that I'm so into you."

"You're so into me?" she asked.

"Very," he said, kissing her on the cheek. "Otherwise, I wouldn't be getting ready to get out of this very warm bed to play in the snow. The extremely cold snow."

Kandace stroked his cheek, wishing she was brave enough to tell Solomon that she felt as if she was falling for him. But the fear of his reputation and the distance between them kept her mouth closed. What if she did tell him how she felt only to turn on E! in a few days and see him kissing another supermodel? How did she know it was even safe to entertain being in love with him? Carmen was still out there and she was obsessed with him.

"Well," Kandace said. "I guess we'd better get dressed."

Solomon stopped her from getting out of the bed. "What's wrong?" he asked.

"What do you mean?"

"I told you how I felt about you and I got the silent treatment," he said.

"Solomon, we can't know that anything will happen . . ."

He placed his index finger to her lips. "I don't want to hear that anymore. I can make anything happen and we're not over when your vacation ends."

"Please don't disappoint me," Kandace said as she swung her legs over the edge of the bed. "I've seen and had enough disappointment in my life and I don't want anymore. I don't know if I could take it."

"I'm going to tell you something that I've never told another woman. I would never do anything to hurt you. You opened up something inside me and I care about you." Solomon stroked Kandace's back. "I'm not going to let you down."

Kandace turned around and faced him. "Don't make promises that you can't keep."

"I don't make promises. If I say it, it will be done," he said as he pointed his finger at her chest. "What about you? I got a heart too."

"I told you, I'm not a heartbreaker," she said. Solomon pounced on Kandace, pushing her back on the bed.

"I hear you, but prove it to me," he said, then kissed her on the neck.

"I will, as soon as we get outside, now get off me!" she said as she pushed against his shoulder.

"All right, all right." He laughed as he rolled off her.

After they were dressed and bundled in their coats, hats, and gloves, Solomon and Kandace headed over to the beginner's ski mountain. While some more advanced skiers had taken to the slopes, Kandace and Solomon were basically alone in the snow. When he wasn't looking, Kandace made a snowball and tossed it at his back.

"Hey, that's not a snow angel," he said as he turned around armed with his own snowball. He threw it at Kandace and she ducked out of the way of the first one, but Solomon's second shot hit her in the midsection.

"I'm going to get you," she said as she rushed toward him and pushed him. Solomon fell and pulled Kandace down on top of him.

"I think I got you," he said as he rolled over on top of her and kissed her. Kandace wrapped her legs around his waist as he brushed his nose against hers. "Are you wet yet?"

"This suit is incredibly warm," she said with a laugh. Solomon rolled over on his back beside Kandace.

"All right, let's do this," he said as he extended his arms and began making a snow angel.

Kandace followed suit and laughed like a little girl as she watched Solomon. She rose to her feet at the same time that he did. "I think my angel looks better," she said.

"That's because she has a cute little figure," Solomon said. "Let's build a snowman."

"Who's the kid now?" she asked with a sweet laugh.

"Still you, because you're the one who started throwing snowballs when we got out here," he said as he started rolling snow for the base of the snowman.

Kandace started piling snow and shook her head. "You know, I had the VHS tape of *Frosty the Snowman* and I remember telling my mom that I wanted to build a snowman and bring it to life. She said if we ever got snow in Guam, it probably would come to life."

"I bet," he said. "We never played in the snow in New York. Richmond was too busy sitting in front of the fireplace reading Shakespeare when it was snowing outside, and my parents wouldn't let the nanny take me out because she said I'd probably pound her with snowballs. So, I was stuck in the house with my brother."

"Were you and your brother ever close?" she asked as they raised the midsection of the snowman on top of the base.

"Not really. Richmond always wanted to tell me what to do and I don't follow orders," he said.

"I'm so surprised to hear that," she said sarcastically, then broke out in a fit of laughter.

Solomon stood back and looked at their handiwork. "This snowman looks like he would ride a short bus to the North Pole."

"Maybe that's because it doesn't have a head?" she said.

Solomon shook his head. "We suck at building a snowman," he said as he rolled a ball for the head.

Kandace cocked her head to the side and looked at the pile of snow. "I guess you're right," she said. "That is one ugly snowman."

"It's probably going to scare the kids, too."

"So, the great Solomon Crawford can't do everything," she said with a laugh. "I wish I had a camera."

"I'm glad you don't," he said. "You probably have a Facebook page that you would post this picture on."

"Actually, we have a Facebook profile for the

restaurant and I'm pretty sure the page hasn't been updated since I've been gone," she said.

"Were you all work and no play before this vacation?" he asked as he leaned on the snowman.

"According to my friends, yes. And, honestly, I was. I'd work nearly thirteen hours a day because I didn't have anything else. Jade's a newlywed and a new mom. Serena's trying to pretend she's not falling in love, and Alicia is trying to make everyone who didn't believe in her see that she is everything that they said she'd never be."

"Wow, you don't seem to be the kind of women anyone should take lightly."

"We're not, but people make that mistake all the time," she said as she crossed over to him.

"If you have a snowball in your hand, it's on."

"What if I was coming over here to kiss you?" she asked with her hand behind her back.

Solomon met her in front of the snowman and she tossed her snowball at him. "Dirty," he called out as she hit him in the stomach with her hidden snowball.

"I'm done, I'm done," she cried out as Solomon lifted her in his arms and spun her around.

"But I'm just getting started," he said, then captured her lips.

Carmen fought tears as she watched from the woods and saw how happy Solomon looked as he played with Kandace. She'd never seen him act that way and she knew there was something different about the way he felt about Kandace. But he was giving his feelings to the wrong woman, again. Just like the woman he'd almost married, Kandace wasn't good enough for him. Her friends wanted to use him and they'd probably sent Kandace to the resort to seduce Solomon, get him to come down there, and bring national attention to that business crap the other woman was talking about on the phone. Carmen swore that she wasn't going to let those bitches hurt the man she loved. More than that, she wasn't going to stand by and watch Solomon fawn all over this woman who didn't know him or love him the way she did. She inched closer to the line of trees next to the hill where Solomon and Kandace were. As he kissed her, Carmen dug her nails into her hand and fought the urge to scream. He should be kissing her, frolicking in the snow with her, and smiling at her the way he did with Kandace.

I hate her. I hate her! she repeated in her mind over and over. Reaching for her blanket, the gun she'd been carrying fell on the ground. She ran her finger across the cold black steel. "I could kill her right now," she muttered. "She deserves to die."

Carmen picked up the gun and pointed it at Kandace's back, but before she pulled the trigger, Solomon spun her around and dipped her as if they had been dancing. Carmen dropped the gun as she saw that firing it would strike the man she loved. "Solomon, why won't you give me a chance?" she whispered.

She took off toward the resort and crept around to the employee entrance. Luckily for her, the door was cracked open. Earlier in the evening, Carmen had discovered that her pass key card didn't work. She pushed the door open and walked into the locker room. She glanced around the corner, making sure no one was inside to see her. Carmen grabbed a pass key card from one of the housekeeping carts and headed to the stairwell. Resting against the wall, she took a deep breath. It felt good to be inside, but she knew she had to move fast before someone saw her. Carmen wondered if Solomon and Kandace were staying in her suite or his. This was going to end tonight one way or another. Carmen checked her waistband to make sure the gun was still there. As she was about to walk up the stairs, she heard the door open. Carmen quickly ducked underneath the stairs as she heard two housekeepers walking up them.

"It's a shame about Anita," one of the women said. "And the police still don't know who did it."

"I miss that bossy woman," the other woman said. "Whoever killed her should just come forward and confess. She never bothered anybody."

Oh please, shut up. If that woman hadn't gotten in my way, she'd be alive, Carmen thought as she listened to the women walk up the stairs. When she finally heard the door close behind them, Carmen came out from underneath the stairs and dashed up to the fifth floor. She entered the Wonderland Suite and saw that it was empty.

"I should've known she moved into his suite. I bet she's been telling him how she's so afraid and needs him to protect her," Carmen muttered.

"Well, no more. I'm getting my man back and she's just going to have to deal with it."

Kandace sighed as she sipped a hot latte in the café with Solomon. Her hair stuck to her neck as the snow melted from all the rolling around they'd done on the hill. "I had so much fun," she said as she leaned over the table and touched the back of his hand.

"Fun? You wore me out," Solomon said. "You're worse than a kid."

Kandace smiled. "I know you're not one to talk about wearing someone out. You've been doing that to me since we met."

"Whatever," he said with a grin. "I dare you to say that you didn't like it."

She stroked his hand. "I never said I didn't. But, I need to get out of this suit and wash my hair." Kandace sopped up water from her neck.

"I told you, incredibly wet," he said, then tweaked her nose.

"Let's go upstairs so that you can take my clothes off and warm me up even more," she said with a wink.

Solomon dropped a few bills on the table to pay for their drinks, then he and Kandace quickly headed up to his suite.

Once they made it inside, Solomon kicked off his boots before turning to Kandace and unzipping her ski suit. He pushed the garment off her shoulders and kissed her neck as he continued to take the suit off. When she was standing there in just her thermal underwear, Solomon sighed. "You seriously have on too many clothes."

"Did you really think I was going to roll around in the snow in just the ski suit? I'll be naked when I get in the tub if you get it started now," she said. Solomon winked at her as he pulled his clothes off and headed into the bathroom.

Kandace slipped out of her thermal underwear and followed him into the bathroom, where he was filling the whirlpool tub with water and bath oil. She slipped behind him and kissed him on his neck.

"What did I do to deserve that?" he asked, turning around and smiling at Kandace in her birthday suit.

"Everything," she said. "I had a lot of fun with you and . . ."

"It's not over," he said. "I was thinking that I should go back to Charlotte with you at the end of the week."

"Don't you have work to do?" she asked.

"I'm the boss. I work when I want to," Solomon said as he pulled her into his lap. He dipped his hand in the tub and sprinkled water on her stomach. "After everything that's been going on, I don't want to go back to New York right away."

Kandace wrapped her arms around his neck as he turned the water off. "Are you all right?"

"Sometimes when I sit down and think about Danny and Carmen, I can't believe how things have changed," he said. "I don't want to get caught off guard again. I want to live in the moment and spend many of those moments just like this."

"Naked on the edge of a tub?" she quipped.

"With you in my arms, yes," he said, then kissed her cheek.

"All right, then, I'd love for you to come back to Charlotte with me, but I have to warn you, my friends are going to give you a hard time because they can be pretty tough," Kandace said as she slipped off his lap and into the tub.

Solomon turned the jets on low and climbed in behind her. "Ever made love in a hot tub before? I've dreamed about doing this with you since the first day I saw you in the lime green bathing suit in the grotto," he said as he dipped down underneath the water and between Kandace's thighs.

"Solomon, you're insatiable," she said when he came up and rested his head between her breasts.

"I know," he said as he took her hand and placed it on his throbbing desire. "But you're the cause of this."

"Oh, you would try to blame me," she said with a smile.

"Can I help it that you're the most desirable woman that I've ever met and when I see you naked all I want to do is bury myself inside you until the sun comes up?" he asked.

"Okay, babe, that was the corniest but sweetest thing you've ever said to me."

"Corny? Now, I've been called a lot of things, but corny has never been one of them."

"Oh, so I guess I need to stroke your ego now and give you a list of other adjectives that I would use to describe you," she said, then kissed him on the cheek.

"No, just do that again, only right here," he replied, pointing to his lips. Kandace kissed him soft and slow, slipping her tongue into his mouth, savoring the sweet taste of him. He pulled her deeper into his kiss, enjoying the swell of her breasts against his bare chest. Lifting her out of the water, Solomon broke the kiss and sat her on the edge of the tub. He smiled at her as he slipped his hand between her thighs. Kandace's body responded to his touch instantly. She felt a tingling from the tips of her toes to the crest of her thighs. Solomon parted her legs as he pressed his finger inside her, searching for her throbbing bud of desire. She trembled as he fingered her most sensitive area and arched her back so that he could have better access to the center of her desire.

"Solomon," she moaned as his finger was quickly replaced with his tongue. He nearly brought her to climax as his tongue danced inside of her, turning her into a pool of lust. Solomon gripped her hips as he continued his sensual assault of her body. Kandace pounded her hand against the marble surrounding the tub as she could no longer hold off the explosion between her thighs.

"You taste so good," he said as he licked his lips. "I could feast on you all day."

Kandace eased back into the tub, smiling ever so slightly as her body rippled with pleasure and satisfaction. "And I'm willing to let you," she said as she grabbed his chin and kissed him. The mix of his sweetness and the taste of herself was incredibly arousing. Hungrily, she deepened her kiss and pressed her body against his and immediately felt his erection against her thighs. Kandace inhaled sharply as Solomon tore his mouth from hers and began kissing and sucking her breasts until her nipples were harder than diamonds and more tender than her lower regions. She gasped when his tongue grazed her nipples.

"I want you," she said. "Need. You. Inside."

Solomon didn't respond to her request verbally, he just lifted her from the tub and took her over to the marble bench near the shower. Kandace wrapped her legs around his waist as he sat her down and ground her body against his. Solomon's knees quivered as he felt the heat from her opening at the tip of his penis. He wanted to bury himself inside her immediately, especially when she kissed him, slipping her tongue between his lips and making him groan with anticipation. It took every ounce of self-control in him to pull away from her and dash into the bedroom to get a condom. But when he returned to the bathroom, sheathed and ready, he laid Kandace across the bench and dove in between her legs.

She expelled a cleansing breath as she and Solomon became one. She thrust her hips into his as he slowly ground his body against her, touching every spot to make her scream. And she screamed his name over and over again as she dug her nails into his caramel shoulder.

"Yes, baby," he said as he plunged deeper. "Oh, you feel so good. So damned good."

"You do too," she moaned as he lifted her into a seated position.

"Ride me, baby," he requested. Kandace locked

her legs around his waist and moved her body like a belly dancer, slowly and sensually as Solomon held on to her waist. He'd never felt so good with someone else being in control of his pleasure. He matched Kandace's rhythm as he rotated his hips in concert with hers. Kandace threw her head back as she felt the rush of her orgasm settling in her hot valley.

Solomon was also on the brink of his own climax and when he felt the heat of Kandace's desire spilling down to his thigh, he couldn't hold back any longer. He released a guttural groan as he came and hugged her against his chest. She closed her eyes as she rested her head on him, and neither of them had the energy or desire to move.

It was nearly an hour before Kandace and Solomon dried off, put on robes and ordered room service. While they waited, Kandace lay against Solomon's bare chest and stroked his smooth skin. "This is nice, but what is taking room service so long? I'm starving," she said.

"It's probably busy tonight," he said. "But I can call and check." As Solomon reached for the phone there was a knock at the door. "Right on time." He hopped off the bed and headed for the door.

"Make sure it's room service," Kandace cautioned. Solomon nodded as he looked into the peephole. When he saw the waiter standing there, he opened the door.

"Sorry it took so long, sir," the young man said as he wheeled the dinner cart into the suite.

"Not a problem," Solomon replied. "We found a way to pass the time while we waited."

The waiter smiled as he looked at Solomon's robe. "Do you need anything else, sir?"

"No," Solomon said as he reached into his pocket and handed the waiter a tip. "Actually, on your way out, put the DO NOT DISTURB sign on the door."

The waiter nodded and headed out the door with the sign in his hand. Solomon rolled the cart into the bedroom where Kandace was waiting. "Dinner is served," he said.

"Great," she said. "I didn't even think to ask you what you ordered."

"Grilled salmon," he said as he lifted the cover off the main dishes. "Green beans with almonds, wild rice, and for dessert, chocolate cake or me, take your pick."

She smiled as she scooted to the edge of the bed where the cart was. "I'll let you know after I eat," she said.

CHAPTER 22

Carmen closed her eyes as she leaned back on the bed. Now that she was warm, she had a chance to get her plan together. If Kandace was in the suite with Solomon, she was going to have to figure out a way to get him away from her. Maybe she should call Richmond and tell him that Solomon was in trouble. *That wouldn't work,* she thought. *Richmond doesn't give a damn about Solomon. No one cares about him the way I do. Why can't he understand that?* Carmen pulled out her gun and stroked it. She was going to kill Kandace. There was no other way to get that leech away from her man. With Kandace out of the way, Solomon would have no choice but to love Carmen.

"I know he didn't mean what he said the other night. He was just confused because we've been friends for so long," she said to the walls. "But when I make him remember, he's going to see that we belong together and how he's always loved me. I'm going to show him and he's going to be so glad that I stayed in his life after that bitch hurt him at his wedding. He'll see, yes. He'll see that I'm the only woman he could ever love."

Carmen crossed over to the door and looked out the peephole to see if the halls were clear. Unfortunately, one family was entering their suite and another was gearing up to leave. She was tired of waiting, but she couldn't risk being seen, not when she was so close to her man. So close to having Solomon's arms around her and feeling his lips pressed against her.

Then a lightbulb went off in her head. Frances could get Solomon out of the suite. Carmen would make sure Frances did just what she wanted. Carmen tucked the gun in her waistband and headed toward the door. She caught a quick glimpse of herself in the mirror and was mortified by her appearance. Her hair was disheveled and stringy, she had dark circles underneath her eyes, and her face was pale. "Oh my God, Solomon is never going to want me if he sees me like this." She ran her hand across her forehead, then dashed into the bathroom. Carmen splashed hot water on her face hoping to get the blood flowing to her cheeks. But she still didn't like the reflection she saw in the mirror.

"You're ugly. I wish you'd never been born and now you come up with these lies about the only man who's ever loved me? What do you want me to do, put him out and get stuck in this house with you?"

"But, Mama, he touched me down there," she'd cried as her mother raised her hand and slapped her.

She tried to cover her face, but her mother grabbed her hand and pushed her against the wall. "You're going to stop these damned lies!"

Tears poured from her eyes as her mother glared at her with hate. "I should've never had you. I shouldn't have waited so long to have that abortion. You're nothing, just like your father. He walked away from me because of you."

"I hate you!"

"I hate you too! I always have hated you and I'm not going to let you cost me another man. Not this time. Get out of my sight before I do something to you."

She ran as fast as her skinny legs would carry her to her bedroom. When she got in her room, he was in there waiting for her. "I told you she wouldn't believe you, little bitch."

"Get out of my room."

"This is my damned house. Every room and everything in it is mine," he hissed through his yellow teeth. His breath reeked of cheap wine and cigarettes. He lunged forward and grabbed her, ripping her shirt. She struggled against him as he threw her on the bed.

"No, no," she cried out as he pulled her pants down. Fed up with being a victim, she brought her knee up and struck a blow to his private parts.

"You fucking bitch," he screamed out in pain. She pushed him to the side and ran downstairs and out the front door. Her mother didn't even look at her ripped clothes and disheveled hair. She stopped running when she made it to the storage shed in the backyard. He kept a gas can for the lawn mower back there. They were going to pay. They weren't going to hurt her ever again. When she opened up the storage shed, she grabbed the ax and the gas can. She dashed back into the house and found him sitting on the couch with her mother wrapped around him.

"You aren't going to hurt me again," she yelled as she swung the ax. He and her mother screamed and ran toward the basement. She followed them swinging the ax and yelling obscenities that they'd hurled at her every day. When they got into the basement, she heard them lock the door. At first she tried to chop the door down, but then she started pouring the gas throughout the house.

"Do you smell that? Do you?" she screamed at the basement door. "Neither of you will ever hurt me again."

"Chelsea, don't you do this," her mother called out. "It's all a misunderstanding."

"Go to hell!" She ran over to the sofa and poured the rest of the gas on it. Then she grabbed his cigarettes and lighter. She lit a cigarette and tossed it on the gas-soaked couch. She had expected it to burst into flames immediately like on all of the TV shows she'd seen. But it smoldered, smoked, and finally, she saw the flames. As she opened the front door, the flames started spreading. They were fast and furious just like her rage and anger.

And when she saw her reflection that night, she didn't like what she saw.

Just like today. "He can't see me like this. He can't think I'm ugly and hurt me like they did." Carmen slapped her cheeks and tried to stop the tears from falling. "Solomon has to love me. He has to love me."

When she pulled herself together and felt that she didn't look like that little girl from all those years ago, Carmen combed her hair, tucked the gun in her waistband, and headed out of the room to find Frances.

"I'm stuffed," Kandace said as she polished off the last bit of Solomon's cake.

"You should be. I wanted that cake," he said as he kissed a smidge of chocolate icing from her bottom lip.

She smiled and rubbed her stomach. "If you're slow, you blow," she said with a laugh. "It was oh so good."

Solomon hugged her tightly and kissed her on the neck. "You're too much," he said.

Kandace crossed her leg on top of Solomon's as they lay back in the bed. "You're still on the hook to take me out to dinner and I promise I won't eat your cake."

"All right," he said as his cell phone began to ring. Solomon grabbed the phone and answered it. "Crawford."

"Mr. Crawford, it's Detective Myer. We found something on the surveillance videos that you should know about."

"What's that?" he asked as he sat up in the bed.

"Someone did enter the building that same night as Danny Jones. It was the woman you know as Carmen De La Croix. We canvassed the neighborhood near your office building, and the bartender at Jimmy Walker's remembered seeing the two of them there the night of the murder. According to the time stamp on the tapes, Danny returned to the office at twelve-thirty. Fifteen minutes later, Carmen entered the building and went up to the executive floor. She didn't sign in and there was no sign of her leaving the building."

"What do you mean by the woman I 'know as Carmen De La Croix'?" Solomon asked.

"I ran a background check on Carmen after she lied to me. She said that she was in Atlanta scouting property for your hotel chain. But we triangulated her cell phone signal to North Carolina. We have since lost the signal because she probably turned her phone off. I got her employee file from your brother, and the Social Security number that is on that file belongs to a dead Puerto Rican woman who would've been sixty-five years old had she lived."

"What?" Solomon said in disbelief. Kandace mouthed, "What's going on?" and he held his finger up.

"Her real name is Chelsea Washington. She had extensive plastic surgery to alter her appearance, but you can't change your fingerprints," he said.

"How did you get her fingerprints?"

"After we took another look at the video, I sent a crime scene unit over to Chelsea's office and they dusted for fingerprints. She came up in the system."

"Why was she in the system?"

"Mr. Crawford, Chelsea Washington is a disturbed woman. She was arrested about four years ago in connection with the death of her aunt, a caterer named Lucy Smith."

"That name sounds familiar," he said.

"It should; she was the caterer at your wedding.

After Chelsea was released, she disappeared when evidence surfaced implicating her in the murder of her aunt. I'm guessing Danny found out the truth about Carmen's true identity. I contacted the local police and they're looking for her because this woman is dangerous. The police chief there said he's going to have his officers comb the resort and post security outside your room or wherever you're staying."

The phone in the suite rang. "All right, my other line is ringing and I'm guessing that's the police," Solomon said, motioning for Kandace to answer the phone.

"Hello," she said when she picked up. "Okay, hold on."

"I've got to go," Solomon told the detective. He ended the call on his cell phone and took the room phone from Kandace.

"Yes?" he said.

"Mr. Crawford, it's Frances. I need you to come to my office. There is a situation."

"Is it Carmen?" he asked.

"No, it's about our guests. We've had a lot of checkouts and a few people are asking for their money back because of all the police activity."

"Frances, can this wait until the morning?"

"It's pretty important and I'm off tomorrow," she said. "I wouldn't bother you if I knew how to handle this situation."

"All right, I'll be down shortly." Solomon hung up the phone and turned to Kandace.

"What's going on, Solomon?" she asked.

He pulled her into his arms and hugged her

tightly. "This thing with Carmen is a lot more dangerous than I could've ever imagined," he said.

"How so?"

"First of all, her name isn't Carmen De La Croix, it's Chelsea Washington. Her aunt, who the police believe she killed, was the caterer at my wedding. I think I met Chelsea. She was a kid or so I thought. After everything blew up in my face, I got drunk. I mean, falling down drunk. There was this waitress who helped get me out without having to look at my guests or anything. She took me somewhere and I passed out. When I woke up the next morning this kid was staring at me with a huge smile on her face. I couldn't remember anything but the fact that I got stood up at the altar. I told her thank you, offered to give her some money for her troubles and she said no problem. I took a cab home and never thought anything of it."

"And that woman was Carmen?"

Solomon nodded. "Only she changed everything about herself, took this dead woman's identity, and became my right-hand woman. When she applied for the job, her credentials were impeccable. I guess Carmen De La Croix did work in the hospitality industry before she died."

Kandace stroked her forehead. "This is crazy," she said. "So, she's been fixated on you for a long time."

"Obviously. The police think she killed Danny and her aunt. And I'm beginning to think that she killed the housekeeper here too," Solomon said.

"Why would she kill the housekeeper?" Kandace asked.

"Maybe she got in her way. I don't know, but I'm thinking you should leave," he said.

"What?"

"Carmen, or whoever she is, is dangerous. If she wants me, she probably thinks you're what's standing between us. I don't want her to come after you or see you get hurt because of this."

"But, Solomon, what about you? She might come after you and she could kill you too," Kandace said.

"You can't stop her and I'm not putting you in harm's way," Solomon said. "The police are putting a guard on me until they catch that woman, whatever her name is."

"Then I guess I'll leave in the morning," she said. "Why don't you leave too?"

"I think I might, but hopefully the police will take her into custody soon. Shit, I told Frances that I would come down to her office and help her deal with some disgruntled guests. Looks like my fabulous opening has been marred by all the police activity that's been going on."

"Solomon, don't go," Kandace said.

"I'll call our security staff and get them to post up outside. I won't be gone long."

"You're worried about me and I'm just as worried about you," she said.

"I'll be fine and"—he tossed her his BlackBerry—"you keep this with you."

Kandace caught the phone and smiled. "Thanks. Be careful out there."

"I'm just going downstairs," he said as he headed to the door.

* * *

Carmen slammed Frances's face into the desk. "Where is he?"

"I—I don't know. You heard me when I called him," she stammered.

Carmen sucked her teeth and slapped Frances across the face. "Call him again."

"All right, all right, but don't hit me again," Frances exclaimed as she picked up the phone and dialed Solomon's suite.

"Hello?" Kandace said when she answered the phone.

"Is Mr. Crawford there? This is the front office manager, Frances," she said as she watched Carmen stalk back and forth.

"He just headed downstairs to your office."

"Okay, so he's on his way. Thank you." Frances hung up the phone, then turned to Carmen. "He's coming now."

"You better not tell him I was here." Carmen ran out of the office and headed for the employee stairs. Now that she knew Kandace was alone, she was going to get rid of her.

CHAPTER 23

When Solomon walked into Frances's office, she was trembling like a frightened kitten and her face was red and swollen.

"Frances, what happened?" he asked.

"She's crazy. My God, that woman is crazy," she exclaimed. "Carmen was here and she slapped me around until I called you and got you out of your suite."

"Call the police," Solomon yelled, then dashed out of her office. He ran to the employee stairs and bolted up to the eighth floor. When he got to the hall door, he tried to open it, but something was blocking it. Solomon pushed against the door to no avail. He ran back down one floor, then hopped on the service elevator. When he got up to the eighth floor, he ran to his suite. The door was cracked open and he heard Carmen yelling.

"He's my man and you're not going to keep him away from me!"

"Please, put the gun down," Kandace said.

"No, no. Not until I get rid of you."

Solomon burst through the door and ran into the bedroom. "Carmen," he called out.

She turned around and looked at him with a wild expression in her eyes. "Solomon, what are you doing here? You—you can't see me like this."

"Listen, you have to put that gun down," he said as he made a move toward her.

"No, stop right there," she said as she pointed the gun at him. "You can't be here."

"I know what you did, what you did for me when my wedding fell apart," he said, attempting to diffuse the situation.

"Then you know how long I've loved you," she said. "How can you let this tramp come between us?"

Solomon took another step toward her. "Carmen, why don't you let Kandace go?"

"No!" she barked as she pointed the gun at Kandace. "She's no good and if she's around she's going to try and get you back. I'm not going to let anyone come between us."

"She won't," Solomon said. "I don't want her. She's just another woman."

Kandace leaned against the wall with her eyes closed and Solomon could feel her fear as he watched her tremble.

Carmen shook her head. "You don't mean that," she said with tears welling up in her eyes. "I saw how you looked at her. I know you've treated her better than any of those other women you used to tell me about. There is something different about her. That's why you brought her up here. But she doesn't love you the way I do." She haphazardly pointed the gun at Kandace and Solomon jumped. "Why won't you give me a chance?"

"I will, if you put the gun down," he said as he extended his hand and reached for the gun. "Carmen, we can't do anything while you're waving that thing around."

She sniffed and wiped her nose with the back of her hand. "Then you tell her to get out, go back to wherever she came from. Her friends want to use you, Solomon." Carmen turned back to Kandace. "Look at me, bitch!"

Kandace opened her eyes and focused on Carmen. As she looked at her, Kandace silently prayed that she wouldn't shoot her. "Carmen," Kandace said, "I'll leave so that you and Solomon can be together. You're right, I do just want to use him."

"Shut up, you liar. See, Solomon," Carmen said. "She only wanted you for her own business. She doesn't love you—you heard her. She doesn't care about you and she can't take care of you the way I have and the way I will."

"I know. I can never be what you are to him," Kandace said, fear rolling down her spine like ice water.

"You don't know anything!" Carmen barked, pointing the gun closer to Kandace for emphasis. Solomon took two steps closer to Carmen, then he reached out and touched her arm, forcing her to focus her attention on him.

"Carmen," he said. "Let her go."

She looked into Solomon's eyes and lowered the gun. "Do you love me, Solomon?" Her voice sounded like a wounded child begging for her parents' love.

"You know how I feel about you," he fudged.

Carmen lifted the gun and pointed it at him. "Say it. Say it so that she can hear it and know that there is no chance for her to try and steal you away from me," Carmen ordered.

Solomon swallowed. So many things ran through his mind as he looked at the barrel of the gun pointed at his chest. Richmond had warned him that he'd find himself looking at a woman holding a gun over him one day.

"You can't keep playing with women's emotions because you got hurt," his older brother had said when stories about Solomon's flings ended up on Page Six.

Heather Williams had told Solomon that she loved him, and he'd replied, "Too bad." Then she'd thrown a lead crystal vase at his head.

"I hope I'm around the day some woman cuts your balls off," she'd screamed as he'd pulled his jacket on and strolled out the door.

Maybe this was karma. The universe had given him a woman he could love, a woman he wanted to love, and now, with a gun pointed at his heart, he was a slip of the tongue from losing his life or costing Kandace hers.

"Say it," Carmen demanded again.

"I—I love you," Solomon stammered.

Carmen rushed into Solomon's arms, holding the gun at her side as he closed his arms around her. He looked at Kandace and mouthed, "Call the police."

Kandace had forgotten that she stuck Solomon's BlackBerry in the pocket of her robe. She quickly pulled the phone out and dialed 9-1-1. Before she could bring the phone to her ear, she saw that Carmen was looking directly at her.

"What are you doing?" Carmen demanded. "Put that phone down or I will blow your brains out."

"Carmen, Carmen," Solomon said as he grabbed her shoulder. "She's not important."

She whirled around with fury floating in her eyes. "You're trying to trick me. I'm not going to allow you to do this to me. You're not going to trick me," she bellowed, then pointed the gun at Kandace, who had dropped the BlackBerry on the bed.

Solomon stood in front of Carmen. "If you want to shoot her, you're going to have to shoot me first," he said. "Put the gun down and we can talk about this."

"Talk? Talk about what, Solomon? I've seen you with so many women in and out of your life. Women who you didn't even bother to say good-bye to. I waited and waited until you realized that I was the only woman in your life who loved you. You still don't see it. You lied to me to save her, a woman you barely know. What's so good about *her*? What does she have that I don't?"

"Carmen, please, put the gun down. You don't want to hurt anybody. I know you don't," Solomon said.

"Answer me!" she yelled.

"Carmen, please!" Solomon exclaimed. He looked up and saw two police officers rushing in the room with their guns drawn.

"Drop your weapon and put your hands where we can see them," one of the officers yelled from behind Carmen. She turned and faced him, but kept her gun trained on Kandace.

"Solomon, tell them to go away," Carmen cried. "Tell them to leave us alone so we can be together."

"Drop the gun, lady," the officer ordered again. Carmen glared at Kandace as if they were the only two people in the room.

"This is all your fault," Carmen said to Kandace. "You told him lies about me, just like Danny told lies about me. Do you know what happens to liars?"

"Carmen, please, I don't even know you," Kandace said. The officers behind them continued to order Carmen to drop her weapon and Solomon wanted them to shoot her, get her out of the way. Carmen slowly started walking sideways as if she was trying to get a clear shot at Kandace.

"Ma'am," the officer yelled. "This is the last time. Put your gun down."

"No," Carmen said without turning to face the officer. "I'm not putting anything down. Everyone is out to get me."

"Carmen, the police will shoot you if you don't put that gun down," Solomon said. He wanted them to shoot because he could see it in her eyes that she was going to shoot Kandace. Her finger trembled on the trigger. "Please, do something," Solomon yelled at the officers.

Carmen looked at him, her face darkened in a fit of rage. Then she pulled the trigger. With lightning fast reflexes, Solomon flung himself in front of the bullet as the two officers opened fire on Carmen.

Kandace rushed to Solomon's side as blood poured from the bullet wound in his shoulder. She touched his face as she cried. "You saved my life," she said. "Solomon." His eyes rolled back in his head as he cried out in pain. The officers called for an ambulance on their radios, but Kandace couldn't compute what they were saying as she focused on Solomon's pain and the blood. "Oh my God, please, be all right," she said with her hand hovering over his wound.

"Ma'am, you have to get back," the officer said as he knelt down on the other side of Solomon. "Sir, look at me."

"Grr," Solomon groaned as he tried to focus on the officer. "Damn, it hurts."

"When is the ambulance getting here?" Kandace asked. "You can't let him sit here and bleed to death."

Moments later, four emergency service workers burst into the room. Two of them rushed to Carmen's side and the other two rushed to Solomon. "Give us some space," the paramedic said to Kandace.

"Don't go," Solomon said faintly, trying to hold on to her hand.

"I'm right here, baby," she said.

"Sir, we need to get you out of here and we can't do that if you don't let your wife's hand go," the paramedic said. "She can ride to the hospital with us."

Solomon nodded and let Kandace's hand go. Then the paramedic got to work, cutting the sleeve of his shirt off and examining the wound. "We've got to stop the bleeding and get some antibiotics in his system. Sir, are you allergic to penicillin?"

Solomon shook his head, then his body started shaking and his breathing became shallow. "He's going into shock," the paramedic yelled to his partner.

"What's happening?" Kandace asked. "Is he going to be all right?"

"Load him on the gurney and let's get some oxygen started and an antibiotic drip going." As the paramedics pushed Solomon out the door, Kandace followed behind them, not caring that she was only wearing a bloody hotel robe.

She didn't glance sideways at the paramedics working on Carmen, didn't care if Carmen lived or died. She just knew that Solomon had to live because she loved him. The paramedics loaded Solomon's gurney in the ambulance and then one of the men helped Kandace climb up. He motioned for her to sit near Solomon's good shoulder.

"How is he?" she asked.

"Blood pressure is low and he's in shock, though the wound doesn't seem that deep," the man said.

Kandace held Solomon's hand, which felt so cold. *Dear God, please save him. Please don't let him die,* she silently prayed.

The ambulance rolled into the emergency department at the Watauga Medical Center and Solomon was rushed in to a trauma unit. When Kandace tried to follow the doctors inside, a nurse placed a hand on Kandace's shoulder. "You can't come back here. Do you want me to track down some scrubs for you to put on?" she asked as she looked at Kandace's bloody robe.

"Yes," she said as she wiped tears from her eyes with the back of her hand. The nurse waved for an orderly, then told him to take Kandace to get a pair of scrubs.

"No, no, I don't want to leave him," she said as she looked at the doors of the trauma unit.

The nurse nodded. "He'll bring them here and there's a restroom around the corner."

Once the nurse entered the trauma unit, Kandace paced back and forth, fighting the tears welling up in her eyes. What if he died? What if he lost his arm?

"Ma'am," the orderly said when he returned to Kandace, "here are the scrubs."

"Thank you," Kandace said though her tears.

"Can I get you something to drink?" he asked. "You look kind of faint."

Kandace shook her head and wiped her eyes. "I can't believe this is happening," she murmured.

The orderly led Kandace to a bench, then waved for a nurse. "She looks like she's going to pass out," he told the nurse, who rushed over to them.

"Ma'am, my name is Kelly. Can I take your blood pressure?" the nurse asked.

Kandace nodded and tried to take a deep breath to calm herself down. The nurse sent the orderly to get a blood pressure cuff while she listened to her heartbeat.

"Your heart is racing," she said. "What happened to you?"

Kandace's hands shook and words wouldn't form in her mind or her mouth. "Get a gurney," the nurse yelled. "She's crashing."

Solomon opened his eyes and the first thought on his mind was Kandace. Where was she? Was she all right? Then his mind tried to comprehend where he was. The room began to come into focus, the machines, the blinking lights, the doctors surrounding his bed.

She didn't get shot, I took the bullet. She has to be all right, he thought.

"Mr. Crawford, I'm Dr. Rivers. Are you with us?" he asked.

Solomon nodded and coughed as he attempted to say yes. "We were able to remove the bullet from your shoulder with minimal damage. But you did lose a lot of blood."

"K-Kandace," Solomon croaked. "Wh-where is she?"

The doctor placed his hand on Solomon's arm. "She's fine. She's resting right now because you gave her quite a scare."

"Not hurt?"

"No, not at all," the doctor said.

Solomon coughed and the doctor instructed the nurse to bring Solomon some water. She rushed to his side with a cup of water with a straw. She pressed the button to raise the bed so that he could drink the water. Solomon took a sip of the water, then said, "Want to see her."

"Not just yet," Dr. Rivers said. "We have to get your fever down. You have a slight infection."

"Don't care," Solomon said after taking another sip of water. "Want to see her."

"Look around, Mr. Crawford. You can't get out of bed right now," Dr. Rivers said as he pointed to the IV in Solomon's arm. Solomon rolled his eyes at his doctor and reached for the tube in his arm. Dr. Rivers grabbed Solomon's hand. "Don't do that. You need to rest and let the medicine work."

Solomon groaned. "I need to see her."

"Your wife is all right, sir. I wouldn't lie to you," Dr. Rivers said. He turned to the nurse and told her to check on Kandace. The woman nodded and left the room. "You must really love her, because if you pull that IV out, it is going to hurt a lot."

"I do," Solomon said.

About twenty minutes later, the nurse returned to the room with Kandace in tow. Solomon smiled when he saw her.

"Oh, Solomon," she said as she rushed over to his bedside. "I was so worried about you and so scared." Kandace brushed her fingers across his forehead. "How are you feeling?"

"Like somebody shot me," he said in an attempt at a joke.

"That's not funny," Kandace said as she grabbed his hand. "I was really worried about you. I can't believe you did that."

"I thought I was Superman."

"Stop trying to make light of this," Kandace said with tears in her eyes. "She could've killed you."

"Or she could've killed you," Solomon said as he reached up and wiped a tear from her cheek. "Don't cry, baby. We're fine."

"Yeah, we are. How long are they going to keep you in here?"

"I don't know, but I was ready to snatch the IV out and come find you. Where were you?"

Kandace pointed to a bandage on her arm. "Getting my own IV. I passed out in the hallway."

"I knew something was wrong," he said. "Are you sure you're all right?"

She kissed him on the cheek. "Yeah. I mean, I'm not the one who took a bullet, right?"

"You're trying to make me laugh? It kind of hurts when I do that."

A nurse walked into the room and smiled at the couple. "I'm glad to see you made it in here, Mrs. Crawford. He was moaning and calling your name for the longest time before he came to. You don't see a lot of love like that in marriages these days."

Kandace opened her mouth to tell the nurse that she wasn't Mrs. Crawford, but Solomon placed his finger to his lips and Kandace just smiled at the nurse.

"We're going to move him to a private room in a little bit. The doctor wants to make sure the fever goes away before sending him home," the nurse said as she checked the machines.

"All right," Kandace said. "We'll be ready."

The nurse touched Kandace on the shoulder. "And there will be a roll-away bed in the room for you to sleep in, Mrs. Crawford."

"Thanks," Kandace said.

Mrs. Crawford sounds good on her, Solomon thought before he drifted off to sleep.

CHAPTER 24

When Carmen opened her eyes, she wished she was dead. She wished the bullets that the officers had shot at her had killed her. Solomon didn't love her and he didn't want to be with her. She knew he'd never love her now that she'd shot him. And she was sure the police had figured out what she'd done — every desperate act. Tears rolled down her cheeks and she couldn't wipe them away because she was chained to the bed like an animal.

Oh, Solomon, how could you betray me for that woman? You told those cops to shoot me. You're just like my mother, wanted me out of the way so that you could have what you wanted. No one ever cares about what I want and what I need. Damn it, damn it all to hell. I swear, I'm going to make him pay. I'm going to take what he values most if it's the last thing I do, she thought as she shifted in the bed.

The room door opened and a doctor walked in with two detectives. "It looks like the patient is finally awake," the doctor said.

"Suspect," Detective Myer said as he walked over to Carmen's bed. "Hello, Chelsea."

"My name is Carmen," she said. "Chelsea died a long time ago."

"A lot of people seem to die around you, *Carmen.* Tell me about Danny Jones."

Carmen rolled her eyes and kept silent. Detective Myer leaned in to her. "You can tell me now or when we fly you back to New York where you will be charged with his murder, Chelsea. And then there is the death of your aunt. You're still facing charges in that case. Was he worth it?"

She narrowed her eyes at him and clenched her fists. If she wasn't shackled like a stray dog, she'd teach this pompous ass a lesson. "I'm not going back to New York," she said.

Detective Myer threw up his hands. "You're facing serious charges right here too. Either way, you're going to prison for a long time, Chelsea."

"Stop calling me that," she shouted.

"Is it your temper that causes you to kill?"

Carmen turned her back to him. *I'm not telling him a damned thing,* she thought.

"Detective," the doctor said. "I need to check her vitals."

"Don't take those cuffs off, because this is a dangerous woman," he said as he and his partner headed out the door.

"Good news, Mr. Crawford," the nurse said. "Your temperature is ninety-eight point six. The meds are working."

"Great, now I can make my tennis game," he quipped.

The nurse laughed and Kandace rolled her eyes. They had been in the hospital for two days waiting for Solomon's temperature to return to normal. Kandace had gone back to the resort and gotten Solomon's BlackBerry and a change of clothes. When she'd walked back into the suite, her mind returned to the night of the shooting. She saw the blood, felt the fear again, and trembled as she grabbed her clothes. Kandace hadn't been able to get out of there fast enough.

"Are you all right over there?" Solomon asked after the nurse left. "You have this strange look on your face."

"I was just thinking that I should call my friends and let them know what's going on," she said, not wanting to say what had really been on her mind.

"Did you get my phone?" he asked.

"Yes," she said as she reached into her overnight bag and retrieved it. She handed it to Solomon. He turned the phone on and shook his head as he tried to read his messages with one hand.

"This thing is not easy to work with one hand," he said. "Forget it, I'm sure Richmond can handle everything and the press surrounding my shooting."

"I wonder if your shooting made news in Charlotte, because if it did—" Kandace wasn't able to finish her statement before the door opened and Jade, Serena, and Alicia walked in.

"Kandace, you'd better be glad you're alive, otherwise I'd have to kill you," Serena said.

Jade rushed over to Kandace and hugged her tightly. "No more vacations alone for you," she said when she released her friend. Alicia stood near the door shaking her head.

"This would've never happened if you'd gone someplace tropical," she said.

"Well, hello to you all too," Kandace said. "What are you guys doing here?"

Serena rolled her eyes and folded her arms across her chest. "Let's see, some crazed murderer was stalking the resort where you were staying. No one knew where you were and we had no way of contacting you."

"What did you expect us to do?" Alicia asked.

"Excuse me," Solomon said. "I'm the one who got shot. But, I am feeling better, thanks."

Kandace turned to Solomon. "You have to excuse them, they lack manners."

"How did this all happen?" Serena asked Solomon. "Was this one of your many women stalking you?"

"Serena!" Jade, Alicia, and Kandace shouted.

She sucked her teeth. "What? I'm supposed to be nice because he's in the hospital? He nearly got our best friend killed."

"It wasn't his fault, Serena," Kandace said. "He can't be held responsible for what that nut did, and if it wasn't for Solomon, I might be dead."

"What do you mean?" Jade asked.

Kandace squeezed Solomon's hand and looked down at him with a slight smile on her lips. He brought her hand to his lips and kissed it, despite the daggers Serena had been shooting at him with her intense glare.

"That bullet was meant for me," Kandace said. "Carmen was trying to kill me and Solomon jumped in front of the bullet."

Jade, Serena, and Alicia looked at him. "Wow," Alicia said. "I'm shocked."

"Speechless," Jade said.

They all looked at Serena. "Okay, okay," she said. "You did a good thing." Serena pointed at Kandace. "But when were you going to let us know that you were all right?"

"Who told me to leave my BlackBerry in Charlotte?" Kandace asked. "Who told me they didn't want to hear from me for two weeks?"

"Yeah, but this was a special case," Jade said. "And by the way, James said he doesn't appreciate his child's godmother trying to get herself killed."

"Tell James I wasn't trying," Kandace said.

"Well," Jade said, looking at Solomon, "it better not happen again."

"Trust me," Solomon said. "I'm not going to let anything happen to my woman."

Jade, Alicia, and Serena exchanged puzzled yet amused looks. "Your woman?" Alicia said through her giggles.

Solomon stroked Kandace's arm and smiled at her. Kandace returned his smile, but inside her mind was reeling. *Post-traumatic stress. He didn't mean that,* she thought.

"Then you shouldn't have a problem getting your woman's friends a room for the night," Serena said. "We're a package deal."

Solomon laughed, then looked at Serena and shook his head. If Danny was still alive, he'd fall head over heels for her. Then again, the woman seemed like she was more than a handful. "I'll call the resort and get you ladies a suite."

"Why don't you just put them in the dungeon so that they will leave tomorrow?" Kandace suggested.

"Dungeon? What in the . . ." Jade said.

"She's joking," Solomon said as he tugged at Kandace's hand.

After Solomon called the resort and made arrangements for Kandace's friends, he thought they were going to leave, but the women stayed in the room and focused their questions on him.

"I would lie to you and tell you that they're not always like this, but they are," Kandace said after her girls had peppered Solomon with questions about his womanizing headlines (Serena), his business acumen (Alicia), and his intentions with Kandace (Jade).

"Ladies," Solomon said, "you should really get some rest in the suite I reserved for you."

"In other words, get out," Kandace said.

Jade looked up from her phone and rolled her eyes at Kandace. "James just sent a picture of Jaden," she said, and flashed the phone at Kandace. Jaden was splashing in the baby tub and smiling.

"He's so cute," Kandace said as she took the phone from Jade's hand. "Are you sure you can spend the night away from him?"

"First, you try to get us to leave the hospital, now you want us to leave town?" Jade joked. "We get the message."

"But I have more questions," Serena said. "Solomon, did you date all of those women you were linked to or was it just an overactive PR department?"

"That's the past," he said.

"That was last week," Serena said. "You know, I'm not as nice as these two."

"I figured that out," he said flatly.

"And," Serena said, "I don't want to see my friend hurt, so you better take care of her or I'll take care of you."

Kandace looked at her friend in disbelief. "Did you just threaten him?" she asked.

"She's joking," Alicia said as she grabbed Serena's arm. "She's hungry and tired. Ignore her. But, Solomon, I would love, love, love to have you speak at my seminar in two months. You think your shoulder will be healed by then?"

"Get out, get out, get out," Kandace exclaimed as she rose to her feet and pushed her friends out the door. "You guys are unbelievable."

"Bye, Kandace," Jade said. "Solomon, we'll talk."

He shot the ladies a thumbs-up signal but he saved his wide smile for the moment Kandace closed the door and returned to his bedside. "Wow," he said.

"Yeah, I guess I deserved that. We gave Jade's husband a really hard time in Vegas when they first met."

"Come here," he said. Kandace climbed into the bed with Solomon, careful to stay clear of his wounded shoulder. With his free hand, he stroked her cheek. "I like your friends. I see why you guys are so close. Are you sure you all aren't sisters?"

"Funny," she said as she turned her head and kissed his hand.

"I don't get the feeling that Serena was joking," he said. "She's a tough one, huh?"

"That's what she wants us to think, but underneath all that is a softy that you wouldn't believe."

"You're right, I don't believe it," he said.

"How are you feeling?" she asked as she placed

her hand on his chest. "I know you're going crazy in this bed."

"Right now, this bed feels pretty good," he said with a smile.

"Does it?"

"And if I wasn't hooked up to all of these monitors, I know how I could make it feel even better."

"Not so fast, tiger," she said. "When your shoulder is better, I have something really special for you. But right now, you need to rest."

"So do you. That cot can't be comfortable. Why don't you go to the resort tonight and sleep in a real bed after you and your friends talk about me behind my back."

Kandace shook her head. It wasn't that she didn't need the rest or the chance to sleep in one of the plush beds at Carolina Serenity, but every time she walked in to the resort, the night of the shooting replayed in her mind. She wasn't going to rest there because she'd see Carmen's face and think she was hiding in every shadow.

"I'm just fine right here," Kandace said.

Solomon rubbed her shoulder. "You're not going back there, are you?"

She shook her head. "How can I? Solomon, you could've died, I could've died. Seeing all of that blood . . ." Kandace said as she shivered.

He held her as tightly as he could with one arm. "Baby, I wish I could take that fear away from you. This should've never happened, but we made a lot of good memories there."

She closed her eyes and thought about all of the things they'd done, the places where they made love and played in the snow. But as she thought about the good things, Carmen's face haunted her and sent chills down her spine.

"Have you heard about Carmen?" she asked.

"No. I'd imagine that she's in custody. I'm sure the cops will come by to talk to me since I'm off the high-powered pain medication," Solomon said.

"What can you tell them? I think the officers who shot her saw that she was unstable and if they'd had better aim, this would all be over," Kandace said angrily.

"Calm down, babe," he said. "Carmen or Chelsea will not bother us again. She's facing murder charges in two states. We're going to be fine."

"I hope you're right."

Solomon kissed her on the cheek. "I'm always right. I knew I'd get you and look at us now."

She pinched his cheek. "You had no idea," she said. "Actually, you should thank Serena for this."

"Serena? And how do I owe her a debt of thanks?" Solomon asked.

"Because I was going to ignore you for the rest of my vacation, but Serena said I should give you a chance. And I was just as surprised as you look right now," she said with a laugh when she saw the expression on his face.

"I'm surprised she didn't tell you to go to another resort," he said.

"That's why I called her, hoping that she would," Kandace quipped.

Solomon rolled his eyes. "You would've been back."

"You're pretty confident about that, huh?" she asked. "I don't think I would have."

"Sure you would've stayed away," Solomon said. "I knew you wanted me the moment you saw me."

"You're lucky you're lying here with a hole in your shoulder. Otherwise, I'd have to hurt you for being such a jerk. You came on way too strong at first."

Solomon smiled. "But it worked."

"No, it was the massage that got me," she said.

"Then I know what I have to do from now on to keep you," he said.

Kandace raised her eyebrow. "Keep me?"

"That's right. You're mine. I haven't felt this way about a woman in forever and I don't want to lose this feeling. Kandace, I'm falling in love with you."

"Solomon," she said softly.

"Listen, if you don't feel the same way, I understand, but I'm going to make you fall in love with me every day of your life."

"Are you sure this is what you want?" she asked. "Because if I fall in love with you, I'm going to want forever. I play for keeps."

"I'm a keeper," he said. "But you already know that."

Kandace laughed. "I guess you're right about that," she said, then leaned her head on his uninjured shoulder. "You are a keeper."

CHAPTER 25

When Solomon drifted off to sleep, Kandace slipped out of his bed and grabbed his BlackBerry to call her friends.

"Hello?" Jade said when she picked up her phone.

"Put me on speaker," Kandace said.

"I was wondering who this was," Jade said. "Hold on."

"What are you doing to that man?" Alicia asked when Jade put the phone on speaker.

"He's sleeping. You women are crazy," Kandace said. "Especially Serena."

"I'm here and I can hear you. Sue me for looking out for you," Serena said. "This guy has quite the tabloid reputation."

"And if you were rich, so would you," Kandace said.

"Not anymore," Alicia said. "Serena is a changed woman."

"Shut up, Alicia," Serena barked. "We're not talking about me, we're talking about Kandace."

"So, who was this psycho woman?" Jade asked.

"More importantly, where is she now?" Serena asked.

Kandace sighed and replied, "She's in a secure wing of the hospital. Too bad she's not in the morgue."

"That's harsh," Jade said.

"Well, what do you expect?" Alicia asked. "She tried to kill her."

"Yeah, because of Solomon," Serena said. "How could he not know she was obsessed with him? Men can't be that damned dense."

"Are we still talking about Solomon? Because if we are, she was really good about hiding who she was," Kandace said. "She had plastic surgery and took the identity of a dead woman."

"This is like a bad Lifetime movie," Alicia said. "But did he say anything about my seminar?"

"What is it with you and this seminar?" Kandace asked.

"Nothing," Alicia said quickly.

"She's trying to prove a point," Jade said.

"To who?" Kandace asked.

"Look," Serena said, "are you serious about Solomon Crawford?"

"Maybe he's serious about me," Kandace replied.

"Aww, hell," Serena and Alicia shouted in concert.

"Guys, I think it's sweet," Jade said. "Maybe you two ought to go on vacation. Then, Serena, you can stop obsessing over Antonio. And, Alicia, you can get a life and stop trying to prove how successful you are to the man who broke your heart in high school."

"Okay, what has been going on since I left?" Kandace asked.

"Nothing," Serena said.

"Jade is just being dramatic as usual," Alicia said.

"Well, I'll deal with you guys when I get back to town," Kandace said.

"Are you going to come over here tonight?" Jade asked.

"Umm, no. I'm going to stay with Solomon," Kandace said, not wanting to tell her friends why she didn't want to go back to Carolina Serenity. That place was anything but serene to her now.

"So, you're going to sleep in that hospital room when we have this lovely suite? It's even named," Alicia said. "What's the name of it?"

"The Wonderland Suite," Jade said.

"That's okay," Kandace said.

"Did something happen here?" Serena asked.

"Ah, not really. That was just the suite I was staying in when I first arrived."

"Oh, because if this was where the shooting happened, we were going to have to move," Alicia said. Kandace could almost see the disgusted look on her friend's face.

"All right, I have to go before the nurses put me out for talking on the cell phone."

"Kandace," Jade said, "we're really glad you're all right."

"Yeah," Serena said. "That was pretty scary hearing about the shooting here and not knowing if you were safe."

"Okay, guys, no need to get mushy," Kandace

said. "I'm going back in to Solomon. But I'll come by for breakfast in the morning."

"See you then," Alicia said. Kandace ended the call and hugged herself tightly. She was so glad to have her friends around.

Carmen didn't know what time it was, but she could tell that most of the hospital staff was gone from the wing she was in. If she could break free of the handcuffs, she would get out of the hospital and find Solomon. She would make him pay for what he did to her. Then she would go after that bitch. Kandace stole Solomon's love from her and she was going to take him from her.

She closed her eyes as the door to her room opened. The nurse walked over to her and checked her vital signs.

"Help me," Carmen whispered to the nurse.

"What?" the woman asked.

"My hands hurt so badly," she said. "Can you take the cuffs off?"

"I can't," the nurse said. "You're in police custody."

"But I'm in pain," Carmen whined.

The nurse pulled her hand from Carmen's and nodded. "I'll talk to the police officer," she said.

"Thank you," Carmen replied. *I wish I knew the police were outside the door. Even if that dumb nurse takes these cuffs off, how am I going to get out of here?*

Moments later, the nurse and an overweight police officer walked into the room. "We can take the cuffs off for five minutes," the officer said through a yawn. "But don't try anything. I'm going to be right outside the door."

Carmen rolled her eyes. Her back ached from the bullet wounds and her shoulder throbbed from the surgery, so she played up the pain hoping the officer and the nurse would buy it.

The officer unlocked the handcuffs and walked out of the room. It was a move that shocked the nurse and Carmen. "Officer," the nurse called as she quickly followed him out of the room. Carmen swung her legs over the side of the bed and realized that escaping out of the room wasn't going to be easy. She was hooked up to a blood pressure machine, a heart monitor, and an IV. Removing any of the equipment would set off alarms that would send everyone in to her room before she had a chance to do anything. *Damn it. How am I going to get out of here?* she thought as she looked at the maze of wires and tubes.

"Time's up," the officer said when he returned to the room.

"Five minutes couldn't have gone by that fast," Carmen said.

"No, but I just got a look at your charges. You're not going to be uncuffed again," he said. "Lie down."

Carmen did what he said. As he stood beside her to recuff her to the bed, her eyes were drawn to his service revolver. With her free hand, Carmen knew she could grab the gun and shoot her way out of the hospital. But she didn't chance it. Instead, she allowed herself to be chained to the bed like an animal.

In time, I'll make them all pay, she thought bitterly as the officer walked out of the room.

The next morning, Kandace left Solomon's hospital room while he was being examined by the doctor. Jade met her at the hospital to take her to the resort.

"I can't believe you're leaving your man to have breakfast with your friends," Jade said as Kandace slid into the car.

"I'm just going to the resort to tell you guys goodbye," Kandace said with a smile.

"What if we want to stay and play in the snow?" Jade joked.

"Yeah right. I'm sure after one night away from Jaden you're ready to get back to Charlotte as soon as you finish your coffee."

Jade laughed. "You know me so well. I'm sure Alicia and Serena are going to complain about how I spent last night talking and texting James. But the pictures he sent of my baby sleeping were so cute."

"I bet," Kandace said. "Motherhood looks good on you."

"You think so? All right, tell me the truth. Are you really serious about Solomon?"

"I-I don't know. Maybe it's because of what we've been through but I feel this real connection with him and I believe we can be happy together," Kandace said with a slight smile on her lips.

"What about his reputation and the fact that he

lives in New York? How can a relationship work with you two?"

"Let's see, he has a private jet. And anything worth having is worth working for," Kandace said. "So I'm going to make him work for me."

"That's what I'm talking about," Jade said. "But seriously, are you sure that you can trust this guy?"

"Did you ask all these questions about James before you married him?"

"Are you thinking about marrying this guy?"

"No, silly. But come on, I thought you would understand our unconventional relationship."

Jade shrugged as she headed down the street. "I just don't want to see you hurt, and honestly, I was hoping for a reunion with you and Devon."

"That was never going to happen," Kandace said. "Once bitten, twice shy."

"But he's changed and I know he wants you. I can't tell you how many times he's asked when you're coming back," Jade said as they pulled into the parking lot of the resort.

"Why is he worried about me now? And, Jade, I hope you weren't encouraging that mess."

Jade threw her hands up after putting her car in park. "I plead the fifth."

Kandace hopped out of the car. "So, that means yes. What were you thinking? I don't want to be with a cheater."

"But you're falling in love with an international playboy," Jade pointed out as she followed Kandace in to the lobby. "Makes a lot of sense."

"Jade, let me handle my love life on my own. I

stood up for you and James when Serena and Alicia told the man to stay away from you."

She nodded. "Okay, you did. But . . . never mind."

"No, say it."

"This guy has a lot more baggage than James came with, and I can't help but wonder if you're not in over your head," she said, her voice filled with concern. "However, you're a grown woman and whatever you decide to do, I have your back."

"That's good to know, because I really believe I'm falling in love with him. And he told me the same thing last night. Before you ask, he's not on the heavy pain medication anymore."

Jade laughed. "I wasn't even thinking that. But it's good to know."

They headed in to the resort café where Serena and Alicia had already started eating breakfast.

"Wow, thanks for waiting," Kandace said.

"The aromas in here were so amazing and Jade drives so slow," Alicia said in between bites of her homemade banana nut muffin.

"Yes," Serena said as she took a sip of her latte. "She is slow."

"Oh, shut up," Jade said as she swiped a piece of Serena's blueberry muffin.

The four friends ate breakfast and to Kandace's surprise, neither Serena or Alicia said anything about her relationship with Solomon.

"I guess we'd better check out and head back to Charlotte," Alicia said after the women finished eating. "Looks like everything is under control here."

"Great, because I really miss my baby," Jade said as

she sipped a glass of milk. "And I don't appreciate you guys drinking all of this coffee around me."

"No one told you to turn your body into a milk factory," Serena said as she polished off her second latte. "Let's get our bags and go."

Kandace froze in her seat. She didn't want to enter the lobby or ride up in the elevator to the floors with the suites. The reminders of the shooting would be too fresh. Were there still bullet holes? *Calm down. The hotel staff has probably patched everything up and there's no sign of the horror that happened in that suite,* she thought as she slowly rose from her seat.

Alicia saw the look on Kandace's face and nodded toward Serena and Jade. "You know what, I think I want more coffee," she said. "You want to join me, Kandace?"

"Sure, I'll even buy," Kandace said as she walked over to the counter.

Solomon smiled as the nurse removed his IV, but his happiness was short lived. A moment later Detective Myer entered his room.

"Mr. Crawford, you're looking well," the detective said.

"Yeah, I feel like a million bucks. What did I do to receive a visit from New York's finest?"

"Well, we're working this investigation with the Avery County officials since we all have serious cases involving the suspect," he said. "We have Chelsea dead to rights on the murder of her aunt and Danny

Jones. Right now, she's facing attempted murder charges in this jurisdiction and she's a person of interest in the murder of the housekeeper."

"So, what do you want from me?" Solomon asked.

"Do I need to leave? I was going to give Mr. Crawford a sponge bath," the nurse said as she unplugged the IV machine.

"That can wait," Solomon said as he pushed the button to raise his bed.

The detective nodded. "Yeah, I don't want to see that much of him."

The nurse smiled and left the room. Solomon turned to Myer. "So, again, what do you want from me?"

"I need a statement. You feel up to it?"

"She shot me. End of statement. I'm trying to put all of this behind me and Kandace," Solomon said.

"I'm going to need her statement too. Here's what I don't understand. How could you hire her and not know that Carmen De La Croix was an assumed identity?"

Solomon rubbed his eyes. "Her references checked out. What more could I have done? Maybe I acted hastily because I wanted to show up my brother. Carmen was my first big hire after taking over the business."

Myer shrugged. "I guess I can understand that. She's not talking and I was hoping you could give me some insight into how I could get her to talk. She seems to think you two had a relationship, and I know your reputation of being a ladies man."

"Wait a minute," Solomon said. "What does that have to do with anything?"

"Were you involved with her? Did you spur her on?"

Solomon cocked his head to the side and rolled his eyes at Myer. "I thought Carmen, Chelsea, or whoever she is, was my friend. We hung out, we worked together, but this goes back farther than her coming to work with me."

"What do you mean?" Myer asked as he pulled out his notebook.

"Few years ago, I was getting married," he said, then pursed his lips when he saw the look of disbelief on the detective's face. "Look, I wasn't always the ladies man you think I am. Anyway, things fell apart and this waitress helped to get me out of the reception hall."

"Chelsea?"

"Yeah. I had no idea she was so disturbed."

Myer scribbled in his notebook. "Wow, I can't believe Mr. Page Six was going to get married."

"Hey, what else do you need from me?" Solomon asked.

"I think that's it," he said. "The district attorney will be contacting you when the trial comes up."

"Knock, knock," Kandace said as she walked into the room. She looked from Detective Myer to Solomon. "What's going on? She didn't escape, did she?"

"No, ma'am," Detective Myer said. "I'm just collecting statements."

Kandace released a sigh of relief and walked over to Solomon's bed. "Good," she said.

"I do need to get your statement," the detective said.

Kandace's face blanched. "Can we do this later?"

"Well, I kind of need to wrap up this part of the case," Myer said. "I only have a few questions."

Solomon took note of the pained look on Kandace's face and waved the detective off. "Can you give us a minute?" he asked as he rose from the bed and took Kandace in his arms.

"Sure."

When they were alone in the room, Solomon lifted Kandace's chin. "Babe, what's wrong? You're shivering."

"I just don't want to think about that night. Why do we need to say anything?" she asked as she held on to Solomon.

"It's just part of the police investigation. They need all the information they can get to make sure they can put Carmen away," he said in a reassuring tone. He ran his finger down her cheek. "You don't have to be afraid, Kandace."

"I just want this to end," she said. "Had I known the detective was here, I might not have shipped my friends back to Charlotte."

"Your girls might have gotten you arrested," Solomon said with a low chuckle. "I'm here and it's going to be all right, okay?"

She nodded. "Then I guess I'd better get the detective."

"You don't have to go right this minute. Let me do this first," he said as he captured her lips and kissed her with a soft, but intense passion. Kandace lost herself in his kiss and forgot about the detective waiting outside the door or the fact that they were in a hospital room.

"Ahem," Myer said when he walked into Solomon's room. "Sorry to interrupt. Miss Davis, are you ready to give your statement?"

Kandace turned and faced the detective. "Yes," she said. Solomon stroked her shoulder as Detective Myer began his inquiry.

"Miss Davis, what happened when Chelsea came to the suite you were staying in?"

Kandace closed her eyes, going back to the moments she'd prayed she'd forget one day.

Kandace had lain back on the bed waiting for Solomon to return from his business downstairs. Her body had still tingled from the aftershocks of their lovemaking and she couldn't wait for his return. Just as she had been about to shrug out of her robe, she heard the suite door open.

"Solomon," she'd called out. "That was quick." Kandace had hopped off the bed and headed for the door with her robe open. "I was thinking that . . . It's you!" Kandace had quickly closed her robe when Carmen had pointed her gun in Kandace's face.

"So that's how you did it, you bitch? You parade around naked and let Solomon have his way with you? You're not the first woman he's done this with. You're nothing."

"Carmen, wh-what are you doing here?" Kandace had asked as she tried to back away from Carmen.

"I could kill you right now, shoot you and let you die. No one would give a damn because Solomon loves me. He only lusts after you like all men lust after sluts," Carmen

had spat. She'd closed the space between her and Kandace, grabbing her face with her cold hands. "You know you're nothing but a slut. A damned slut who doesn't have much more than her looks to offer. Solomon will grow tired of you, just like he did with every other woman. Every other woman but me. He needs me and he loves me." Carmen had pushed Kandace in the corner and pointed the gun at her chest. "Tell me, what am I going to have to do to get you to leave Solomon alone?"

"Shouldn't that be his choice?" Kandace had asked before thinking.

Carmen had slammed Kandace's head into the wall. "Shut up, bitch. Solomon is my man. He's mine and I'm not going to let you have him."

Carmen had backed away from her, but kept the gun trained on her chest. "He's my man and you're not going to keep him away from me!"

"And then," Kandace said, "Solomon burst into the suite."

Detective Myer stopped writing and looked up at Kandace, who seemed to be reliving the terrifying night.

"Is that all that happened?" the detective asked.

Kandace's eyes grew wide. "What more do you want me to say? Do you know how scared I was as I stood there with that gun in my face?" Kandace's voice rose as she spoke. Solomon stroked her back softly.

"Calm down, babe. It's all right. She's gone now. Detective Myer, I think you have enough," Solomon said.

"Yes, I do. Thanks, Miss Davis. Your statement is

going to go a long way in convicting her in North Carolina and New York."

Kandace fell into Solomon's embrace as she cried silently. Neither of them noticed when Detective Myer left the room.

CHAPTER 26

Later that afternoon, Solomon was released from the hospital and he and Kandace headed back to the resort. When the car that the resort sent to the hospital to pick them up arrived at the resort, he could feel Kandace tense up. The driver got out of the car to open Solomon's door.

"You want to go home?" he asked her when she gripped his hand tightly.

"You don't think I should go in there and face my fears?" she asked as she looked up at the building.

"I think you should do whatever you feel comfortable with. I can have a porter bring your things down and we can head to Charlotte right now."

"We?" Kandace asked. "What do you mean, 'we'? You have to recover from your gunshot wound."

"I can get quality health care anywhere. And the doctor referred me to the clinic the Carolina Panthers and other NFL teams use to help me heal my shoulder. Guess where this place is?"

"OrthoCarolina?" Kandace said, remembering

Jade's brother-in-law, Maurice, having to go there after the football season ended to deal with an injury.

"That's the place," he said. "But if you feel like you have to go in here and prove something to yourself, then I'm standing right beside you."

She took another glance at the entrance of the resort. "Okay," she said. "I'm a big girl, I can do this."

Solomon got out of the car first, then he stood aside as Kandace slowly climbed out. He wrapped his good arm around her waist and led her inside the resort.

"Good morning, Mr. Crawford. Glad to see you back," the front desk clerk said.

Solomon smiled and nodded at her as he and Kandace headed for the elevator. "Are you all right?" Solomon asked as they stepped on the elevator cart.

Kandace took a deep breath and squeezed Solomon's hand. "I'm fine," she said. "So far, anyway."

"That's good. Remember, I'm right here for you." The elevator doors opened on the eighth floor and Kandace took another breath.

She could almost hear the officers and the gunshots as they walked to the door of the suite. Kandace's knees felt as if they were going to buckle underneath her. But she pressed on and walked in to the suite behind Solomon. Kandace half expected to see bloodstains on the floor, but she had to remind herself that nothing happened in Solomon's suite. Still, the specter of Carmen's insane actions floated around Kandace's mind and in every shadow at the resort. Blinking, she tried to clear her mind of the morbid thoughts.

Solomon tried to pull his garment bag from the

closet, but he caught a sharp pain in his shoulder. "Damn," he muttered, bringing Kandace out of her thoughts. She turned to him and crossed over to the closet.

"You have a staff that can do this for you," she said as she lifted the bag out of the closet and tossed it on the bed.

"You know me. I had to see if I could do it myself first," he said as he sat down and expelled a breath. "That really hurt."

"I'm sure it did," she said, thumping him on the forehead. "Knucklehead."

"Hey, I already said I was in pain and you cause me more," Solomon joked. "That's just wrong."

Kandace winked at him as she picked up the phone and called the front desk. "Want me to kiss it and make it better?" she asked as the phone rang.

"Then let me tell you what else hurts," he replied with a wily smile.

Slowly, Kandace found herself relaxing in the room. Her mind recalled all of the things she and Solomon did during her vacation—the kissing, the flirting, the lovemaking—things that far outweighed the terrifying moments when Carmen held that gun on her.

Kandace hung up the phone after making arrangements for the staff to come and take their things downstairs. "I have to tell you, my living situation in Charlotte doesn't come with a staff or a lot of space," she said, thinking about the two-bedroom town house she'd been renting since moving to North Carolina.

"You're there, right?"

"Yes."

"Then that is all I need to get on the road to recovery. Just make sure you keep your girl Serena away from me."

"I think she should be back in Atlanta by the time we get to Charlotte," Kandace said, remembering the cryptic conversation she and Serena had when she'd first arrived at Carolina Serenity.

"Good. She's scary."

"No, she isn't. To know her is to love her," Kandace said with a laugh.

"I'll take your word for it," he said. Moments later there was a knock at the door and members of the resort's porter staff entered and began taking the couple's luggage downstairs.

"You can't drive, can you?" Kandace asked.

Solomon shook his head. "Doctors orders."

"Good thing I have a driver's license and a car," she said as he rose to his feet.

"Well, your driving isn't the only thing I need you for," he said. "But you're going to have to take it easy on me when you get me into bed."

"What did the doctor order about your other activities?" she asked.

Solomon wrapped his good arm around her waist. "I don't always follow doctor's orders," he said before kissing her with a smoldering passion that caused her legs to quake.

"Is that so?" she asked when they broke the passionate kiss.

Solomon winked at her. "Yes, because I want

you so bad right now, I don't give a damn about this shoulder."

"We'd better get on the road," she said as she placed her hand on his chest, stopping another kiss. "Or we're not going to make it out of here today."

"Would that be such a bad thing?"

"Yes," she said as she took a step back from him. "So, let's go. I'll even spring for dinner tonight."

"Says the woman who owns a restaurant," Solomon said as they headed out the door.

Carmen sat up in her hospital bed as best she could, straining to hear what the detectives outside her door were saying.

"New York has the more pressing charges," she heard the NYPD detective say.

"But our district attorney has ordered that she gets evaluated in a mental hospital," said the Avery County detective. "And she's still a suspect in a murder case in our jurisdiction."

"She's a fugitive from New York," the detective boomed.

"Well, if you'd done your job, she wouldn't be here and we wouldn't have a dead woman on our hands."

The door to the room opened and a nurse walked in to check her vital signs. The woman looked as if she was nervous to be alone with her.

"I don't bite," Carmen said. "This is all a misunderstanding between me and the man I thought loved me."

"Okay," the nurse said as she placed the blood pressure cuff on Carmen's arm.

"Have you ever loved someone and then they betrayed you? Told someone to hurt you?"

The nurse removed the cuff and wrote the reading on the chart. "I can't say that I have."

"Well, I'm going to make them all pay," Carmen said. She grabbed the nurse's hand. "I'm going to win."

"Ugh, okay," the nurse said as she pulled away from Carmen and dashed out of the room.

She heard the nurse tell the police that "the patient in there is crazy as a loon." Carmen smiled. Her plan was working. If she could convince the North Carolina authorities that she belonged in a mental hospital, she could get to Solomon and that woman. *Then they will pay.*

Solomon wiped his mouth with the cloth napkin at Hometown Delights, the restaurant that Kandace and her friends owned in Charlotte. Yes, the food was good, but he wasn't feeling the chef, who kept coming to their table to specifically check on Kandace. It was obvious to Solomon that Devon Harris had designs on his woman.

"How was dinner?" Kandace asked Solomon.

"Great. But next time, we're ordering takeout," he said.

"Why?"

"That way we can eat without the interruptions,"

Solomon said as he watched Devon walk over to their table again.

Kandace placed her hand on Solomon's thigh. "Are you jealous? You have nothing to be worried about."

"Kandace," Devon said when he stopped at the table, "how was the meal?"

"It was terrific, as usual," she said.

Devon rocked back on his heels and smiled. "You were always my muse," he said.

Solomon cleared his throat and said, "The chicken was a little dry."

Devon glanced at Solomon. "Thought you had the steak?"

"I thought you were the chef and not the waiter," Solomon said. "But here you are at the table again."

"What's your problem, man?" Devon asked. "Kandace and I work together. And because of you she's been through hell."

Kandace rose to her feet and said, "Hey, what's going on here?"

Solomon shook his head and sprung from his seat. "Ask your chef," he said as he bolted out the door.

Kandace sighed with frustration and looked at Devon. "You have been overly attentive," she said. "What gives?"

"Are you sure you should be with this guy?"

"That's rich coming from you."

"That was a long time ago and I was young and made mistakes. I took this job hoping that we could reconnect," he said.

"I don't go backward," Kandace said as she

grabbed her keys and purse. "But to answer your question, I am sure I should be with Solomon." She sprinted out the door and found Solomon leaning against the wall. "Solomon," she said, placing her hand on his chest, "why are you acting like a baby? And if this is how things go when we run into each other's exes, I'm guessing I need to wear track shoes when we go out in New York."

"I know I overreacted, but I could see what that dude was doing. Besides, I remembered you telling me that you two had something going on, and he looks like he wants to get it started again."

"It doesn't matter, because the only person I want to start something with is standing right here," she said as she pressed her lips against his.

"Make sure he knows that," Solomon said.

"You want some dessert?" she asked.

"What do you have in mind?"

Kandace grinned. "It involves a lot of licking. And it is packaged to go."

"I'm in love with this idea," he said as they headed to her car.

As they got in the car, Kandace caught a glimpse of Antonio Billups walking into the restaurant. She wondered briefly if he was there to meet Serena. Kandace really wanted to see those two work out the issues between them. She knew her friend was falling hard for Antonio, no matter how she tried to deny it.

"I have to make a quick call," she told Solomon as she cranked up the car. Kandace grabbed her Black-Berry from her purse and dialed Serena's number.

"Hello?"

"Serena, there's a situation at the restaurant you need to take care of."

"Are you working when your *boyfriend* is in town?" Serena asked.

"We had dinner there. Just get over here. I'll talk to you tomorrow." Kandace ended the call, then turned her phone off.

"What are you up to?" Solomon asked.

"Just meddling in my friend's life," she said. "The usual."

Solomon shook his head and laughed. "You guys are too much," he said.

"I'm going to show you too much," she said with a smile.

Solomon leaned back in the passenger seat of her Lexus IS. "I would've never taken you for a sports car driver," he said as they pulled up to Kandace's place. "I figured you as a practical SUV woman."

"That was just a rental," she said. "I have a need for speed."

"Not always. There is one thing you do really slowly," he said.

"And what would that be?" she asked as she shut the car off.

Solomon took her face in his hands. "You kiss me really slowly," he said, then leaned into her and pressed his lips against hers. Kandace took Solomon's bottom lip between her teeth and ran her tongue across it. She slowly kissed him, her tongue swirling around his until they were both heady with desire and anticipation. Kandace pulled back from him, looking into his eyes. She saw desire, passion, and it spurred her own want.

"Can we quickly get out of the car?" she asked as he dropped his hand from her face.

"Yes," he said as he opened his door. Kandace followed Solomon to the door of her town house and fumbled to find her house key. Once she opened the door, Solomon backed her against the wall and untied her trench coat. He loved the fact that winter in Charlotte didn't mean women had to dress in heavy layers. He removed her black sweater dress in one quick motion, but he left her black knee-high boots on.

"Damn, so sexy," he said as he drank in her image. Solomon ran his hand down the center of her chest. Her skin was like the finest silk underneath his fingertips. "You're more than sexy, you're beautiful."

"Solomon," she moaned as she took his hand and kissed his fingertips. "I want you so badly."

He slid his hand down to her lacy black panties, his fingers dancing around the waistband, and she trembled as he slipped his hand inside. "You have me, now and forever," he said as his finger found its way to her wetness.

Kandace moaned as he parted her wet folds of flesh. He teased her sensitive bud with his finger, stroking her slowly and deliberately until she screamed out his name.

Her love rained down on him and he pulled his finger out, licking her sweetness as if it was the nectar from mythical Mount Olympus. Solomon doubted he could make it upstairs to Kandace's bedroom, because he wanted her now. Wanted to dive into her sticky sweetness. Taking her hand, he led her to the stairs and backed her against the third one from the bottom. He pulled her legs apart and planted himself between her thighs, licking desire until she shook from satisfaction. Kandace squirmed against him, lifting her hips into his kiss as he greedily licked and sucked her.

She moaned his name over and over again as she exploded against him over and over again.

Kandace tugged at the button and zipper on Solomon's pants and used her feet to pushed them down to his ankles. Solomon inched up her body, licking his lips. Kandace shivered as she felt his erection against her thighs. "Solomon," she moaned as she pressed her body against him. For a second, Solomon thought about taking her without protection, taking her and possibly filling her belly with Solomon Jr.

Not until you marry her, a voice said in his ear. It startled him, made him pull back from her and stare down into her angelic face. *She's the one. She's the woman I've been looking for.*

"What's wrong?" she asked when she opened her eyes and saw Solomon staring at her.

He stroked her cheek, then leaned down and kissed her lips gently. "Nothing's wrong," he said when he broke the kiss. "Everything is right. I love you, Kandace."

"What?" she asked, not trusting her ears.

"I love you," he said as he kissed her neck. "I love you."

Kandace knew logic should've taken over. How could he love her? How could he love her after such a short time? *The same way you love him,* she thought. Kandace wrapped her arms around his neck as his mouth covered hers. She wanted to tell him that she was in love, wanted to tell him that she loved him too, but fear stopped her. Caused her to keep her mouth closed around his lips. Kandace wrapped her legs around his waist, deepening her kiss and hoping that she could convey her feelings to him without saying a word.

Solomon pulled back before he lost his control. "Protection," he said. "And since it's in your room, let's take this to the bed."

"All right," she said as she rose to her feet and walked slowly up the stairs. Solomon smiled as he took in the sight of her shapely bottom and quickly followed her up to the bedroom. A sliver of silver moonlight shone through the thin curtains and the light danced off Kandace's skin, giving her an angelic glow that made him harder than he ever thought possible. Solomon nearly tripped over his feet as he rushed to his overnight bag and snatched a condom out of the pocket.

When he was covered, Solomon bolted to the bed and joined Kandace as she unsnapped her bra and tossed it on the floor. "Lie down," she told him. "I wouldn't want you to strain your shoulder."

"Yes, ma'am," he said as he lay on his back. Kandace mounted him, guiding his erection into her wetness. Solomon moaned as he felt her tighten herself around his pulsating manhood. She rocked her hips and rolled her body against him. Up and down she thrust, and Solomon mirrored her movements. Fast, then slow like Coltrane's sax, and intense like Miles's horn. She was so wet and so hot. Solomon relished the feeling as he wrapped his arms around her waist and held her tightly. Kandace ground against him until she felt as if she was about to explode. Solomon could feel her body tremble against his as she leaned forward, pressing her breasts against his chest as the pleasure of her orgasm rippled through her body. She rubbed her lips against his collarbone and sighed.

Solomon stroked her hair and kissed her cheek. Kandace followed a bead of sweat down his chest with her fingertip. "Is it really possible for us to be this happy?" she asked.

"You don't think we deserve it?" Solomon asked. "And if you think this is happy, you haven't seen anything yet."

"I love you, Solomon," she said.

He smiled brightly, happy to hear those words slip from her lips. But in true Solomon Crawford fashion, he said, "Why don't you tell me something I don't know?"

"Ooh, you're lucky you're still nursing a wound or I would kick you out of this bed," she joked.

"But I have no doubt you'd welcome me back," he replied.

Kandace laughed. "You're too much. Still the same cocky asshole I thought you were."

"But you love me," he said as he kissed her gently on the lips.

CHAPTER 27

The Superior Court judge in Newland, North Carolina, read the documents on his bench and then cast a glance at Carmen. She didn't look capable of such horrible crimes, but after twenty years on the bench, he'd seen baby-faced killers and beautiful women who had committed horrific crimes. He cleared his throat, then said, "I'm ready to render my ruling."

Carmen's public defender tapped her fingers on the table as she waited for the judge to issue his ruling.

"I'm ordering that the defendant enter the Behavioral Health Center in Charlotte for a thirty-day evaluation. At the end of the evaluation period, I will take the doctor's findings into consideration before ruling on the defendant's extradition to New York," he said.

"Your honor," the assistant district attorney from New York County said as he stood up. "New York County has the most serious charges against this defendant. We can have our doctors examine her, but she needs to face the—"

"Mr. Becoats, I understand you have serious charges against the defendant, but I have a concern for her mental state. Before she goes anywhere, she will be evaluated. I don't want to hear anything else on the matter," the judge said, then banged his gavel. "Next case."

Carmen hid her smile. This was even sweeter than she imagined it could be. Going to Charlotte would put her close enough to Kandace to make her suffer. After she disposed of her, then she'd get back to New York and make Solomon pay for turning his back on her. Still, she'd get the one thing she always wanted from him before she slit his throat. *Maybe I can steal some Viagra from the hospital and spike his drink. Then he'll have no choice but to make love to me,* she thought as the sheriff's deputy led her to a holding cell.

Carmen didn't pay attention to her public defender telling her what the ruling meant and when she could expect to be shipped to the hospital. Carmen was too busy imagining jabbing a knife into Kandace's chest.

Solomon sat in the waiting room of the clinic wishing he could skip physical therapy today. Despite the fact that he was on time for his appointment, he still had to wait for some reason. *This would not be happening in New York,* he thought as he walked up to the receptionist. "Excuse me—how much longer?" he asked.

"I'm not sure," she said. "Your doctor is working with one of the Panthers right now."

"Oh great," Solomon said sarcastically. As he went back to his seat, the door opened and Carolina Panthers star wide receiver Maurice Goings walked into the waiting area. *Hope this means Philadelphia is going to win Sunday,* he thought, looking at Maurice as he talked on his cell phone.

"Nah, coach, I'm cleared to play," Solomon heard him say.

"Damn," Solomon muttered as he picked up an old copy of *Sports Illustrated.* Maurice glanced over at him and nodded as if he thought Solomon was a fan. Before Solomon could say anything, he was called back to the exam room.

"Sorry about the delay, Mr. Crawford," Dr. Elis Sanford said.

"Yeah, I've been waiting an hour." Solomon tried to keep his tone even since this man was about examine him.

"I would suggest that you schedule your appointments for Tuesdays. It's a lot slower here then."

"I'll keep that in mind," Solomon said. The doctor began the examination of Solomon's shoulder but didn't start therapy that day because he felt the shoulder wasn't healed enough to begin rehabilitation.

"The last thing you want to do is rush a tendon injury," Dr. Sanford said.

"I'm just hoping to get better sooner rather than later," Solomon said.

"Well, I think we can make that happen with my course of treatment. I'm going to prescribe you a mild pain reliever," the doctor said as he wrote a prescription. "And I'll see you in a week."

"On a Tuesday," Solomon said.

The doctor nodded and smiled. "Yes, next Tuesday," he said as he handed Solomon the prescription slip.

Solomon walked up to the front desk, paid the fee for the service, and then pulled his phone out to call Kandace.

"Hello?" he heard Kandace say.

"Hey, babe, I'm all done at the doctor."

"All right, I'm wrapping things up at the restaurant, so I'll be right there. What did he say about your shoulder?"

"It's too soon to start rehab, so no lifting you up on the wall tonight."

"Funny," she said. "I'm leaving now."

Solomon ended the call and headed outside. He was surprised to see Maurice Goings signing autographs for some nurses out front.

"Hey, guys," Maurice said, "make sure you check out Hometown Delights when you get ready for lunch. The food is great."

"I've been there," one of the women said. "I was hoping to see that fine Devon Harris."

The other two women laughed. "Me too," another woman said.

Solomon leaned against the wall and muttered, "Should've been there last night."

Maurice turned around and looked at Solomon. "You say something, my man?"

"No, just talking to myself," Solomon replied.

One of the nurses looked up at Solomon. "Aren't you Solomon Crawford?" she asked. "Oh my God, I see you on E! all the time."

"What is this, famous man day in the Queen City?" one of the other nurses asked.

"I wouldn't say that I'm famous," he said.

"I would," Maurice said. "If you're looking for property, I should put you in touch with my brother."

Solomon smiled as he saw Kandace's Lexus pull up. "You know what. Let me give you my card and we'll set a meeting up. I think expanding in Charlotte is a great idea."

Kandace hopped out of the car and shook her head as she watched Solomon hand Maurice a business card. "Now, this is scary," she said.

"What's up, Kandace?" Maurice said, then gave her a quick brotherly hug.

"What are you two plotting?" she asked as she took Solomon's hand in hers. The three nurses sucked their teeth and walked away.

"I should've known Solomon Crawford was waiting on a woman," one of them said.

"You two know each other?" Maurice asked. Solomon remembered that Jade was married to Maurice's brother.

"Yes," she said. "But you still didn't answer my question."

"Just talking about some possible land deals," Solomon said. "Maurice, it was nice meeting you and good luck next Sunday."

"Next Sunday?" he asked. "We have a game this Sunday."

"I know. McNabb's my man, I can't go against him," Solomon said.

It was about three P.M. when Carmen arrived at the Behavioral Health Center. She looked at the doctor asking her questions about her mental state, but she didn't say a word at first. *I know what they want me to say, what they want me to do, and I'm not going to play this game right now. Then again,* she thought as she looked at the baby-faced doctor, *I know just what to do.*

"Chelsea, we can sit here and say nothing, but I really want to help you," Dr. Hovis Clarke said.

"Please don't call me that. My name is Carmen," she said in a soft voice.

"Why don't you want to be called by your given name?" Dr. Clarke asked as he scribbled in his notepad.

Carmen sighed and bit the inside of her lip until tears sprang into her eyes. "No one loved Chelsea," she said once she stopped biting her lip.

"What's the difference between Chelsea and Carmen?" he asked.

Please, you have got to be kidding me, she thought as she stared at him with a blank look on her face. *What does he want to hear? What is going to get this man out of my face?* She dropped her head in her hands and pretended to hyperventilate.

Dr. Clarke dropped his pen and rushed to her side. "Carmen, are you all right?"

She made her body go still, and Dr. Clarke called for a nurse and a doctor on his cell phone. In her mind, Carmen was wearing a huge grin because she hadn't expected things to work this well.

Poor Dr. Clarke, she lamented. *Apparently young and not very bright. North Carolina must be desperate for doctors.*

The nurse and the doctor rushed into the room and checked Carmen's vital signs.

"She's unresponsive," the nurse said as she shone a penlight in Carmen's eyes. "What should we do, Doctor?"

Carmen began to pretend she was having a spasm, hoping to spur the doctor into action.

"Call for transport to CMC," the medical doctor said. "Clarke, you're going to have to ride with her and let the staff know what she's in here for."

"All right."

Within seconds, Carmen felt herself being secured on a gurney. She tuned out the conversation the paramedics were having as they loaded her in the ambulance.

As the paramedics hooked her up to machines and tested her blood sugar and took her blood pressure reading, Carmen prayed they wouldn't figure out that she was faking everything and send her back to her padded room.

"This is weird," one of the paramedics said. "Everything is checking out as if its normal."

"Doc, what were you two doing when she crashed?" the other paramedic asked.

"Just talking. It's possible that she has a psychosomatic condition," he said. "But just to be safe, I want her to be examined thoroughly."

And, Dr. Clarke, if you don't get in my way, you might survive, she thought as she felt the ambulance stop.

Kandace watched Solomon typing on his laptop while she was supposed to be typing a press release about Alicia's business seminar. He looked so focused as he worked. Every now and then he'd grunt and start typing faster. One thing she could say about her man was he was intense when he worked. *My man,* she thought. *I can't believe this. Never would I have imagined that I was going to have a date for Thanksgiving dinner.*

"Damn," he muttered, then picked up his cell phone and made a call. While Solomon talked to his New York office, Kandace finished the press release and e-mailed it to Alicia for her to approve. Two weeks ago, she would've moved on to her next project and buried herself in more work, but right now, all she wanted to do was bury herself underneath Solomon.

The door to her office swung open and Jade walked in with Jaden in her arms. "Kandace, I'm glad you're still here," she said. "I know I was supposed to be here for this dinner party tonight, but

Jaden has a fever. Can you please stay here until Serena comes at eight?"

Jaden whined in his mother's arms. "We sure can," Solomon said as he hung up the phone and walked over to Jade. He placed his hand on the little boy's forehead. "You get him out of here and don't worry about this place."

"I was wrong about you," Jade said. "And I'm glad."

"Call me and let me know how my godson is doing," Kandace said as Jade rushed out the door. When Jade was gone, she turned to Solomon with a wide smile on her face.

"What?" he asked.

"That was so sweet of you," she said. "I was planning on taking you home and rubbing your shoulder."

Solomon closed the space between them and wrapped his arms around Kandace. "Had I known that, your friend would've had to stay here with the sick baby," he joked.

Kandace pinched his cheek. "Such a liar. I saw how concerned you looked when Jaden started crying. I guess Solomon Crawford isn't the big bad wolf he wants all of New York to believe he is."

"Shh, woman. If someone hears that, I'm going to have to try and tear down a playground or some-thing to rebuild my image."

Kandace gently kissed his lips, then said, "You wouldn't dare."

"No, I wouldn't," he said. "I got a soft spot in my heart for kids."

She cocked her head to the side. "Really?"

"Yes. One day, I hope that I have a few kids of my

own," he said, revealing a thought he'd never shared with another woman.

"You're showing me a side of you I never thought I'd see," Kandace said. "Where was this guy in Sugar Mountain?"

"Oh please, had you met him, you would've succeeded in trying to ignore me," he said, then squeezed her bottom. "Is your chef here?"

"I'm sure he is," she said. "But all I have to do is sit in this office in case a problem arises."

Solomon let her go and walked over to the door and locked it. "Is that so?"

"Umm," she said as she began unbuttoning her blouse. "You must be reading my mind because I was wondering when you were going to get around to locking that door."

She shrugged out of her blouse, revealing a leopard print bustier. Solomon expelled an appreciative breath. "Lovely."

Kandace unzipped her skirt and revealed a black garter belt holding up her sheer black thigh-highs. "Damn," he said as he walked over to her and held her hands above her head as he drank in her stunning image. He ran his hand down her chest, down to her shapely hips, and pulled her against his throbbing body. Just the sight of her made him hot and hard with desire. "I want you so bad right now," he said.

Kandace pushed him backward onto the small sofa where she had slept many nights after spending more than twelve hours at the restaurant.

With Solomon in the seated position, he opened

his arms to her. Kandace sauntered over to him with a smile and planted herself on his lap. "You know," she said as she wrapped her arms around his neck and legs around his waist, "I've never done this before."

"Well, I'm so glad I'm the one to break your office cherry," he said as he felt himself hardening against her thighs.

"So am I," she said as she reached down and unbuckled his belt, then unzipped his pants. Kandace slipped her hands inside his boxer briefs and massaged his hardness until she felt the first drops of his desire pooling.

"Mmm," he moaned as she continued to stroke him back and forth. She lowered herself onto his erection and Solomon was enveloped in her warm wetness. Kandace threw her head back as Solomon gripped her hips and drove deeper into her, reveling in her heat and her wetness. Kandace moaned in pleasure as she ground against him. Solomon's mouth found its way to her chest. He pushed her bustier down, exposing her perky breasts, and sucked and licked her nipples until her body vibrated with desire. She tightened herself around him and brought him to the brink as she rode him like a prized steed. Just as Kandace reached her climax and Solomon exploded, there was a knock on the office door.

"Oh my goodness," Kandace whispered.

"Kandace, are you in there?" Devon called out.

"Shit," Solomon exclaimed.

"Ah, just a minute," Kandace said as she scrambled to put her clothes on. "What's wrong, Devon?"

"I had something I wanted you to taste. Is everything all right in there?"

Solomon zipped up Kandace's skirt, then adjusted his pants and opened the door.

"We're good," Solomon said, offering a sly smile to Devon.

"I didn't know you were busy," Devon said when he walked in and placed a tray of food on her desk. "This is a new dish I was thinking about putting on the menu."

"Oh," Kandace said.

"You two enjoy it," Devon said dejectedly, then walked out of the office.

Kandace looked down at her poorly buttoned shirt and slapped Solomon on his chest. "You could've told me about my shirt," she said.

Solomon rubbed his chest. "I didn't even notice," he lied. "Food smells good."

"You're dirty, Solomon," she said. "You might as well broadcast what we were doing."

"I think you already did," he said as he pointed to a bright red passion mark on her chest.

"My goodness," she said as she rebuttoned her shirt. "This is going to look real nice when I'm acting as hostess tonight."

Solomon took a plate of food and started eating the jasmine rice and beef tips. "I was minding my business and you took off your clothes and got in my lap. This is actually good."

Kandace laughed and took a bite of the food. "It is good," she said.

About an hour later, Kandace and Solomon were out front seating a group of veteran Carolina Panthers players into a private dining room.

When Maurice spotted Solomon, he laughed and said, "What's the McNabb fan doing here?"

Rumbles rippled though the crowd of football players. Many of the things they said would've made the rowdy crowd at Lincoln Financial Field blush. Solomon fanned them off as he helped Kandace hand out the menus.

"All right," Kandace said. "You can't blame the man for being on the wrong side. He's from New York. But if you could keep it down so that you don't get a bunch of fans and groupies back here."

"Hey," Walter Homer, a defensive lineman said. "The only dude trying to stay away from groupies is Mo. See some fine ones with an ass like yours, send them back here."

Kandace stepped in front of Solomon when she saw his fist close and his jaw clinch in anger. "Just walk away," she said.

"Who is that fat . . ."

Kandace placed her hand over Solomon's mouth, then ushered him out of the dining area.

Once they were out of earshot of the players, Solomon swore. "How often do you have to deal with that?" he asked.

"First of all, you're overreacting. Homer is harmless and he flirts with everybody," Kandace said.

"That was disrespectful," Solomon said.

Kandace shrugged her shoulder. "It means nothing because," she said as she grabbed his hand and placed it on her bottom, "this is all yours."

"I like the sound of that," Solomon said. "Just tell me that you don't have to go back out there."

"No, I don't." She leaned in and kissed him on his chin. "You know we only put up with them because Maurice is Jade's brother-in-law and those guys are good for our bottom line."

"Seems like some of them are worried about your *bottom line*."

"Solomon," she said in an exasperated tone, "green doesn't look good on you."

"Whatever."

Carmen opened her eyes after she was wheeled into a room at Carolina's Medical Center. Dr. Clarke was sitting in a chair near the door drifting in and out of sleep. She checked her wrists and was a bit surprised that she hadn't been shackled to the bed. She had an IV in her arm, but no heart monitor this time. Quietly, she pulled the IV out of her arm, then she slipped out of the bed, stretching her arms above her head. Pretending to be in and out of consciousness for the last five hours had been taxing on her, but she had a mission and she wasn't going to stop until she completed it. She pulled one of the tubes from the IV machine and crept over to Dr. Clarke, who was sleeping soundly now.

"Sorry about this, Doc," she whispered. "I thought I could spare you, but you're in the way." Carmen wrapped the thin tube around his neck and choked him before he had a chance to scream for help. She continued to squeeze until she felt the life slip from his body. Satisfied that the doctor was dead, she dragged his lifeless body into the bathroom. She stripped his clothes off, hoping that she would be able to wear them. When she put the pants on they were about three sizes too big and the shirt was ill-fitting around her shoulders, but she knew she needed them until she could get a pair of scrubs to get her out of the hospital.

Once she got outside, Carmen figured she could find her way back to Kandace's restaurant and then she would make the bitch suffer. She reached in the doctor's pocket and saw that the man had about eighty dollars in cash on him. That would be enough to get her around if she needed a taxi or to hop on the bus.

She turned to the doctor's dead body and shook her head. "Thanks for the cash, Doc. You know, you asked me why I didn't want to be called Chelsea and I guess it's because Chelsea was a weak, poor excuse of a woman who allowed people to walk all over her. Chelsea died when I lit that fire. She was worthless just like my mother and that man she thought was more important than her own child. Carmen is a woman of action, but you already know that." She smiled coldly and walked out of the bath-room, closing the door behind her.

Carmen crept to the room door and opened it just a bit, seeing that the halls were clear. The nurse's station was at the other end of the corridor near the elevators. Since it was so quiet on the floor and no nurses roamed the halls, Carmen was able to walk down the hall and find a utility closet. She smiled as she saw green scrubs folded on the shelf. She closed the door behind her, stripped out of the doctor's clothes, and pulled on a pair of scrubs. She grabbed a pair of paper shoe covers and put them on her feet.

When Carmen walked out of the closet, she saw a nurse walking in to what had been her room. She tore off toward the elevator. As she pressed the down button, she heard a bloodcurdling scream and the two nurses at the nurse's station took off down the hall without giving her a second look. Once she stepped on the elevator, Carmen knew that she was going to get away without a problem.

CHAPTER 28

Kandace shook her head as Solomon, Homer, and Maurice sat at the restaurant's bar laughing and drinking rum and colas. She found it hard to believe that less than three hours ago, Solomon wanted to bash Homer's fat head in. Though she was happy the men were getting along, she was ready to close up shop. *I am going to kill Alicia,* she thought. Her friend never showed up and when Kandace had called her to find out what was going on, the only excuse Alicia had given was that something had come up.

"All right, guys, unless you want to pay the bartender and the sous chef overtime, get out," Kandace said as she leaned on Solomon's good shoulder.

Maurice looked down at his watch. "Damn, it's later than I thought. Kenya is going to kill me."

"Don't you think you need to call a cab?" Kandace suggested. "I don't think you're going to play on Sunday if you get arrested tonight for DUI."

Maurice pointed at Solomon and laughed.

"You were trying to set me up so McNabb would win, huh?"

"I don't need to do that. I've seen what your quarterback has been doing this season. I'll call a car for you two and make sure everyone gets home safely with no charges," Solomon said.

"Babe, you're not in New York. I'll call Crown Cab."

"I can drive home," Homer said as he struggled to stand up. Maurice grabbed his keys from his hand.

"I know you're stupid, but I didn't know you were a damned fool," Maurice said. "We'll take that cab."

Kandace picked up the phone from behind the bar and called the cab. Solomon followed her behind the bar and wrapped his arms around her waist after she hung up with the taxi company. "Those guys are pretty cool," he said.

"It wasn't always like that, but that's a story for another day," she said. "I'm going to tell Raymond he can take off. Once their taxi gets here, we can go."

"Do we have to wait out here with them? I can't get my mind off that sofa in your office," he whispered in her ear.

Kandace turned around and stole a quick kiss from him. "Tell me about it," she said.

"Ugh," Homer exclaimed. "Is it something in the water around here? And if so, where's my cup?"

Kandace glanced at Homer over her shoulder. "What are you muttering about?"

"Why don't you hook me up with your friend? You know, the loud one." Homer said. "Then I can be as sickening as you two and Mo and Kenya and James and Jade."

"Shut up, Homer," Maurice said. "You're the one with an allergic reaction to being with one woman."

Solomon laughed. "I used to have that allergy," he said, then he looked into Kandace's smiling face. "Then I met the right woman."

"Spare me," Homer said, making a gagging sound.

"Cab's here," Maurice said. "Let's go, Homer."

The big man followed Maurice out and Kandace walked over and locked the door. "I thought they would never leave," she said after pulling the blind down.

"Me either," Solomon said as he crossed over to her. Kandace wrapped her arms around his neck and brushed her lips against his.

"I cured your allergy, huh?" she asked.

"Yes, you did, and I'm enjoying the treatment," he said as he slipped his hands underneath her skirt. "Forget the sofa. Let's get out of here and make use of that big bed in your bedroom."

"All right, I'm going to check the kitchen and then we're out of here," Kandace said.

Solomon headed to her office and Kandace took off for the kitchen. While he waited for her, he shut down her computer and packed up her laptop. Moments ticked away and he wondered what was taking Kandace so long in the kitchen. "That damned chef had better not be trying to make a move on her," he muttered as he bolted out of the office and headed for the kitchen.

"Kandace, babe, what's the hold up?" Solomon called from the hallway.

"Don't you move," Carmen hissed as she pointed the sharp blade of the knife at Kandace's throat. Kandace's eyes focused on the blood dripping from the blade of the knife, blood that proved Carmen was a homicidal maniac. Raymond Martinez's body lay in the corner in a pool of his own blood. Raymond had just graduated from Johnson and Wales University and had been excited for the chance to work with Devon Harris. Now that opportunity had cost him his life.

Looking down at the blade wedged against her throat, Kandace fought the urge to scream. She was sure Solomon was walking into his death. Kandace had seen his potential as a pastry chef and she enjoyed the treats he would sneak to her when he worked late trying to come up with new recipes. He reminded her of Devon in the early days when he'd been finding his footing as a chef, before their relationship had fallen apart. Kandace had seen the same kind of drive and determination in Raymond as she saw in Devon. She had been looking forward to seeing his star rise and now he was dead.

"Hey, Kandace. Are you in here?" Solomon called out as he stepped into the kitchen.

Carmen looked away from Kandace, shocked to see Solomon there. Kandace took a chance to get away from her and jabbed her knee into Carmen's midsection, knocking the breath out of her.

Carmen flew backward into the stainless steel counter, sending the knife clanging to the floor. "SOLOMON!" Kandace yelled as she attempted to run. Carmen grabbed a pan and threw it at Kandace, hitting her in the center of her back.

Solomon flew over to the counter in time to see Carmen, dressed in the green hospital scrubs, reaching for the knife as Kandace fell to the floor. He kicked the knife out of her reach and stomped on Carmen's hand.

"How could you?" Carmen screamed. "You ruined my plan, Solomon."

He snatched her up by her shoulders and Kandace ran to the utility closet in the hall outside the kitchen. "Your cook isn't the only thing that got cut," Carmen said, then delivered a sharp blow to Solomon's family jewels. While Solomon clutched himself in pain, Carmen grabbed the knife from the floor and ran after Kandace.

Kandace held her breath in the utility closet as she heard feet padding down the hall. When she stuck her hand in the pocket of her skirt, she was relieved to find her BlackBerry, but when she pulled it out, she saw that she didn't have a signal in the closet. Sticking the phone back in her pocket, Kandace looked around for a weapon, but before she could find one, the door swung open and Carmen stood in the doorway with the knife in her hand.

"Did you think I wouldn't find you?" she sneered.

Kandace took a step back as Carmen moved forward and pointed the knife at her face. When she tried to stab Kandace in her shoulder, Kandace ducked, but the point of the knife nicked her face. When Kandace saw the blood drop on her shirt, she lunged at Carmen's knees, knocking her down on the floor. Then she kicked the knife out of her hand and scrambled to pick it up.

"Where is Solomon?" she demanded.

Carmen spat in Kandace's direction. "Don't worry about Solomon. I took care of him."

Anger surged through her body and Kandace delivered a kick to Carmen's head. "If you hurt him," she exclaimed as she kicked and kicked. Carmen rolled into a ball and reached out and grabbed Kandace's ankle, pulling her down to the floor. She pounced on top of Kandace and tried to wrest the knife from her hand, but Kandace pounded her back with her free hand while trying to keep the knife out of her reach. Carmen tried to grab Kandace's hair and slam her head into the floor, but Kandace brought her knees up and slammed them into Carmen's midsection. She rolled over on her side in pain and Kandace rushed to her feet and ran to the front of the restaurant. "Solomon, Solomon," she screamed.

"Kandace," she heard a breathless Solomon call back from the dining room. She rushed to him, looking over her shoulder for Carmen.

"Call the police, please call the police," she said frantically. Solomon and Kandace rushed for the front door while he dialed 9-1-1. Just as Kandace had the door unlocked, a knife came flying her way. She and Solomon quickly ducked and the sharp knife lodged in the wall. Carmen came out of the shadows armed with what seemed like every knife from the kitchen.

"Drop the phone or I won't miss her with the next one," Carmen exclaimed.

Solomon dropped the cell phone with the operator still on the line. "Think about this, Carmen. You don't want to hurt anybody else," Solomon said as he took a step toward her.

"Yes, I do," she said madly. "I loved you and you turned your back on me for her. I have bullet wounds because you told the police to shoot me so you could save her."

Carmen dropped all of the knives except for the meat cleaver she held and then she rushed toward Kandace. Solomon ran in front of Carmen and grabbed her as she swung the cleaver wildly.

"Why didn't you give me a chance? Why couldn't you love me?" Carmen screamed as she struggled against him. Solomon squeezed her wrist with all of his might but she wouldn't let her weapon go. He sidestepped her as she tried to kick him again. "I loved you."

"You're sick, Chelsea."

Carmen stopped moving for a brief second. "Chelsea is dead and soon you will be too." She brought the cleaver down on his shoulder and Solomon dropped to the floor.

Kandace ran to the pile of knives and grabbed one. As Carmen lifted the cleaver to strike another blow to Solomon, Kandace lunged forward and drove the blade of the butcher's knife into Carmen's chest. The meat cleaver clanged to the floor as Carmen fell.

She gasped and gurgled for her next breath as blood poured from her chest. Kandace kicked the meat cleaver across the floor out of Carmen's reach, then rushed to Solomon's side.

"Are you all right?" Kandace asked frantically.

"Yeah," he said as he touched his shoulder. "She just nicked me." They both looked at Carmen as she lay dying on the floor.

"It's finally over," Kandace said as she heard the sirens in the distance. Solomon slowly rose to his feet and took Kandace's face in his hands. He saw her cut for the first time.

"Did she hurt you?" he asked as he ran his thumb across the dried blood on her face.

Kandace shook her head, then broke down sobbing. "I thought she'd killed you when she found me in the closet, Solomon. I can't lose you. I love you too much."

"I love you, too," he said as they waited for the officers to enter the restaurant.

It took two hours for Solomon and Kandace to give their statements to the police. When they were finally ready to leave the restaurant, three television reporters were outside waiting for them and the police.

"Shit," Solomon whispered when he saw the reporters coming their way. "Don't say anything to them."

"This is going to be bad for the restaurant," Kandace said as she trembled in Solomon's arms.

"Miss Davis, what happened?" one of the reporters called out.

"Was this a robbery?" another reporter asked.

Solomon held up his hand. "Can we give you guys a statement in the morning? We're tired and a little bloody right now."

Solomon ushered Kandace to her car, ignoring the other questions the reporters were hollering out. "Are you going to call your friends?" he asked when they got in the car.

"I'm willing to bet one of them was watching the news and that means all of them are going to be waiting for me," she said as they drove to her house. When they pulled into the driveway, Kandace pointed to the two cars parked on the side of the road.

"Alicia and Serena are here."

"It's good they have your back," he said as they got out of the car.

"But I'm regretting that I gave them a spare key," she said as they walked up to the front door. Kandace didn't even bother to take her house key out because Serena opened the door and enveloped her friend in a tight hug.

"My God, please tell me that psychopath is dead," Serena said as she glared at Solomon.

"Can we do this later?" Kandace asked as Serena led her over to the sofa. Alicia came from the kitchen with a mug of tea and a plate of chocolate chip cookies.

"Are you all right?" Alicia asked as she set the plate and the mug in front of Kandace.

Kandace touched her cheek and nodded, though she wasn't all right. She didn't think she'd ever get the image of Carmen dying out of her head. Especially since she was the one who had killed her.

But I had to. If I hadn't killed her, she would've killed me or Solomon. This was never going to end with her alive, she thought as she took a sip of the cinnamon tea Alicia had made.

Solomon eased on the couch beside Kandace and wrapped his arm around her shoulder. His touch was so comforting that he didn't need to say a word to put her mind at ease.

Alicia walked over to Serena, who was standing by the door as if she was looking for someone. "We should go," Alicia said in a loud whisper.

"All right," Serena said, then she turned to Solomon. "You need to walk us out."

"Are you going to be okay?" Solomon asked Kandace.

"You're not going that far," Kandace said as Solomon stood up and walked her friends to the door.

Once Solomon, Serena, and Alicia were on the front porch and out of earshot of Kandace, Serena turned to him and said, "You'd better take care of our friend."

"That's all I want to do right now," he said.

"That's good," Alicia said. "What happened in the restaurant tonight?"

Solomon ran his hand over his face and glanced at the blood on his shirt. "It was very ugly. Carmen killed one of the chefs and she would've killed me and Kandace if Kandace hadn't stabbed her."

"She killed her?" Alicia asked as she hugged herself while rocking back and forth.

Solomon nodded. "She had to."

"And where were you when all this was going on?" Serena asked.

"I had a meat cleaver in my arm," Solomon said as he shot an aggravated glance at Serena. "I didn't want anything to happen to Kandace and I didn't want her to have to do what she did."

"You need to go back to her," Alicia said. "Come on, Serena."

Serena turned to Solomon and offered him a faint smile. "Thank you for protecting our girl." She gave him a sisterly hug, then she and Alicia got into their cars and headed home.

Solomon walked into the house and found Kandace curled up on the sofa asleep. She moaned softly as if she was having a nightmare or reliving the real life nightmare that happened to them moments earlier. He placed his hand on her shoulder and gently shook her. "Kandace."

She jerked awake and uttered a quiet scream as Solomon pulled her into his arms. "The blood," she muttered. "I keep seeing all of the blood."

"Baby, it's all right. It's over and no one will ever hurt you again," he said as Kandace clung tightly to him. "Let's get you to bed. Do you want to take a shower first?"

She shook her head. "I just need you to hold me," she said as she rose to her feet. Her eyes zeroed in on the bloodstain on Solomon's shirt. "Don't you think you should have your shoulder looked at?"

"It's not bad. Besides, I'm more concerned about you, Kandace. I'm so sorry you had to go through this. But it is over," he reassured her again. "I will never let anything or anyone else hurt you."

As they headed up to the bedroom, Kandace felt safer. And when she got into bed and Solomon wrapped his arms around her, she felt secure.

CHAPTER 29

For the next three days, the media descended on Kandace and Solomon with a relentless force. After the local stations revealed that Solomon Crawford was at the scene of Carmen's murder, the New York reporters came to Charlotte and camped out. And after the media discovered that Maurice Goings was the brother-in-law of one of the restaurant's owners, the frenzy intensified.

Luckily, the Charlotte-Mecklenburg Police ruled that Kandace was justified in killing Carmen, which put an end to all the legal questions surrounding Carmen's death and the restaurant was free to open. Police also linked Carmen to the death of Dr. Hovis Clarke and the murder of the housekeeper at Carolina Serenity. With each detail of what a monster Carmen was, Kandace's blood just ran cold.

Solomon walked in to the living room as Kandace was watching CNN reporters refer to his connection to Carmen's murder spree. He took the remote from the table and shut the TV off. "You need to get out of town," he said.

"What?"

"I think you need another vacation," Solomon said.

Kandace shook her head. "A vacation started all of this," she reminded him.

Solomon cocked his head to the side and frowned at her. Kandace covered her face. "You know what I meant," she said. "When is this going to be over? We released a statement and those damned reporters are still digging. What more do they want?"

"Unfortunately, this is a sexy story," Solomon said as he sat on the sofa beside Kandace and pulled her into his arms. "It'll go away as soon as something else happens. The Macy's Thanksgiving Day Parade will knock this out of the headlines."

"Damn, I forgot all about Thanksgiving," she said. "This year we were supposed to have a dinner for the homeless and then we all were going to have a big dinner with everyone."

"Where?" he asked, looking around Kandace's small home.

"At the restaurant. But now, I'm not sure."

"Why not? I know it's hard right now, but you can't stay away from your dream because of what Carmen did. She was a sick woman and I'm sorry that she ever hurt you," Solomon said. "But you can't let her overshadow all your good memories and what you've worked for."

Kandace sighed. "You're right. Believe it or not, they used to have to pry me out of the restaurant."

"And you haven't been back since this happened."

"How can I? Every time I think about that place, I see Raymond and Carmen."

Solomon stroked her cheek gently. "Then you need new memories there. Think about how much good you are going to do for the less fortunate. And I'll help you guys in anyway I can. I'll even be nice to your chef for a day."

A small smile touched her lips and she patted Solomon on his knee. "How's your shoulder."

"Fine," he said. "At my appointment this morning the doctor said I should be ready for rehab next week."

Kandace ran her hand across her face and leaned against Solomon's strong chest. "Will you go to the restaurant with me today?" she asked.

"Of course," he said. "Anything you need."

"Right now," she said as she held tight to his arm, "I need you to hold me."

"Always, baby," Solomon said as he kissed her on the forehead.

A few hours later, Kandace and Solomon headed to Hometown Delights and much to their dismay, the press was waiting outside for them.

"Mr. Crawford, Mr. Crawford," one of the reporters called out as he and his colleagues ran up to Solomon and Kandace. "How did you find out that Carmen De La Croix was living under an assumed identity?"

"Were you two lovers?" a female reporter yelled out as Solomon opened the door to the restaurant and ushered Kandace inside.

Kandace froze at the door. "This was a mistake,"

she said as she turned to exit the restaurant, but Solomon stopped her.

"Either face this or a bunch of reporters. You're stronger than this. I know you are."

Kandace took a deep breath and walked forward. This was her restaurant. She and her friends had worked too hard, jumped through too many hoops to build this place and make it a success. She couldn't let Carmen rob her of that.

"Kandace?" Jade said as she appeared from behind the bar. "I'm glad you're here."

"Hi," Kandace said.

Jade rushed over to her and hugged her friend tightly. "I would've come by sooner, but Jaden is just getting better," she said, then turned to Solomon and gave him a hug. "Thanks for getting her here."

"How's the baby doing?" he asked as the trio walked over to the bar.

"All better and acting like his father. I had to sneak out of the house while they were both asleep," Jade said as she pulled out three coffee cups. Kandace looked around the restaurant hoping that she wouldn't see Carmen's face or Raymond's dead body. Every shadow made her shiver. Then she felt Solomon's hand on her knee.

"You all right?" he asked.

Kandace smiled. "I'm getting there."

Jade smiled at them. "The police finally cleared this place as a crime scene and Devon's been working hard on the dinner. I stole some corn bread." Jade lifted a small aluminum pan from underneath the bar.

"He's going to get you," Kandace said as she took

a square of bread from the pan. Solomon took a piece of bread as well and as much as he didn't want to like it, it was delicious.

"I was thinking," Jade said after she polished off a second piece of corn bread. "After Thanksgiving, we should have Antonio redo this place."

Kandace nodded. "I like that idea."

"Good, then you can tell Serena," Jade said, then took a long sip of coffee.

"Tell me what?" Serena asked as she walked into the restaurant. "And I want you all to know that I got rid of those reporters."

"Good job," Solomon said. "Somebody named Antonio is going to redecorate the restaurant."

Jade and Kandace looked at him as if he'd lost his mind. He shrugged, not knowing what the big deal was.

"What?!" Serena shrieked. "Have you all lost your damned minds? There are more contractors in Charlotte than Antonio Billups."

Kandace crossed over to her friend and wrapped her arm around her shoulders. "Why don't you just calm down. You can't deny that Antonio did a great job with this place the first time," she said.

"Oh, shut up," Serena said. "I know what you two are doing and I don't like it. Antonio doesn't want me and I'm sick of his mixed signals. Besides, who's going to pay for this renovation?"

"I will," Solomon said.

Everyone looked at him. "We can't allow you to do that," Serena said. "We've paid for everything in this restaurant and we're not . . ."

"Serena, I'm paying for it," Solomon said with finality.

"And what? You get a stake in our restaurant?" Serena asked.

He furrowed his brows. "No, you just stay away from my chef in the mountains," he said.

"What?" Jade asked.

"Nothing," Kandace said. "Solomon, this is too much."

"Nothing is too much for you," he said.

"My God," Serena groaned. "You two are getting just as sickening as Jade and James."

Kandace rolled her eyes at her friend and sauntered over to Solomon and planted a huge kiss on his lips. "Thank you," she said.

He winked at her and took another piece of corn bread. "You can really thank me later," he said.

"So," Serena said, "are we opening today or what?"

Jade looked at Kandace. "What do you think?" she asked.

Kandace sighed and looked thoughtfully at Solomon. He stroked her cheek and smiled. "You can do this," he whispered.

"All right, let's do this. Otherwise Solomon might change his mind about paying for the redesign," she said jokingly.

"I hope he does," Serena muttered as she walked over to the bar and swiped Kandace's coffee cup and a piece of corn bread.

EPILOGUE

THANKSGIVING DAY

Solomon couldn't remember the last time he shared such an enjoyable Thanksgiving meal, despite the fact that his blood relatives weren't around the table and everyone sitting there was tired from serving over three hundred homeless families. Solomon was shocked that Maurice Goings and many of his Carolina Panthers teammates showed up and worked hard to feed the people. He'd kept looking for reporters to show up, but they hadn't. Maurice had told Solomon that he knew things were still raw for Kandace and he hadn't wanted to ruin her Thanksgiving plans by not showing up and helping out. Solomon knew he'd be cheering for the Panthers from now on as long as they weren't playing his beloved Eagles. Solomon had even buried the hatchet with Devon Harris. He totally understood why the guy was hung up on Kandace. She was the most beautiful woman in the world and if he'd allowed her to slip through his fingers, Solomon knew he'd want her back too. It was too late though, because Kandace Davis had done the impossible—she'd opened his heart to love. She'd erased the memories of the wedding that had fallen apart years ago. She'd replaced the faceless and nameless women he'd wasted so much time with. Solomon glanced at Kandace as she poured ice tea for everybody.

"I'm sorry," Homer said. "Is this Long Island ice tea? After all that work we did, we need some alcohol up in here."

"That's the last thing you need," James Goings said as he rocked his sleeping son. "Besides, Kenya and Jade can't drink."

"So," Serena said as she stood up and headed for the bar, "what's your pleasure, guys?"

"Can you pour yourself into a glass?" cornerback Davis Simmons called out.

Maurice kicked him under the table and shook his head at him, saying, "She will hurt you."

"I want her to," Davis said.

"No you don't," Jade said as she placed a basket of fresh corn bread in the center of the table. "Just let it go."

Davis stood up and followed Serena in to the bar area. Alicia shook her head. "He'll be back in five."

"Four," Jade said.

"Three," Kandace said with a laugh.

"Damn," the group heard Davis exclaim after hearing a loud smack.

"I tried to warn him," Jade said.

"Defensive players don't listen," Maurice said. "Hell, he should've known if Homer wasn't hitting on her that she wasn't to be messed with."

"Why don't you take your daughter and change her?" Kenya said as she placed two trays of clam dressing on the table.

"Come on, Robi," Maurice said as he lifted the little girl from her carrier seat and took her to the bathroom to change her.

"It isn't lost on any of us that we're serving and you guys are just sitting here," Alicia said, then she took her seat. "I'm done."

"Me too," Kandace said as she sat down beside Solomon and pinched his thigh. "Get to work, baby."

Davis slunk back to the dining room holding his jaw as the guys stood up and headed for the kitchen. James handed Jaden to Jade after she sat down, then he kissed her cheek. "We'll be back with the turkey," he said.

As Solomon walked in to the kitchen, James grabbed him by his good shoulder. "Welcome to this crazy family," he said.

"You know what," Solomon said as he reached into his jeans pocket, "I'm ready to make it official." He flashed James the four-and-a-half carat, emerald-cut diamond ring.

"Damn, that's blinding. You know, we're really going to hate you," James said as he held the ring up. "The rest of those women are going to expect us to step up now."

Solomon took his ring back and laughed. "Hey, my lady deserves the best. Besides, I'm going to have to knock her up to keep up with you and your brother."

"That's the easy part," James said as he took the turkey from the island and Solomon grabbed a pan of macaroni and cheese.

The men headed back to the dining room with the final parts of dinner and placed them on the table. Solomon was happy to see that Serena had brought a bottle of champagne in a bucket of ice and two bottles of ginger ale for the mothers.

"Are we ready to eat now?" Jade asked as she slipped Jaden into his carrier seat.

"Just a minute," Solomon said, eliciting groans from Homer, Serena, and Davis. "I won't take up a lot of time, I swear." He took Kandace's hand in his and kissed it. "I can't remember the last time that I celebrated Thanksgiving like this. Most people would think that I have a lot to be thankful for because of my business success, money, and stunning good looks."

Maurice tossed a piece of corn bread at him. "Man, get to the damned point."

"The point is," Solomon said as he swatted the flying bread, "Kandace, I love you. I never thought that I would meet someone like you who challenged me, forced me to be real with her, and opened my world up to what a real love is, and I want to keep this feeling going for the rest of my life."

Tears welled up in Kandace's eyes and she stood up to face Solomon. "Solomon," she murmured, "I love you too."

Jade leaned her head on James's shoulder and

fought back her own tears. Kenya beamed and squeezed Maurice's hand. Alicia watched Solomon and Kandace with her elbows perched on the table. Serena just looked disinterested as she sipped her vodka sour.

"Kandace," Solomon said as he reached into his pocket and pulled out the engagement ring. "Will you marry me?"

She looked down at the large stone and took in a sharp breath. "Solomon," she said as tears poured down her cheeks.

"I need an answer, babe," he said as he took her left hand in his.

"Yes, yes, I'll marry you," she said as he slipped the ring on her finger. Solomon hugged her tightly, then kissed her as if they were the only two in the room. Everyone at the table broke into applause, even Serena, who quickly wiped a stray tear from her eye.

"I love you so much," he said as he let her go.

Kandace smiled brightly at her fiancé and stroked his cheek. "I hope you're ready for all this," she said. "We're crazy all the time, not just during the holidays."

"It doesn't matter, because I'm crazy in love with you," he said.

If you enjoyed *No Other Lover Will Do*, don't miss

Lessons from a Younger Lover
by Zuri Day

Coming in March 2010 from Dafina Books

Here's an excerpt from
Lessons from a Younger Lover . . .

CHAPTER 1

There are two things Gwen Smith never thought she'd do. She never thought she'd move back to her rinky-dink hometown of Sienna, California, and she never thought she'd come back as a forty-year-old divorcee. Yet here she sat in the middle seat of a crowded plane, at the age where some said life began, trying to figure out how the boring and predictable one she'd known sixty short days ago had changed so quickly.

The first hitch in the giddy up wasn't a total surprise. Her mother's dementia had become increasingly worse following the death of Gwen's father, Harold, two years ago. Her parents had been married forty-four years. It was a tough adjustment. At the funeral, Gwen told her husband that she knew the time would come when her mother's welfare would become her responsibility. That she thought Joe would be by her side at this crucial time, and wasn't, was the fact she hadn't seen coming.

But it was true nonetheless. Joe had announced

his desire to divorce and packed his bags the same evening. Two months later she was still reeling from that okey doke. But she couldn't think about that now. Gwen had to focus on one crisis at a time and at the moment, her mother was the priority.

"Ladies and gentlemen, the captain has turned on the seatbelt sign indicating our final descent into Los Angeles. Please make sure your seatbelts are securely fastened and your seats and tray tables are in their upright and locked . . ."

Gwen stretched as well as she could between two stout men and tried to remove the crook from her neck. Still, she was grateful she'd fallen asleep. Shuteye had been all too elusive the past few weeks, when ongoing worries and raging thoughts had kept true rest at bay. Fragments of a dream flitted across her wakened mind as they landed and she reached into the overhead bin for her carryon luggage. Gwen didn't know if she wanted to remember it or not. Lately, her dreams had been replaced by nightmares that happened when her eyes were wide open.

"Gwen! Over here girl! Gwen!"

Gwen smiled as a familiar voice pierced the crowd roaming the LAX Airport baggage claim area. She turned and waved so that the short, buxom woman wearing fuchsia cut-offs and a yellow halter top straining for control, would know that she, God and everyone within a five-mile radius had heard her.

"Gwendolyn!" Chantay exclaimed, enunciating each syllable for full effect as she reached up and hugged her childhood friend. "Girl, let me look at you!"

"You just saw me last year, Tay."

"That visit went by in a fog. You know the deal."

Gwen did, and wished she didn't. Her last time home was not a fond memory.

Chantay stepped back, put her hand on her hips and began shaking her head so hard her waist-length braids sprayed the waiting passengers surrounding them. "What are we going to do with your rail thin behind? You couldn't find enough deep-dish pizzas to eat in Chicago? No barbeque or chicken and waffle joints to put some meat on your bones?"

Gwen took the jab good-naturedly. Her five-foot seven, size six body had caused her heftier friend chagrin for years. No matter that Gwen had never mastered how to show off her physique, put on makeup, or fix her hair. The fact that she could eat everything, including the kitchen sink, and still not gain a pound, was a stick in Chantay's craw.

Chantay enveloped her friend in a big bear hug. "You look good, girl. A day late and a dollar short on style with that curly-q hair straight out of *A Different World*, but overall . . . you look good!"

Gwen's laugh was genuine for the first time in weeks. "You don't look half bad yourself. And opinionated as always I see."

"Honey, if you want a feel good moment, watch Oprah. I'm going to tell you the truth even if it's ugly, and speaking of the "u" word, those Leave-It-To-Beaver pedal pushers . . ."

"Forget you, Tay! C'mon, that's my luggage coming around."

A half hour later, Gwen settled back in Chantay's Ford Explorer as they merged into highway traffic for the two hour drive to Sienna. The air conditioner was a welcomed change to the ninety degree July heat.

"I still can't believe you're here."

"Me either."

"You know you've got to give me the full scoop. First, I never thought you'd ever get married and if you did, you'd never, *ever* get divorced!"

"Obviously life wasn't following your script," Gwen muttered sarcastically.

"Oh, don't get your panties in a bunch, sista, you know what I'm saying and I'm not the only one. Who did everyone vote the least likely to, uh, get married?"

"I believe the exact description in the high school yearbook read 'would die an old maid'."

"Well, I was trying to save you the embarrassment of quoting it verbatim but . . . who was it?"

They both knew the answer was Gwen. But rather than help make the point, Gwen answered the question with one of her own. "Who did they say would probably have ten kids?"

"Humph. That's because those nuckas didn't know that fornicate does not equal procreate. After being stuck with raising one *accident* and another *oops* by myself, I had my tubes tied. I told the doctor who did the procedure that if a "baby I pulled out" number three showed up in my pee sample, his would be the name in the father line. So believe me, if there's a sperm bad enough to get past the Boy Scout knot he tied, then that's a baby that deserves to be born."

Gwen looked out the window, thought about

Chantay's two daughters and watched the world whirl by while Chantay pushed past seventy and flew down the surprisingly light 405 Freeway. While Chantay had often said she didn't want kids, Gwen had always looked forward to motherhood. She was still looking, but couldn't see any bassinet or baby bed because a divorce petition was blocking the view.

Chantay scanned for various stations on the radio before turning it off altogether. "Why are you making me drag the details out of you?" she whined, exasperation evident in her voice. "What happened between you and Joe?"

The name of Gwen's soon-to-be former husband elicited a frown. "You mean *Joey?*"

"Who the hell is that?"

"That's what he calls himself now."

"I call him bastard, but I digress. What happened?"

Gwen sighed, sat up, and spoke the truth straight out. "He met somebody else."

"You have got to be kidding. Corny-ass Joe Smith, the computer nerd who could barely pull the garter off at y'alls wedding?"

"That would be him."

"What fool did he find to listen to his tired lines?"

"You mean besides me?"

"Girl, I didn't mean that personally. Joe has some good points. He seems to know his way around a computer better than anybody."

"That's one."

"We've got ninety minutes of driving left. I'll think of something else."

Gwen laughed, appreciative of the levity Chantay brought to a sad situation.

"So . . . who is she?"

"Her name is Mitzi, she's twenty-two and works in his office. They both like motorcycles, Miller Lite and poker. He tattooed her name on his arm and moved into her studio apartment last month. But I don't want to talk about him right now."

"Whoa, chick! You're sure going to have to talk about him later . . . *and* her. That was way too much information to leave me hanging. But I can wait a minute, and in the meantime change the subject to somebody you can talk about . . . Adam 'oh, oh, oh, oh' Johnson!"

"Chantay, you are too silly! I haven't thought about that line since we left high school." Gwen, Chantay and a couple other misfits used to substitute his first name in Ready For The World's hit, "Oh Sheila." Chantay would hum it as he passed in the halls and the other girls would break into hysterical laughter, making them all look like fools.

"That is the single welcomed surprise I've had these past few weeks. That Adam is the principal at Sienna. Can you believe it?"

"No, because I never thought a brothah with that much weight in his lower head would have any brains in his upper one."

"Well there's that, but even more is the fact that he's back living in our home town. After being such a standout at Texas A&M and going on to play for the Cowboys? I guess a lot happened to him since the last news I heard, that he was sidelined with an injury and forced to retire early."

"I can't believe his wife would agree to move back

to such a podunk town. She looks too hoity-toity for Smallville; but I only saw her one time on TV."

"They're divorced."

"What? Girl, stop!"

"Yep, he told me that when we talked. He was nice actually, not the cocky, arrogant Adam I remember. He wouldn't admit it, but I know he's the reason why, to use his words, my getting this post is 'in the bag'."

"Don't give him too much credit, Gwen. You're a first-rate teacher, and it's not like our town has to beat off qualified educators with sticks."

"Maybe, but the way everything happened . . . I'm just happy to know I have a job secured, or at least I will after my interview next week. Mama has some money saved up but that's all going to her assisted living expenses. I still need to support myself, and pay half the mortgage on the condo until it's sold."

"How's Miss Lorraine doing?"

Gwen shrugged. "Mama's about the same, I guess."

"Isn't she a bit young for what the doctors say is happening to her?"

"From what I've learned, not really. The disease is usually associated with aging, but can actually occur at any time, from a variety of causes. The medical community usually gives it a different name when it occurs in someone, say, under fifty-five. But whatever the title, the results are the same—a long-term decline in cognitive function."

"Just be glad she's still here," Chantay replied. "You can still hug her, whether she knows you or not."

"Oh, she knows you, and remembers more than

she lets on, I'm thinking. But I hear what you're saying, Chantay, and I'm grateful."

They were silent a moment before Chantay changed the subject. "Joe's a lowlife. He could have stayed in the condo and split the rent with the fool he's sleeping with until somebody bought it. He's just an asshole."

"That would have been too much like right. But it is what it is. Don't get me re-pissed about it."

Chantay started humming "Oh Shiela." "Wouldn't it be ironic if you move back to town and snag its star player after all these years? Now, we'll have to give your dated butt a makeover, but by the time I'm done with you . . . you'll move all those other silicone stuffed heifas in town out of the way."

"I wonder who else from our class still lives there."

"Girl, it don't even matter, keep your eye on the prize." Chantay gave another sideways look at her friend. "Um-hum. If it's Adam Johnson you want, trust, I can help you get him."

Gwen had thought about Adam, and what a nice balm he might be for the hurt Joe had caused her. Not that she'd get into anything serious right away. It would be months before the divorce came up on the backlogged Illinois court docket and was finalized. But since speaking to Adam, she'd fantasized a time or two about the heartthrob she remembered: tall, lanky, chocolate, strong, with bedroom eyes and a Jherri curl that brushed his shoulders. She never dreamed she'd get another chance with someone like Adam. But as she'd learned all too painfully in the past few months—life was full of surprises.

More of the Hottest
African-American Fiction from
Dafina Books

Come With Me J.S. Hawley	0-7582-1935-0	$6.99/$9.99
Golden Night Candice Poarch	0-7582-1977-6	$6.99/$9.99
No More Lies Rachel Skerritt	0-7582-1601-7	$6.99/$9.99
Perfect For You Sylvia Lett	0-7582-1979-2	$6.99/$9.99
Risk Ann Christopher	0-7582-1434-0	$6.99/$9.99

Available Wherever Books Are Sold!

Visit our website at **www.kensingtonbooks.com**.